"Do you believe in old sayings?"

When her eyes clouded with confusion, Steven went on, "The kind that spilled forth from the mouths of wise old men?"

"I suppose so. Why?" Brandy fell into his silver-lined trap.

He stepped forward and captured her face between his hands. "Then you belong to me now. Save a life and it's yours." He dropped his bombshell, searing with his burning lips her parted ones.

Caught by surprise and trapped within his strong embrace, Brandy swayed against his hard frame and surrendered to the intoxicating kiss. Her arms eased around his waist, beneath his dinner jacket, and wandered up the muscled back. Steven's mouth greedily devoured the sweet abandonment of hers. He hadn't planned on this and it stunned him. His arms tightened around Brandy, almost fiercely and painfully. His lips became insistent, demanding, ravishing.

With more than twenty-one million copies of her books in print, Janelle Taylor has secured her place in the hearts of readers as one of today's best-loved storytellers. This *New York Times* bestselling author began writing in 1977 while working as a research technologist at a medical college. *Valley of Fire* was Janelle's first contemporary romance novel.

JANELLE TAYLOR

Valley of Fire

MIRA BOOKS

FOR:

Linda M. and Mary C.,
my wonderful sisters and friends

AND

Adele, my indispensable "Casey"
and marvelous friend.

ISBN 1-55166-309-0

VALLEY OF FIRE

Printed in U.S.A.

Chapter One

Brandy's shaky fingers mopped the continual beads of perspiration from her forehead and upper lip for seemingly the millionth time; an unnatural crimson flush was visible beneath her golden tan. Her respiration was labored and shallow; she hadn't realized that oppressively high heat made it difficult to breathe and to remain alert. Her dark emerald eyes were glazed with a torment never before experienced, unspeakable fear glittering within their expressive depths. Tawny hair clung to Brandy's moist neck and stuck to the edges of her face; her damp shirt and jeans were glued uncomfortably to her sleek body. For the first time in her life, Brandy Alexander was literally petrified, a feeling which played havoc with her normal self-assurance in handling a trying situation, a feeling which assailed her too often these days.

With nerves on edge, Brandy irrationally berated the reflective glare from the freshly washed hood of the rented Cadillac de Ville. She also fumed at the mechanic who had failed to notice the impending trouble spots which had led to the car's breakdown, including the vital air conditioner. Without it, the black Caddy was like a brick oven, baking her flesh and roasting her brain.

To instill new hope into her rapidly vanishing spirits, Brandy cautioned herself against overdramatizing this strange and precarious situation. She should not allow herself to readily accept the dire fate which was nakedly glaring her in the face, much like a threatening stare from one of the deadly villains in her novels.

On the last weather report, the man had stated the temperature for Las Vegas was one hundred and eighteen degrees, but it seemed more like one hundred and fifty degrees in the scenic Valley of Fire where she was helplessly imprisoned in a steaming, useless vehicle. The heat was now unbearable, yet bear it she must if she wished to survive.

For the past four hours, Brandy had waited and prayed for help to arrive. Her patience and hope had run a race to see which one would give out first. From her vantage point, their perilous race had ended in a tie. The heat had steadily increased within Brandy's expensive confines; yet, she had instinctively known the greater danger of abandoning the car and heading off down that winding, black-topped road that stretched out endlessly before her weary gaze like some deadly, sleeping viper that might awaken any minute and strike at her if she dared to tread upon its stygian back.

Brandy absently promised herself that in the future she would be reluctant to leave the cool protection of her rustic ranch house in the midst of summer. She sighed wistfully as she closed her eyes and envisioned the verdant cedars and the lofty pines with their heady odors and a backdrop of intoxicating blue, the sigh painful to her parched throat. It was easy to picture the massive white oaks and the slender willows which surrounded her home, along with the colorful goldenrods, bluebells, and the bluish-green of the Kentucky grasses dancing in a gentle breeze. Yet, for all of her creative ability, Brandy could not realistically imagine the cool, crisp breeze which stirred her long hair and clothes as she worked on her screened porch or as she walked barefoot in the surrounding fields and woods or waded in the swift-running brook near the house.

At the moment Brandy was too ensnared by this frightful dilemma to worry about her many problems, such as her future commitment to Devon Publishing Company, the assignment which had innocently placed her in this dangerous circumstance. She tried unsuccessfully to recall the name of the man who had suggested the Valley of Fire as the best location to research her new science-fiction novel. Even if Brandy could recall his name, how could she blame him for her accident? In the future, perhaps she should stick to writing romances, mysteries, and westerns; inexplicably, each science-fiction novel written had held uncanny surprises for her.

Brandy felt she could hold the Farley Rent-A-Car Agency responsible for the empty water container in the trunk, if not for the broken air conditioner and radiator hose. Ironically, the man at the rental company had been the very person to warn her against traveling into the desert without "at least one quart of water per person." This predicament should certainly teach her to look out for her own interests and safety in the future, just as she had done in the past. It annoyed her to realize she had foolishly overlooked such a vital matter as her own preservation. Brandy pondered her sudden disappearance of courage, resolve, and stamina which had aided her successful writing career and her independent life-style.

Lately Brandy had permitted too many problems to interfere with her sound judgment and independence. For the life of her Brandy could not justify or rationalize her decision to rewrite her last historical romance novel to suit Webster Books. She had not needed that large advance, nor the sizable royalties from its following landslide sales. Perhaps that was the raw nerve. She had allowed herself to be talked into adding several explicit love scenes and a glorified murder to her original manuscript for *Love's Cruel Arrows,* additions she had vainly argued against as being unnecessary to sales and as too vivid for taste. Plus, Brandy had fretted over offending the Sioux Indians with the harsh changes in several scenes.

But she had watched the novel climb to the heights of the bestseller lists and had even been approached for a movie sale. Even more irritating were the scriptwriter's demands for more drastic changes, more detailed sex, and more gory violence. She had wanted the novel to stand on its own literary merits and to mirror American Indian history, not become a sensational insult to their noble heritage. How could she intelligently argue with what the public demanded from its writers and movie producers? Evidently it was true that an author could write her own book just to a certain point. Maybe that was the crux of her vexation: with the changes, it didn't seem like her book anymore. Brandy wondered if the money and fame were all that important. . . .

Brandy could still hear Casey's final arguments: "Please listen to me, Brandy; you can write all day and toss those manuscripts into a desk drawer if you refuse to give the public what they demand. If they want sex, gore, and realism—close your eyes and let someone else type your final manuscript. What good is all the literary talent in the entire world if no one buys and reads your work? You don't have any choice; the publishers and readers have certain demands which you must meet. When you finish this current science-fiction title, we'll have to settle on the movie rights to *Arrows*. You know they'll refuse its purchase without those specific changes. Think about it long and hard; they won't wait forever for an answer."

Who knows? Brandy thought now; maybe Casey was right. Maybe she did have to furnish her public with juicy romances which left nothing to their imagination. After all, Casey Treavers was the best literary agent around and they had been best friends for years. So far, Casey had never steered Brandy in a wrong or an unprofitable direction. Casey was more than competent. She was dependable, genial, trustworthy, and vivacious. Still, the taste of a sellout lingered in Brandy's pleasingly shaped mouth.

Brandy perched herself sideways on the seat to avoid the full intensity of the sun's rays and to catch any possible breeze which might pass through the car's open doors. The escaping steam had long since ceased its climb into the torrid air. Once the sustained *s* sound had halted, she had been encompassed by total, eerie silence.

There had been no need to burn her fingers by lifting the hood; whether it was the radiator or simply an inexpensive hose, there was nothing she could do. For a woman who had been in sole control of her own life for so long, Brandy was distressed by her recent bouts of helplessness and defeat. It now seemed to her as if other people or novel events were stealing her confidence. Brandy couldn't help but question if success was coming too easily these days. The challenge and love for writing still burned fiercely within her, but something was wrong. Brandy wasn't as carefree and happy as she should be; she wanted more from life and from herself.

With all power gone from the motor, Brandy had not even been able to move the stalled car from its precarious position in the center of the narrow, winding road. To alert any possible motorist of danger, she had opened all the doors. Once it had sufficiently cooled, she had also lifted the hood, then the trunk. Having taken all conceivable safety precautions, Brandy had sat down to await assistance.

It had not taken long for her to become acutely aware of the intolerable heat. Nor had it taken but moments to discover the empty water container in the car's roomy trunk. Numerous realities had quickly settled in on Brandy's astute mind: There was no water available, even though Lake Mead was only miles away; there was no comforting shade other than the minute amount offered by the car; the highway was now deserted; and it was only midday, hours until release from the heat and glare.

The chartered bus tours had made their scenic trips to this particular location as near to sunrise as possible. Most vacationers came to Las Vegas to gamble or to be entertained by extravagant shows, not to tour a deserted wasteland over thirty miles from town. At midday, all intelligent people were surely within air-conditioned enclosures! With luck, new tourists would show up at sunset, hours from now....

Time had passed at a snail's pace since her misfortune. At present Brandy was experiencing feelings of overwhelming solitude which were only natural for these harsh conditions. Leaf-green eyes scanned the rugged terrain which surrounded the car. In all honesty this portentous phenomenon of Mother Nature did provide the perfect panorama for *Twilight over Venus*. This site certainly did seem to be magically transplanted from another world.

Creosote bushes, naked yuccas, and assorted species of small cacti sparingly dotted the otherwise barren, hostile ground. There was not a single tree of any consequence within sight. The ground was covered by a mixture of rocks and gravel of varying sizes and in multiple shades of black and dull white. All except for those imposing dark red mountains surging upwards as if in brazen challenge to the heavens themselves.

This magnificent, uncanny range of peaks and valleys had given this site its more than accurate name. When the rising or setting sun touched those vermilion-colored hills, their surfaces burst into blazing life, as if angrily inflamed from the decades of battling the raw elements of wind, rain, and harsh temperatures. The alert eye could study the striated, pitted surfaces which attested to this merciless attack by the climate and elements, forces which had viciously lashed at their textures and fashioned them into weird or realistic shapes and images, an endless battle which had imbued this valley with an aura of mystery and haunting splendor.

Nervous laughter filled Brandy's chest as strange images and illusions flickered through her susceptible mind. Upon first sighting this area, Brandy had been awestruck by its wild beauty and fascinated by its unearthly presentation. Those craggy surfaces of dehydrated and baked russet clay appeared to be the mischievous works of some playful, alien giant. The shapes and facades had instantly reminded Brandy of the mud-drippings she had made as a child from the red clay that was so abundant in the South. The dying sun fondled those rusty contours with fiery fingers and stirred them to flaming life as if the Phoenix itself were imprisoned within them, fiercely struggling to be reborn. Brandy had been compelled to return again today with her camera and more film in order to capture the Valley's uncanny spell. Too, just standing in the midst of such sights created feelings of wonder and finiteness, and she needed to capture such moods and feelings on paper while experiencing them.

Feeling elated by this timely discovery of nature, she had not felt the slightest hesitation about returning here alone. She had always worked alone, denying the possibility of being influenced by another person's reactions to sights and sounds which she was researching for an upcoming novel. Strange, it almost seemed as if she had been irresistibly drawn back to this valley one more time....

Being a science-fiction author as well as writing in other genres, Brandy chuckled as she contemplated strange mental tuggings to this valley as if by some alien force, as in a recent movie concerning alien encounters. If this was some unearthly test of her mettle or courage, she hoped it would soon terminate. Brandy instantly cautioned herself against such silly dramatics and her overactive imagination, for this situation was very real and very frightening.

Since Brandy refused to wear a watch she had no accurate way of knowing what hour it was. She was annoyed and surprised that the Caddy didn't have a digital clock. However, judging from the sun's position and the season, she reasoned it to be around five o'clock. This being Brandy's first visit at this late hour, she had no way of knowing about the signs which warned against entering this secluded area too close to nightfall, nor could she know of the grounded helicopter which normally patrolled this area.

The heat and the lack of water had taken their toll upon her. By now, she had trouble concentrating upon the rapidly approaching sunset. In fact, she could not seem to think clearly or to focus her attention upon any mind-consuming idea. Brandy's thoughts flitted from one idea to the next like an industrious honey bee darting from one fragrant flower to another in its avid search for nectar. Her head was light and dizzy as if she had hastily consumed too much champagne.

When Brandy attempted to wipe the moisture which gathered on her upper lip and forehead, she thought it strange to find her fingers numb and tingly. A curious limpness washed over her, making movement difficult. She fervently wished her heart and pulse would cease their violent race with each other. Brandy mutely ordered the imaginary bees to move away from her ears and to halt their incessant humming. She had written about death and torment countless times, but she had never contemplated her own death. Just before she lost consciousness, Brandy wondered why it was becoming so dark and dreamy; she wondered if she was indeed dying.

As Steven Winngate topped the steep hill within visual distance of the black Cadillac which was unexpectedly parked in the middle of the highway, his mind was on his upcoming meeting with the executives of the development company he was planning to invest in if his conclusions about an expensive resort in this promising area were correct. A man who usually had several business deals going at one time, Steven was evaluating a future deal while concentrating on an imminent one. He had assumed he had time to check out this area before heading to his dinner meeting concerning a new oil lease and refinery. Sighting the peril before him, Steven struggled to shift gears and to maintain control of his sleek and powerful Harley-Davidson motorcycle. He made an urgent attempt to brake his speed and to halt before crashing into that car. The smell of scorching rubber flew upwards into the infuriated man's flaring nostrils. The ear-splitting screams of melting tires being eaten up by the hot, hungry pavement simultaneously pierced his ears.

Steven was relieved he had cautiously reduced his speed after topping that last hill on this snaking road. He gripped the clutch so hard that the knuckles on his left hand blanched white. His toes ached inside his expensive No-cona snakeskin boots as he rapidly shifted foot-gears and lowered his speed in a wild attempt to prevent his bike from leaving the blacktop road and helplessly tearing off across those cutting rocks, biting cacti, and devouring sands. Still, it would be better to risk the landscape than to collide with a parked car. Steven called upon all of his skill, determination, and brute strength to conquer this unexpected danger.

At last he brought his Harley-Davidson to a stop, within inches of the front bumper of the Cadillac. Unsuppressed fury and rapid breathing caused his nostrils to flare and his well-muscled body to stiffen. Steven angrily gritted his teeth as he jumped off of his motorcycle to challenge some idiot to a battle which might knock some sense into his stupid, reckless head. A booted foot kicked the parkstand down so forcefully that he almost overturned his huge machine. Ocean blue eyes were stormy and threatening as Steven swaggered towards the open door, fists clenched tightly.

Steven assumed this predicament was some childish prank or an ignorant action since the car had obviously not been wrecked or parked on the almost nonexistent shoulder of the highway. He leaned his towering six-feet-four-inch frame over to peer inside the car. The irate man's sole intent was to verbally, or possibly physically, attack its hare-brained occupant. Observing the eye-catching figure of what Steven considered to be a youthful female slumped over on the front seat, he cautioned himself to bring his volatile temper under some civil measure of control until he could analyze this puzzling situation which could have left him crippled.

"Miss? Are you sick?" his deep, resonant voice inquired. When there was no answer or movement, Steven lightly shook Brandy's left shoulder and called out to her again. Still no reaction.

Steven walked around the car and approached the front seat from the right side. When the woman made no attempt to respond, he leaned forward and pulled her limp body out of the steaming vehicle. He gently laid her upon the loose dirt beside the road, knowing the pavement was still full of heat from the day's sunning.

When Steven pushed wet amber hair from Brandy's flushed face and viewed it for the first time, he unknowingly stared into her arresting features which were stunningly surrounded by clingy curls the shade of aged brandy. A pleased gaze appreciatively scanned unblemished, golden skin. Long, lush lashes fanned out on her moist cheeks. She had a pert nose which was neither too small nor too large. Steven lifted one lid to peer into a forest green eye with flecks of yellow, enchanting eyes which reminded him of an exotic jungle cat. For a man who was finding himself too bored and restless these days, this unexpected predicament stimulated his senses. If it was thrills or challenges he needed to enliven and tantalize him, this adventure certainly presented them.

The intrigued man gave free rein to his perceptive mind. Even though this enticing creature was darkly tanned to a golden honey shade, he could easily make out the rosy flush upon her exquisite cheekbones. Her mouth was wide and full with a heartlike dip. Laughing sapphire eyes noted delicate creases around her mouth and eyes which hinted more at a sunny disposition rather than at marking her age, which he approximated at mid-twenties.

Being a handsome and wealthy bachelor who was incessantly pursued by females, Steven's eyes leisurely slid over the stirring figure of this unknown challenge. He assessed Brandy to be around five-feet-five-inches tall, probably weighing in at around one hundred and fifteen pounds, wet. Brandy possessed a supple and firm body, giving the impression of vitality and discretion, qualities which appealed to him.

Brandy's dark blue designer jeans boasted of a flat stomach and slender, shapely legs. Her tapered, poplin shirt with its bold hues of wildflower faces revealed her nicely rounded bustline. Brandy's flushed, yet ashen, features and clammy clothes and body informed the alert Steven of a mistakenly impulsive nature which had gotten her into this predicament.

A capricious grin flickered across Steven's face as he noted the white tennis shoes upon her feet. Somehow those snowy Adidas looked incongruous with her costly jeans and shirt, even more inconsistent with the expensive gold jewelry which she was wearing. He lifted her left hand to check out a nagging suspicion. There was no wedding band there, only an emerald and diamond dinner ring.

Steven shrugged his massive shoulders and decided this somewhat careless female was most appealing and nicely rounded in the right places. He lifted a smooth, graceful hand to check her rapid pulse, detecting the doughy feel of her flesh. He pulled her chest close to his alert ear to listen to her drumming heartbeat, enabling him to catch a whiff of a lingering fragrance which stirred his blood.

Steven noted the excessive dampness of her golden mane as he laid her head upon the ground. He was briefly baffled by her unconscious state. It didn't appear she was visibly injured, and she certainly had not been involved in a wreck. It looked as if she had suddenly halted her car and had fallen over on the seat. He worried when he could not arouse her. If she was drunk, she didn't give off any odor of liquor. If she was drugged, she had rashly overdone it. Feeling obligated to assist her, Steven berated her accidental intrusion into his tight schedule. He glanced at his watch. Fate couldn't have chosen a worse moment to attack this beauty.

Steven walked over to the car to solve this mystery. It was only a few moments before he located the broken hose and the empty radiator. He wondered if she had been left behind by some companion who had gone for help or if she had been traveling alone; either action was dangerous. It was also clear she had either consumed all of her emergency water or she had left town without any: another stupid mistake. Steven scolded himself for his irrational interest in this maiden in distress; he had enough clingy and hungry females pursuing him at present.

Steven Winngate sighed heavily in rising annoyance. He couldn't deny he was partially to blame for his troubles with the opposite sex. The problem was that he was weary of playing games with women who wanted more from him than he was willing to give or to sacrifice. A curious loneliness and restlessness were plaguing him these sultry days. He would admit he wanted a woman to share his life, one who loved and wanted Steve and not "The Steven Winngate." If the missing facet to his life was a compatible woman, why was it so impossible to locate one? He certainly had a lengthy line of conquests behind him. Why was it so annoying to have women drawn to his looks, prestige, and wealth? A self-made man with what he had to offer couldn't help but attract countless females. Now here was another feminine problem dumped into his lap and at a most inconvenient time.

A sensitive, strong-willed man like Steven Winngate couldn't just ride off and leave a helpless female out here alone and ill. Obviously she was suffering from heat exhaustion. Her car was out of commission, and she was sinking fast. In addition, there could be another victim out there somewhere seeking help, but possibly needing it more than she did. It was approaching time for his meeting. There was no way he could meet both obligations if he didn't get moving.

He cursed silently. There was only one humane choice; he would have to lay aside his business and pleasure to take this fetching, troublesome female back to Vegas to the hospital. She was vulnerable and beautiful.... He grinned devilishly. Perhaps she might find some appropriate way to express her appreciation to him for saving her life.

With luck, he might locate a highway patrolman to hand her over to within the first few miles. Steven reached inside the car and pushed the gear into neutral, then forcefully rolled the car off the side of the highway and pulled on the emergency blinkers. Until the battery gave out, that would offer some hint of the vehicle's hazardous location. The patrolman could send someone out to tow her car into town.

Just as a precautionary action, Steven gathered her possessions to lock them in the trunk of the Cadillac. He grinned as he picked up a pair of sporty, canvas sandals with a two-inch heel—shoes which were more harmonious with her obvious taste and status than the running shoes she was wearing. He noticed the camera and briefcase without placing any significance on either item. Steven casually flung her beige canvas shoulder bag into the trunk, without thinking to search it for her identity. However, his curiosity urged him to open the shimmering gold shopping bag which contained a size eight sensuous silk dress in muted shades of blue, green, and purple.

He closed the bag as images of how she would look in that stylish dress flickered in his mind, the fusion of shades perfect for her natural coloring. He slammed the trunk. Aware of the passage of time and his uncommon indecisiveness, Steven dropped the car key into his jeans pocket. He closed the car doors in order to remove the steady drain on the battery from the interior lights, energy the flashing lights would require.

As the towering man walked over to where Brandy lay, a new thought came into his already irritated mind: How could he carry an unconscious female back to town on his bike? Steven stalked over to glare down at her. Then he gathered her light body into his strong arms and headed for his bike.

Sturdy legs agilely straddled the motor in his light blue brushed denim jeans. He sat the girl before him, careful to keep her legs and ankles away from the hot engine and tail-pipe. He placed her left leg across his right thigh and her right leg over his left thigh. He removed his yellow ban-dana which served to entrap his perspiration as well as dress up his western attire. He bound her hands together and slipped them over his head, allowing them to rest around his narrow and firm waist where not an ounce of excess flesh was permitted to exist. The span of his muscular chest and the measured reach of her bound arms brought their heated bodies into close contact. Steven reached backwards and placed her feet within the saddlebags on either side of the back wheel. Steven knew he had no choice but to toss the metal tops off the road: He would worry about replacing the covers later. It was more important to prevent her feet from flaying wildly in the wind. With her secured tightly to his powerful body and her feet prevented from any dangerous mischief, they were ready to move out.

For the first time, Steven realized he had not even re-moved his indigo helmet. Needless to say, his mind had been elsewhere since this adventure began. Suddenly aware of how this confining setup might appear to curious eyes along the way, he quickly struggled to unbutton his sky blue denim shirt with its embroidered yellow designs on the front and back. He certainly did not want to draw any unnecessary attention to either of them. Another intruding newspaper or magazine article about him didn't sit well at all; he was weary of being publicly exploited. Even with his great wealth and power, he couldn't always protect his privacy, but he damn well gave it his best shot. A lazy grin raced across his enticing features as he recalled how he had solved the inva-sion of his privacy by his most troublesome and persistent intruder....

During his attempt to remove his shirt, Steven became acutely aware of Brandy's soft and curvaceous appeal. He grinned as he visually traced her multiple advantages, in-cluding a seductive figure, a mouth which invited searing kisses, exceptionally striking features which teased at a man's dreams, and a dainty chin which offered a hint of youthful mischief. Her skin mutely enticed caressing; her carefree mane the color of ripe wheat compelled fingers to wander freely through it. The admiring gaze waxed serious; Steven's frame grew taut as he caught his train of thought and recognized the discomforting strain upon his jeans. He demanded his logical mind to explain how an unconscious female could have such a potent effect on him. She was too attractive and compelling. No doubt she had broken quite a number of hearts! Women with such looks always used them without mercy!

He placed his denim shirt around her and secured the long sleeves behind his back. He blindly worked to hide her bound hands within its concealing folds. He sighed in relief, for now it would merely look as if she had fallen asleep or as if she was a totally unbridled spirit who was immodestly snuggling up to her lover! But what did he really care about the feelings and thoughts of total strangers? All that concerned him was his privacy and pride, and damn anyone who trampled on them.

The only problems he now faced were no helmet for her and the unknown length of her unconscious state. Of course it wouldn't matter if the police halted him for this precarious riding position or for her missing helmet. He would gratefully hand her over to someone else. The real danger lay in her coming to. If she suddenly awoke and started fighting with him, they could both be thrown from his bike. Still, he had to chance her rescue and get on to his waiting appointment before those impatient executives headed for their private Lear jet at the airport. One would think men accustomed to waiting months for an oil well to come in would learn some patience.

Steven lowered his face shield and kicked back the parkstand. Finding the correct gear with his right foot, he switched on the ignition and gripped the clutch with his left hand. The roar of the engine brought a smile to his sensual lips. Nothing pleased Steven more than a smooth-running, efficient piece of machinery which belonged to him. He pulled on the light switch and eased the motorcycle around. He gradually increased the gas intake to the engine and eased off so smoothly that Brandy didn't even shift an inch within his embrace, not that she could.

Along the snaking blacktop highway, Steven's keen eyes continually scanned the darkened roadside for evidence of a possible companion. If this woman had been traveling with someone, her companion could have gone in the opposite direction towards Lake Mead. As soon as he came into contact with help, Steven would notify the authorities of this strange situation and of her abandoned car.

If one could be grateful for small favors, Steven was extremely pleased with the illuminating full moon which was climbing over the mountains. It was dark now and the heat of the day had become less demanding. They journeyed for miles with the arid breeze nipping at their bodies. Soon, Steven was forced to halt the motorcycle in order to confine her tawny curls within her shirt to prevent their whipping into his line of vision and endangering their safety. He savored the feel of her hair as he imprisoned it.

As he steadied the bike with his strong legs, he berated himself for a stupid oversight. He reached around her and retrieved his water bottle. He forced the thin spout between her lips and then squeezed on the bottle. Most of the tepid water dribbled from the corners of her mouth, but he saw that she was instinctively swallowing some of the lukewarm water. He did this several times until she moaned softly and snuggled up to his hard chest as an injured child to a parent. A curious feeling of protectiveness washed over him, one which warmed him.

Even though the woman had not awakened, Steven knew he had helped her in a small way. He moistened her lips, then replaced his water bottle. He checked her confines and rested her damp face against his light blue, V-neck T-shirt. He unknowingly hugged her tightly. In some mysterious way, he almost felt as if she now belonged to him for all time. Didn't the Chinese have an old saying about if you saved a life you owned it? He eased off once again.

They had traveled for thirty-three miles before he spotted a patrol car just up ahead of them. Steven fed his engine more gas as he hastily attempted to catch up with the car which was beginning to pull away from them. He blinked his headlight time and time again to attract their attention. He pressed his horn with his right thumb. At last the officers seemed aware of his motives and slowed down. Finding a safe location, the patrol car eased off the side of the highway.

Steven pulled over as soon as he was even with them. He turned off his engine to be easily heard and understood. "I've got a problem for you. I found this girl in the Valley of Fire. I don't know how long she's been out. I was taking her to the hospital in town, but you fellows could do it faster. Her car's abandoned beside the road back there: broken hose to the radiator. I left the lights on as a warning, but the battery will be drained pretty soon. I locked her things in the trunk. I've got the key in my pocket."

Steven reached behind him and yanked the shirt from around their joint bodies. He ducked as he pulled her bound hands over his head. He lifted her feet from the metal saddlebags and let them hang free across his legs. Suspicious eyes observed both him and the captive girl.

"Here, take her. She's your problem now. I'm already late for an important meeting as it is," he stated impatiently, the rosy illusion over now and feeling a curious denial which he didn't understand.

The Nevada patrolmen had slowly and cautiously gotten out of their car. Both men studied this arrogant man who was issuing orders like a commanding officer. This was a domineering man and an odd situation which demanded closer scrutiny.

"Not so fast, mister! Who is she? What's your name?" the first officer questioned. He was a big, burly man who brooked no foolishness or intimidation, and positively didn't like inexplicable events like this one.

"How should I know who she is? Never laid eyes on her till she nearly caused me to wreck my bike out there. I came over a hill, and there she was. Stalled right in the middle of the road. Dumb blondes! Since her car was out, I brought her along with me. For all I know, there might've been somebody with her. Seems crazy for a woman like this to be out there alone. I didn't see anyone on my way in, but he could have headed towards Lake Mead—especially if he's a stranger to these parts. Wouldn't hurt to check it out," he advised the two startled men.

"If you don't mind, we'll ask the questions," the indignant officer tersely stated.

"Go right ahead, officer, but please make it snappy. As I said, I'm late for a meeting. This little vixen's already been a load of trouble. I'd be delighted for you to take her off my hands."

"You claim you don't know who she is?" one officer skeptically asked. "You just happened on her out there?"

"That's absolutely correct!" Steven snarled, aware of their doubts and his swiftly fleeing time.

"Where's her purse, her driver's license?" the second man joined in on the irritating interrogation.

"I told you before, I locked her things in the trunk of her car. I didn't think about bringing her purse or ID. She looked in pretty bad shape, so I tossed her on my bike and headed out. I suggest you get her to the hospital in a hurry."

Before the man could reply, Steven cunningly transferred his enticing burden into the second officer's arms. The speechless bachelor gazed into her lovely face. He caught himself before whistling his appreciation of her beauty, but failed to conceal the hungry look within his wide eyes, an offensive reaction Steven didn't like.

"Hold on here a minute. Who are you? How do we know you didn't harm her in some way? Is she drunk? On drugs?"

the first man queried, knowing how it would appear on his record if he allowed a criminal to slip through his fingers.

Steven sighed in annoyance and frustration. "I was only doing a good deed for some female in distress. I have no idea what's wrong with her. I assumed it was heatstroke. I haven't laid a finger on her except to help her," he stated as politely as possible considering his turbulent state of mind and the officers' subtle implications.

"Let me see your license," the first officer demanded.

"Come on, now; I'm late," Steven argued, reluctant to divulge his identity, knowing the media would find this episode amusing.

"The license," the officer insisted, piqued by Steven's smug manner and odd behavior. This muscular rogue wouldn't be released until he was convinced of his claims.

Steven angrily withdrew his wallet and pulled out his card. He handed it to the offensive man who was delaying his progress now that he had completed his duty to mankind. He watched the officer's eyes narrow with suspicion and flicker with alertness. The first man held it up for the other one to scan. The two men locked gazes following their intense study of the man before them and the card in the officer's tight grip.

"Says here you're Steven Winngate. Funny, you don't look like no oil millionaire to me. Got any other proof of your identity? Did you steal this license from Mr. Winngate?" the man scoffed doubtfully, recognizing the name on the imprinted card.

"All the cards in my wallet carry the same name: mine. Just what is an oil man supposed to look like?" Steven snapped in rising aggravation at this ridiculous delay. How dare these men question him like a common criminal!

The second officer injected, "What's she doing all tied up like this? You calling off some joke or kidnapping plot?"

"This is absurd!" Steven stormed. "I've never seen her before in my life. If I was guilty of some crime, would I simply ride up and hand her over to two policemen?" Steven didn't realize that the first officer had just noticed the Colt .38 special wedged into his boot, the snubnose pistol he always carried for protection. He had removed it from the saddlebag to avoid it being bounced out of the open container.

Sighting the weapon, the first officer cautiously drew his gun, intimidated by the towering man before him, painfully recalling when Lieutenant Starnes recently lost his life when responding to an "officer needs help" call. He was also aware that his partner's hands were full, while this man's were now free. He leveled the .357 Magnum on the shocked Steven and softly warned, "Just take it easy until we can check out you and your wild story. Cliff, put the girl in the backseat. Be sure she's really out. See if she has any weapons or ID on her. Then handcuff this man. His tale is a little curious to me. Steven Winngate, huh? After we leave her at the hospital, we'll check out your ID."

"You must be kidding!" Steven angrily exploded. "If you dare to arrest me, you'll be making a terrible mistake! I told you, I've never seen her before tonight. I should've left her out there and called in her location from my hotel! As for her being tied up, how else could I hold her on the bike with me?" he growled, alerting the two men to his dangerous fury. Steven's whirling mind was tallying the cost of this good deed; if he failed to show up within the next hour, he would lose an oil option which would cost him five hundred thousand dollars! No impulsive female was worth that much money. He suddenly wondered if he was being intentionally delayed; after all, the impending deal was worth millions.

"There ain't no need for your smart mouth! If you're telling the truth, you'll be free to go in a little while. If not...." He allowed his silence and tone to slide out meaningfully, clearly doubting Steven's words. The officer had concluded the stranger was much too tense to be trusted, but he didn't mention the partially concealed weapon until his partner's hands were free. Besides, what would a man like

Winngate be doing riding a motorcycle in the middle of nowhere? Winngate was alleged to be one of the wealthiest men alive, a man who had a Midas touch where oil was involved.

They debated for a few more minutes as the second officer put Brandy in the backseat and lightly frisked her for hidden weapons. He pulled out his sharp knife and cut the bandana from her wrists. He stuffed it into his pocket, perhaps as evidence. He returned to his partner's side to handcuff the reluctant, furious man.

Steven was outraged when the first officer ordered him to place his hands on top of his head, but complied when he realized how serious the man was. The officer then told his partner to take Steven's weapon from his boot. Steven was firmly shoved against the car and frisked for other weapons, much to his astonishment and fury. "I have a permit for that gun!" he shouted angrily at this treatment. "It's in my wallet."

"Only if you're really Winngate," the officer sneered. "Cuff him." With that, Steven Winngate was placed in handcuffs.

It didn't help matters when Steven refused to explain his confidential trip into the Valley of Fire or his critical meeting tonight. He vowed to make these two bumbling officers—and the female who had inspired this trouble—rue this day.

The first man had to forcefully guide the hot-tempered Steven to the car and to shove him into the backseat with Brandy. Steven fumed when Brandy slumped against his shoulder. He mentally determined to make all three of these people pay for this humiliating invasion of his privacy and this unforgivable attack upon his masculine pride: all because he had played the Good Samaritan! Right now, Steven's mental wrath was directed at the woman next to him.

The officer radioed ahead to the hospital to inform them of their arrival with a possible heatstroke victim. They also notified another patrol car to check out Steven's story about her car and her accident. After asking Steven several questions, the officer fed his description and those answers over the radio to be checked out by the sergeant on duty.

By the time they reached the Las Vegas Hospital, both men were profusely apologizing to the impatient prisoner in the backseat. After turning Steven over to the hospital officials and answering their countless questions about her, Steven was driven back to his hotel. The second officer hopped out the moment the car halted to open the door for a surly Steven.

Both men pleaded forgiveness for their gross error in judgment. "Sorry, Mr. Winngate. We had no way of knowing you spoke the truth. Men like you ride around in fancy limousines with chauffeurs, not alone in the desert on some motorcycle! Can't blame us for doubting your word. You were carrying a gun and acting mighty strange. If we can be of any assistance to you, don't hesitate to call on us," the first officer stated as he shifted nervously beneath Steven's frigid glare.

Bringing his temper under reasonable control in order to extract a favor from these two men, he smiled genially and declared, "There is one favor you two can do for me. I would greatly appreciate it if you could record one Lance Reynolds as the man who rescued that damsel in distress this afternoon. A man can't be too careful with his reputation and privacy. I wouldn't like the media to get wind of this little fiasco. Do you follow my drift? Publicity? Golddiggers?"

"As far as the records go, Lance Reynolds assisted some stranger in the Valley of Fire this afternoon. You can bet me and my partner won't mention your name to anybody! We'll keep this little incident a secret between us. There's a service bringing in her car right now. By midnight, we'll know who she is and why she was out there. Appreciate your understanding, sir. I'll have your bike delivered tomorrow," he promised with a smile.

"Excellent. And if you gentlemen ever need a favor, don't fail to contact me. In case you talk to that young lady, don't reveal my real name to her either. I have enough females chasing after my money now," he said with a lazy chuckle. He keenly noted the phony smile upon Cliff's face and recalled how this officer had eyed the unconscious goddess.

The patrolmen returned to their car and pulled out. A well-dressed man rushed from the hotel lobby. Steven's sapphire eyes locked on his longtime friend and business partner. It was obvious Brent was sorely distressed, but Brent was always uptight when so much money was involved.

"Where the hell have you been, Steve? I've been at my wit's end to keep those men here until I could locate you! This deal's too big to blow. We have exactly twenty minutes left on that option," Brent Hartley said anxiously; he was the only man who dared to address Steven Winngate in such a bold manner.

Steven laughed before exclaiming, "If I told you, old buddy, you'd never believe it! Just call me Sir Lancelot in the future," he playfully murmured as he headed into the plush hotel for the long-awaited meeting in his rented penthouse, thoughts of the lovely stranger lost for the present.

Chapter Two

"BP, one-thirty over ninety-five.... Respiration, shallow and rapid...heart rate, one hundred b/p/m... Temp., one-oh-four point three.... Pupils dilated, but responsive. EKG readout, normal. EEG readout, normal," came the nurse's report on Brandy's vital readings and tests.

"Call it sunstroke; no, list heatstroke. She isn't sun-burned. Let's lower her body temp. with iced water dips every four hours. When her temp. drops to one-oh-two, start cooling her with wet sheet wraps. See that she gets massages, especially in those hands and feet. Put her on a normal saline solution at two hundred cc an hour. If you spot any infection or loss of circulation anywhere, notify the staff doctor STAT! All we can do is replace those salts and fluids as quickly and carefully as possible."

Dr. Adam Ross turned to the nurse and questioned, "Any word on her identity? We need to know if she has any medical problems or allergies." Adam's hooded eyes furtively eased over Brandy again.

"None yet, Doctor. The patrolman said they would forward that information as soon as they get it."

Dr. Ross gave this enchanting case more thought. Grinning with open pleasure, he issued new orders, "Place my name on her chart. Notify me if there's any change at all, or if she comes to before I complete my rounds. When that officer calls in, have me paged." It just wouldn't be proper to turn such a pretty female over to a mere staff doctor, he smugly mused to himself. Noting the looks which were exchanged between the head nurse and the nosey student nurse, he glared a warning to them. He stalked out of the emergency room like some pompous penguin, ignoring the fact that his last problem was with a lovely female patient whom he had pursued.

"Hold still, miss, or you'll yank the I.V. loose!" came a stern command into Brandy's hazy brain. "Just a few more minutes and I'll get you out of there. You're lucky; your temperature is returning to normal quicker than expected. Just relax, dearie." The voice softened noticeably.

"Re...lax?" Brandy argued weakly. "I'm fr-fr-freezing. What hap...pened? Where...am I?" she stammered amidst confusion and through chattering teeth.

"You're in the Las Vegas hospital. You're suffering from heatstroke. This ice water dip will lower your fever and put some fluid back into your body. There's an I.V. in your left arm, so try to hold as still as possible," she calmly advised.

Thoughts clearing some, Brandy inquired, "How did...I get...here? The last thing I remember...was that dreadful heat out there."

"Some passing motorist found you and brought you in; a Lance Reynolds, I believe. A few more hours and you'd have been in deep trouble," she absently remarked as she checked the connection to the I.V. tubing. She wanted to make sure the girl had not jerked it loose during her thrashing.

"Lance Reynolds?" she repeated, the name meaning nothing to her.

"That's right, honey. A real handsome devil from what I saw. Too bad you were unconscious," she jested to relax the ailing, shaking girl. "What's your name? Reynolds forgot to bring your purse or I.D. along. The state patrolmen are on their way to bring in your car and belongings."

"Katherine Alexander," came the normal reply to a stranger.

"Any medical problems or allergies, Miss Alexander? It is miss, isn't it? There's no wedding ring on your finger."

"Miss. No problems that...I know about. How long...have I b-been here?" she asked as her teeth chattered noisily. She suddenly shuddered violently, sending water and ice over the edge of the short, shallow tub.

"About forty-five minutes or so. What's your address?" the nurse continued with her own line of questions and notations.

"Box three ninety-one, London, Kentucky," she politely replied, waiting for the woman to complete her records before asking any more questions.

"Where's London, Kentucky? Never heard of it."

"It's about midway be-between Lexington and Knoxville...very small and quiet. Wh-what time is it?" she inquired, looking around the windowless room.

The nurse glanced at her watch, then stated, "Near ten."

"Ten o'clock! But you sa-said I had only been here less than an hour! You m-mean I've been unconscious all that time?" she asked, fretting about being handled by total strangers while almost dead to the world.

"That's right, honey," came the less than comforting answer. "Now, I have to notify Dr. Ross that you're awake. He was put on your case when they brought you in." The distraught female was too upset to notice the caustic tone in the nurse's voice when she mentioned Ross's name. For the life of her, Nurse Densely couldn't imagine how that obnoxious, lecherous man kept his medical license! If he wasn't acting like the greatest doctor in the world, he was chasing anything in a skirt!

Brandy glanced down at the white hospital gown which was nearly transparent in its soaked state. Horror filled her at being further exposed to strange eyes, masculine eyes. What did she care if he was a doctor! She instantly argued with that intention, "Couldn't I dry off and get into another gown f-first? This one is mighty revealing in this condition. Besides, I'm c-cold. Please..." she shyly entreated.

The nurse chuckled knowingly and smiled. In an attempt to irritate the arrogant, hateful Dr. Ross, Mrs. Densely grinned and complied. She helped the shaky Brandy out of the tub. Before Brandy could argue with her next intention, the nurse had hastily removed the dripping gown. Brandy realized it had not even been over her left arm, merely held in place with a long strip of surgical tape. She flushed with embarrassment at her nude state, fearing someone would enter at any moment.

"Careful of the water, dearie," the nurse calmly warned. "We wouldn't want you to slip and break a leg or an arm." She quickly toweled off Brandy's shiny, bumpy flesh, then guided her over to an examination table. "Can you make it okay? Hold on to me," she told the shaky Brandy.

Brandy sat on the edge of the padded table while the nurse helped her into another hospital gown, a medium blue one this time. Unable to pass the left sleeve over her I.V. tubing, she simply ran one tie beneath Brandy's left arm and secured it to the other one behind her back. She tucked the loose sleeve into the empty armhole.

"Where are my panties?" Brandy asked with a modest tone to her muted voice, her face a rosy red. It was surprising how naked she felt without panties.

The nurse sighed indulgently. She went to the cabinet and brought out a roll of white tape. She pulled off a long strip to secure the back of the hospital gown to prevent its gaping view of a shapely derriere. "That's the best I can do for you now. Your clothes were drenched. We sent them downstairs to the laundry."

"Thank you. What now?" Brandy asked apprehensively, starting to warm up a little. A blue sheet was placed over her lower body.

"Dr. Ross will need to check you over again. He can answer any other questions you might have. You lie down while I change your I.V. bottle. Try to relax and rest."

A trembling Brandy promptly obeyed her orders. Before she began another task, Mrs. Densley went to the wall phone and had the doctor paged. When he answered, she stated in a professional tone, "The female patient in emergency is conscious now, sir." She listened to his orders and remarks, then gave a succinct, "Yes, Doctor. I'll see to it." Smirking visibly, she hung up.

She returned to Brandy's side. She silently took Brandy's vital readings and recorded them upon the chart she was holding. Too feeble and weary to converse with the domineering, but gentle, nurse, Brandy meekly did as she was told. As the nurse finished her tasks, the wall phone signaled a call.

Mrs. Densley answered it. She only listened to the voice on the other end for a moment or two before stating, "The patient has already regained consciousness and given us that information." She listened patiently for a few more minutes, then replied, "You'll have to ask the doctor when you can speak with her. She's very weak and confused at present." She listened once again, then commented, "That's fine, sir. Good-bye."

She came over to Brandy's side and smiled warmly. "I thought you might prefer some time to clear your head and wits before those officers rush in here with a thousand questions."

Brandy returned her smile. "Thank you, Mrs. —"

"Densley. Emily Densley. I'm certain you've been through quite a scary ordeal today. A little time to think and rest can't halt the wheels of justice too long," she teased jovially.

"You're very kind and helpful, Mrs. Densley."

Brandy anxiously awaited the arrival of the doctor whom Mrs. Densley so obviously disliked. She did not have to linger for very long. He swooped into the brightly lit room like a hangglider coming in for an artistic landing. He flashed her a smile which was anything but genial or professional. Brandy relaxed just enough to give him a wan one in return. Her alert eyes read the navy blue lettering upon his stark white jacket which proclaimed his identity and lofty status.

Adam Ross asked for Brandy's new readings. The arrogant tinge to his voice could hardly be missed. Yet, he grinned mischievously as he ordered the confident Mrs. Densely to ready her for an examination. "Looks as if your blood pressure, pulse rate, and temperature are gradually returning to normal, Miss Alexander. Excellent. The chart indicates no medical allergies or problems.... The EKG and EEG appear to be normal. Any difficulty breathing? Any pain or numbness anywhere?" he inquired as he listened to her heart from several locations on her upper back. "Take a deep breath. Now, let it out slowly.... Again, please...." She only nodded in reply to his queries.

When Dr. Ross moved to the front of her chest, Brandy quickly averted her eyes from his piercing ones. "Mrs. Densley, kindly remove the tape from her gown. I need to listen to her heart." His tone was pleasant, but his eyes hinted at his dislike of this particular nurse.

Mrs. Densley came forward and gently removed the tape from Brandy's backside. She told Brandy to lie down on her back. The gown was lowered to her slim waist and a white towel was placed over her bare breasts. As the doctor moved the cold, flat surface of his stethoscope between her breasts and then under the left one, her face grew redder and redder. Her cheeks burned with the force of her embarrassment, knowing she was totally nude beneath that flimsy sheet. She glued her eyes to the ceiling panels and focused her attention upon guessing images from the varying sizes and shapes of the holes within their rough texture.

Time crawled by and the study continued. Thinking this examination was taking much too long, Brandy risked a glance at his face. Sure enough, his expression said he was concentrating upon anything except her rapid heartbeat. He seemed amused by the scarlet flush upon her neck and upper chest. His eyes were leisurely scanning any area of her slender, golden body that was visible to his wide gaze. Suffused with modesty and anger, Brandy gave a loud and meaningful, "Ah-hem...."

The doctor glanced up at her crimson face and challenging eyes. He easily noted her open annoyance with him. His blue eyes twinkled at her unspoken, but clear, accusation. He casually replaced the towel across her bosom and turned to make some notations upon her chart. He then proceeded to ask her many questions about herself, her solitary trip into the Valley of Fire, and her condition as it had progressed during the day. Brandy didn't question her instant dislike of this man, but something about him struck a note of discord within her sensitive nature.

Brandy answered each question fully or partially, according to how much information she felt the overly curious doctor was entitled to know. She had already decided this man would not be the one to handle her case if it was necessary for her to remain in this hospital; that is, if there was any civil way to get around him. For all she knew, he could be the chief-of-staff! How she wished she was home and under the kindly, gentle supervision of Dr. Crowley and his adorable Nurse Gimble.

Knowing the reaction she would no doubt receive from this kind of man if he learned of her identity, she did not tell him her occupation or her motive for her fateful trip into the nearby desert. She had met his type many times in the past: overbearing, egotistical, aggressive playboys. She had always been wary of men who discovered her real identity— and with good reason. Many of them placed her in the role of one of her heroines or boldly placed themselves in the role of one of her romantic heroes, assuming they could become her dream-man in reality and enchant her into mindless submission. It was easy to detect Dr. Ross's exaggerated opinion of himself, physically and professionally. Even blindness couldn't have concealed his meaningful tone of voice, inviting expressions, and brazen touches. Didn't he realize he was on duty and she was an injured patient? This man definitely fit the pattern for men who believed romance writers were hotblooded, carefree nymphomaniacs who supplied their fantasies in black and white.

She had always found it more relaxing and less demanding if she presented herself as Katherine Alexander, breeder of thoroughbred Appaloosas on a ranch in Kentucky, until they could become better acquainted. While totally true, it prevented many misunderstandings and claims upon her time and her attention. In all fairness to the male sex, these rules usually applied to unknown females as well. She had learned long ago that Katherine Alexander could slip into a cordial group far more easily than Brandy was allowed to do....

She began to edge some of her own questions in between his, a fact which annoyed him. Why, she couldn't determine. He seemed to prefer being the master of any situation, and he didn't take to her being assertive.

"Just a few more questions, Miss Alexander, then you can rest. I was hoping to be able to supply the patrolmen with enough information to leave you alone for a few days," he informed her. "In my opinion, you'll need bed rest for a full week. We'll replenish your salts and fluids gradually. Heatstroke interferes with the body's heat regulation center in the central nervous system. It usually requires about a week to properly restore the body's sweating process," he remarked, hoping to impress this female with his abilities and knowledge.

"I see," she replied softly. "May I make a few phone calls before I'm put to bed for the night? I'll need to alert the hotel to my accident, so they'll hold my room and possessions." That statement sparked another thought. "You did say the police were bringing in the car?"

"That's right," he casually agreed.

"Could you please have them bring me the things I left in it? Also, I'll need to notify the rental agency about the car trouble." Oddly, her thoughtfulness and intelligence irritated him further, which also chafed Brandy. He was getting her subtle messages of discouragement, and was reacting as expected.

"You can take care of those business matters in the morning. Right now, your health and rest are more important. Mrs. Densley, would you see to a room for Miss Alexander? I'll see you in the morning, Miss Alexander," he commented, then hesitated briefly. "Is there any family who should be notified tonight?" he unexpectedly asked.

Too exhausted to discuss any touchy matter at this late hour, Brandy simply shook her head no and said, "Thank you, Dr. Ross. I'll see you in the morning."

Surprisingly his tight expression softened slightly. His blue eyes glowed warmly for a moment. Before he was out of the door, she called out, "Doctor, is the man who found me still here?"

Miffed, he scoffed, "He left right after dropping you off. I'm positive the police have his name and address if you're still interested in the morning."

"I would like to thank him for assisting me. After all, he did save my life, or so you said earlier. Thank you once again, Dr. Ross. Good night."

The nurse called for a stretcher to come and take Brandy to her assigned room. After settling Brandy in that sterile, depressingly colorless room, the nurse checked her I.V. and bid her a sunny good night.

Brandy only hesitated a few minutes after Mrs. Densley's departure before reaching for the bedside phone. She asked the hospital operator to connect her with her hotel. After informing them of her recent accident, she asked them to hold her room until further notice. She also asked if there was someone who could pack a few of her personal belongings and deliver them to her in the morning, with ample payment of course. The hotel manager quickly consented, well aware of who Miss Brandy Alexander was. Knowing it was too late to call Casey in New York or the rental agency in Vegas, she postponed those two calls until morning.

She made a mental note to contact the police for information about her gallant rescuer and for knowledge of her things which had been left in the Cadillac. Exhausted, but pleased with her success and survival, she closed her burning eyes and went to sleep.

Muted noises and muffled voices aroused Brandy that next day. She stirred and attempted to sit up. Feeling like a limp dishcloth, she promptly lay back down. It was not long before she heard a cheery "Good morning, Miss Alexander."

Brandy turned instantly and glanced up at the unfamiliar nurse who was standing near her bed. She murmured a polite, "Good morning." This woman had a sunny, easy disposition, a youthful, pleasing face with a radiant smile and laughing hazel eyes. Brandy liked the way this nurse encouraged a person to feel calm and happy, an enviable trait.

The nurse silently took her temperature, blood pressure, and pulse rate. She marked these numbers upon a pad in her hand. She then changed the almost empty saline bottle. She gently lifted Brandy's left arm and studied the connection to make sure it had not been dislodged during the night. She smiled again, her eyes lucid and sincere.

"Dr. Ross will be in to see you in about an hour. Do you feel up to breakfast this morning?" she inquired, her tone laced with a heavy western drawl.

"Only some juice and coffee if that's all right. I don't normally eat breakfast."

"Fine, Miss Alexander. Fluids are what you really need right now. You should try to consume as much liquid as possible for the next few days," she advised the steadily calming Brandy.

"Why do I ache all over?" Brandy asked about the annoying soreness in her whole body. She felt as if she had been put through the wringer, every inch of her body fussing.

"That's a common reaction to dehydration. You'll feel weak and sore for about a week. Your body received a big shock. Let's just say it's making your abuse of it loudly known to you. Any pains anywhere? Hands? Feet? Chest?"

"None. Has the hotel delivered my suitcase yet?"

"I'll check when I return to the desk. If not, I'll bring it to you when it arrives."

"That's very kind of you. I must admit I feel rather like a fool for permitting such a dangerous accident. The desert is certainly no place for a Kentucky greenhorn," she remarked with a musical laugh.

Taking an instant liking to this fragile but resilient girl, the nurse smiled once again. "I'll have some juice and coffee sent in. If you need anything before I return, just buzz."

Later, Brandy was slowly sipping another serving of fresh orange juice and steaming, delicious coffee. It soothed her sore throat to some extent. She had made her call to Casey, telling her not to worry about her and promising to keep her informed of her progress and condition. Brandy had decided not to call the police just yet. They would no doubt be in to see her later; she could inquire into the identity of one Lance Reynolds at that time.

She sighed lightly. Lance Reynolds.... What a romantic, strong name. Rosy visions danced across her imaginative mind. Rescued just like one of her heroines. How very exciting and unique. She sighed dramatically and frowned. She would be sorely disappointed if he was only seventeen or perhaps fifty with a balding pate and beer-gut. Brandy hastily chided herself; a timely rescue didn't require a handsome and mysterious rogue!

The hotel did send her suitcase over to her as promised. It contained the necessary items for a more comfortable and attractive stay. When Dr. Ross came in, she was just leaving her bathroom. After the nurse had disconnected her I.V. Brandy had bravely denied her lingering weakness long enough to brush her teeth, to wash up, and to change into one of her own gowns: a becoming satin one, in a soft shade of celadon, grecian in style.

The combination of golden tan, milk-white teeth, celadon gown, forest-green eyes, and amber hued tresses which fell loosely around her bare shoulders and tossed in casual layers on the top and sides presented her as the stunning illusion of a Greek goddess. That particular gown not only enhanced her figure but also complimented her coloring.

As she exited the bathroom, she nearly collided with Ross. A look of disbelief and undisguised interest traveled his hawkish features before he could prevent it. His gaze swept over her flawless complexion, scanty attire, her startled green eyes, and tawny mane within a few brief seconds... as did that of the towering man just a few steps behind him.

After a gasp of surprise, her jungle-green gaze instantly passed over Ross to fuse with the hypnotic sea-blue one of the most visually arresting man she'd ever seen. Unable to think clearly, she simply stared at him, her bare feet seemingly glued to the floor. For all she knew or saw, Dr. Adam Ross had suddenly become invisible or nonexistent! She was slowly drowning in those powerful pools of blue, and she didn't even care. There were no such things as time and reality. Little creases edged those potent blue orbs as a sensual grin lazily pulled his lips towards his left jawline. A flicker of astonishment was unhurriedly replaced by undeniable pleasure and amusement.

Brandy was rudely snatched back to cold reality by the formal tone of Adam Ross. "I should have knocked first, Miss Alexander; I didn't realize you weren't dressed. Besides, you shouldn't be out of bed without my permission," he boldly reprimanded her, irrationally vexed by her reaction to the virile man with him. So much for his social plans for her after her release.... Women, he mentally sneered, always pushovers for looks and money! He hurriedly warned himself to tread lightly with this female and this precarious situation; he couldn't afford another black mark.

Brandy's lovely face flushed a deep scarlet at his discourteous chiding before another man, and such a man! The rosy color quickly escaped her face and raced down her golden chest. "Yes, Dr. Ross; you should have knocked before entering a lady's room. I wasn't expecting any visitors since I don't know anyone here in Vegas," she informed him. Since she was confined to a hospital bed, how *should* she be dressed?

Brandy lifted the matching green robe from the bed and began to struggle into it. Before she could do so, the other man instantly came forward and gallantly assisted her. Confused by her magnetic attraction to this total stranger, she flushed again as she stammered a gracious "thank you." Weak and shaky from her exertion, she sat down upon the bed and clutched the edges of the robe tightly together.

She wondered if this magnificent creature was another doctor or if he might be a state patrolman who had come to question her about the accident. His manner of dress told her nothing. She had great difficulty pulling her wayward eyes and straying attention from him as she attempted to converse with the impertinent Ross.

"Who removed your I.V.? I left distinct orders for you to receive five bottles. The chart shows only three given so far," he was saying, needlessly throwing around his weight. Damn, he was tired of people changing his orders and treating him as if he were some offensive disease. Half of the staff here would be delighted to see him tossed out of the medical field. Maybe he should go into private practice; he'd had it with the politics and pressures in hospitals!

Brandy warily eyed the stocky, offensive man before her. She held out her bruised, injured left arm and stated, "The tape stuck to the sheet and jerked the needle loose. The nurse went to bring another connection, I believe she called it. I took advantage of the brief freedom from tubes and needles in order to bathe and put on one of my own gowns, if you don't object, Doctor. After all, your hospital garb is most lacking in looks and in privacy." Brandy focused her attention on Ross, contemplating his nasty manner and unethical conduct. Didn't he realize she could report him for his brazen behavior? Did he even care? More to the point, why was Ross so hateful to her? Everything she said or did appeared to offend or challenge him.

The lazy chuckle from the other man brought her attention back to him. His intensely blue eyes were filled with genuine amusement. His perfectly straight teeth were stark white against his bronzed, irresistibly compelling features. His midnight black hair was vital and full; one thick wave fell over his right temple with just the right hint of wind-blown intrigue which invited feminine hands to stroke it.

His vibrant red crêpe de chine, custom-tailored shirt failed to conceal the virile physique with its snug, vivid confines; in fact, it boasted loudly of the solid, well-developed muscles and brute strength beneath it. Wisps of curly black hair peaked out around the edges of the neckline which had been intentionally left unbuttoned, boldly showing a provocative expanse of a manly chest which caused chills of excitement and fascination to race over Brandy's entire body. His slim hips and firm, long legs were encased in navy blue straight-legged slacks. His camel-colored blazer completed his dashing, intoxicating image. It should be a crime for any man to look like this! She shifted uneasily as she thought: *How would this hunk of manly charm look naked?* Shocked, she hastily dismissed that train of imagination.

Brandy's gaze helplessly eased down his massive shoulders to the thick biceps which declared him to be either a rugged outdoorsman or an extremely active sportsman. No athlete could be in better shape or form! He was easily six-feet-four inches tall. He reeked of self-assurance, charisma, polish, and arrogance. His dark blue eyes possessed that heady mixture of mystery, enticement, and allure. His was clearly a personality that definitely ruled its own destiny and perhaps the fates of many other people—certainly numerous women. Brandy struggled to vanquish the irrational jealousy which oozed through her. He was magnificent and utterly bedazzling.

Brandy hastily decided he was the most attractive, beguiling man she had ever seen. She could not suppress a smile as she mentally added the final touches to her brazen, intense scrutiny: He was the epitome of every hero in her many novels; he was the image which comprised the daydreams of countless women, including herself; he was the very pinnacle of manhood. Perhaps too perfect... She inwardly dreaded to discover the flaws this delightful stranger surely possessed, as all men did.

"Miss Alexander is absolutely correct, Dr. Ross; your hospital gowns are sadly lacking in every way. How do you feel this morning?" the deep, mellow voice lazily drawled in an accent she found captivating, one whose power and depth caused her heart to flutter wildly. If possible, his tone was a mixture of midwestern and Welsh, a sexy combination if there ever was one! His sensual smile left her temporarily speechless as she absorbed its warmth and pull.

"Better, thank you," she finally managed. Unable to be denied his identity and purpose any longer, she asked, "Who are you?"

Before he could answer her, Ross hastily did so. "This is Lance Reynolds, the man who found you yesterday. He wanted to see how you were before I examined you again," he stated, as if trying to insinuate some suggestive point to her handsome cavalier. "As you can see, Mr. Reynolds, she's in fine hands. If you will excuse us, I am in quite a rush this morning."

Ignoring the doctor, Brandy stared at the playful smile upon her rescuer's soft, full, sensual mouth. Her own lips curled up into a natural, dazzling smile; her emerald eyes softened and glowed warmly. It was nerve-shattering to imagine herself being carried and held in that enticing embrace.

"I was hoping to have the opportunity to properly thank you for your help yesterday. If they're right, you saved my life. I must admit it was a most harrowing experience," she confessed, her voice as soft as a summer breeze.

"Someone should have warned you not to venture into the desert without an escort and certainly not without an adequate supply of water," he gently chided her, recalling the stern lecture he had planned and rehearsed countless times; that was, until he had gazed into those bewitching eyes of forest green and seen her enticing figure which was so seductively clad in that sheer strip of green. Her artless, soft aura gave birth to emotions which he had never felt before. He was alert to her disarming manner, subtle magic, and sexual allure—a dangerous combination in a female. She wasn't at all what he had expected to confront this morning. Without awareness, he was being drawn to her, lured as a hungry fish to a delectable bait. There was something different about this woman, but he couldn't put his finger on it. And he was curious about Adam Ross's conduct. Without a doubt, the doctor was just as enchanted as he was, enchanted and rebuffed. Steven grinned, knowing Ross didn't stand a chance against him.

"The missing escort wasn't my problem; the car and an empty water container were," she stated softly, not wanting this man to think her foolish or rash. Brandy had met and known many men, but none to compare with this vital, vivid creature before her dreamy vision. "Next time, I shan't place my life and safety in the hands of a careless mechanic."

He seemed about to remark upon her last statement, then decided against it. "Katherine Alexander, in your debt, kind sir," she politely introduced herself, even though she assumed he already knew that fact. She could not hide her pleasure at his prompt visit and genuine concern for her.

He nodded and grinned. "Your southern accent says you're a long way from home," he stated with an inviting tone to his rich vibrant voice.

"Kentucky does seem another lifetime away from here. Have you ever visited there?" she casually inquired to prolong their first meeting, disregarding the doctor's anxious fidgeting.

"On several occasions. But evidently not in the right area," he joked easily, alluding to disappointment in not meeting her sooner. His gaze lingered upon her mouth, then lifted to fuse with hers.

She smiled in wishful understanding. Unaccustomed to such forwardness and flirtation, Brandy was at a loss with this disquieting man. "Perhaps I can show my gratitude by treating you to a fabulous dinner when I'm released from here," she stated before she could help herself. Somehow the thought of never seeing him again was a pain too great to bear, too unthinkable.

She instantly realized how forward such an invitation might seem. For all she knew, this man could be married. Even if not, he was a total stranger and this was their first meeting. Although it was the 1980s, she was still an old-fashioned girl. Was she really asking him for a date? Before she could come up with some polite way to excuse herself, he stole her chance.

His blue eyes smoldered with some emotion unknown to her. "I would be delighted, Katherine; or do you go by Kathy?" he asked, observing her sudden hesitation.

"Kathy," she murmured, unable to think clearly when he focused that smile upon her. How she wished she could be witty, sophisticated, charming, and beautiful like her heroines....

"If you two could continue this conversation later, I must get on with my rounds," the acidic voice ate into Brandy's dream world.

"Certainly, Dr. Ross," her rescuer mildly answered, never taking his attention from Brandy. "Kathy, it's a treat to find you looking so well this morning; you gave me quite a scare yesterday. I'll visit you again soon, if I may?"

"Anytime, Mr. Reynolds," she murmured in full agreement, utterly captivated by this Apollo in human form, praying she wasn't overly revealing her interest in him.

"Lance, please," he urged with a seductive smile which clouded her reason and dismissed her reserve.

"Thank you for the gallant rescue, Lance," she stated, her eyes saying far more than her words ever could.

She stared at the closed door for a long time after his departure, listening to the steady retreat of his Dingo boots. Forgetting about the nasty doctor in her room, she sighed lightly and smiled secretly to herself. Could such a man be real?

"It isn't every day a Romeo like that rescues you, is it?" Adam playfully teased, wishing that her dreamy smile was directed at him. He was tempted to ask if she was feeling like one of her heroines, but wisely didn't let on he knew her identity, especially since she appeared eager to conceal it. "Is there anything I can get for you, Miss Alexander? Books? Newspaper? Anything?" he asked.

She leveled curious green eyes upon him. "You're very thoughtful, Dr. Ross. Nothing, thank you."

"Please call me Adam," he promptly suggested.

Brandy eyed him secretly, wondering at this abrupt change. He certainly wasn't in a hurry now that Lance Reynolds had vanished. To spare a few moments of time for the man who saved your life was neither foolish nor futile. Still, she prided herself on her manners. Unless he gave her cause, she would overlook his prior rudeness. To reestablish a formal aura, she asked, "How am I doing this morning?"

He smiled and remarked, "You look and sound exceedingly better today. I was rather terse with you last night, Miss Alexander. Please accept my apology."

His confession and apology stunned her. "Perhaps we were both under stress last night," Brandy stated calmly, feeling his apology wasn't honest.

"Would you prefer another doctor assigned to your case, Miss Alexander?" he asked, a hint of tension in his tightly controlled tone. He was clearly backing off, mentally cautioning himself or cunningly testing her emotional waters.

"Whatever you prefer," she said. Obviously they had a personality clash, but why cause trouble when she would be dismissed soon? Other matters demanded her attention and energy....

He smiled and nodded, visibly relaxing. "In such a case, a truce would be in order. I've endured a very heavy schedule lately. Perhaps I was a bit short last night and just now. I suppose I am overtired and short-tempered." He offered a devious excuse for himself, not wanting to be dismissed from a case which might draw the attention of the chief-of-staff. He could do without that trouble again. Besides, he was behaving like a fool, a spurned lover. So what if he hadn't scored right off the bat? As he called to mind her last television interview and sensuous novel he reminded himself she would be around for several more days.

This time when he examined Brandy, he was very careful not to give her any reason to suspect any dalliance or misconduct. If she continued to repel him, he would find some other way to vex this vain female! He was a doctor, not a garbage collector! No one dared to treat him as she had done and go unpunished!

"My suggestions are for plenty of bed rest, one week minimum; lots of fluids, anything you wish; and total relaxation. Any questions?"

"Have the police been here yet? Do they still want to talk with me?" she asked, trying to restore some measure of calm and professionalism into their moods.

"The nurse told me someone would come by this afternoon. If you need anything, just let me or the nurse on duty know."

"Fine. Thank you, sir."

Doctor Ross left her room with plans of an intoxicating seduction flickering through his mind. Beauty, charm, wealth, and fame were enticing qualities in a proper wife for Dr. Adam Ross. Hopefully her knight in shining armor wouldn't return again. If Reynolds did appear for another visit, he would find some way to discourage the handsome rake. Perhaps he should read some of her novels again, just to discover what romantic entrapments appealed to her. One day soon...

BRANDY LAY BACK upon her pillow as the nurse finally came back to reinsert her I.V. In her mind, she was racing along a flower-edged path in pursuit of a human Adonis. His smile could rival the sun for warmth and brilliance. The blueness of his eyes was the shade of a tranquil sea. Such strength and confidence had emanated from him. He was unlike any other man she had met, except in the pages of her books or in her own romantic dreams.

Brandy tried to analyze Lance Reynolds's appeal. It was a combination of all of his traits: his stirring voice, his sensual smile, his confident stance and movements, his dress, his hypnotic eyes, his strong and handsome features, his virility, his charm, and his way of making a woman know she is a woman. He radiated sensitivity and intelligence. He appeared a man who would be at ease with anyone and anywhere, a master of all situations. His clothes and manner told her he had money, probably plenty of it and a very healthy dash of power and influence. Definitely a dangerous and captivating combination.

Brandy received another stunning surprise about midafternoon. She was absently flexing her fingers on her left hand, hoping to reduce their stiffness and chill from being forced to lie motionless for the I.V. solutions. She sighed lightly as she snuggled down into the feather pillow, feeling restive at this confinement. Her eyes were slowly sweeping the scenery beyond her large window.

One good thing about Las Vegas was the panorama; no matter which side of a building you were on, there was always a magnificent view of mountains and desert. It was as if someone had carelessly dropped a load of buildings right in the middle of a desert which was surrounded with mountains of brown, carnelian, black, and purple. This view was a definite contrast to the pine-covered mountains of the

Northeast or the deep South. These nearby mountains were utterly barren, their rough surfaces nakedly exposed to nature's demanding elements.

"Rugged and raw, but it's beautiful, isn't it? I wonder how many secrets those hills have witnessed through the ages." The unforgettable voice softly invaded her peaceful mind, wreaking havoc upon her senses.

She turned to find Lance Reynolds nonchalantly leaning against the beige wall next to her bed, his azure eyes lingering upon the multicolored mountains on the far horizon. She had not even heard his stealthy entry and had no idea how long he had been standing there. Those cerulean eyes lowered to Brandy's pinkened face. She was momentarily speechless once again.

He was dressed in cream-colored linen slacks which fit perfectly. He had changed into a royal blue cotton soft-shouldered sports jacket. He now sported a tailored oxford shirt in a creamy shade with bold splotches of deep blue upon its surface. As before, the top three buttons had been left undone, enticing innocent eyes to that virile chest. The cream and blue color scheme highlighted his bronze skin, blue eyes, and black hair. If ever there had been an irresistible man born, he was standing right before her eyes this very minute. Brandy was all too aware of never having met any man like this one.

Her gaze locked upon the gold rope chain around his neck. The head of a lion with its mane flying in an invisible wind was attached to it: a Leo zodiac symbol. She smiled and almost remarked upon the appropriateness of his powerful sign. Instead, she stated softly in a strained voice, "That's a most unusual Leo; it's beautiful." Where were her creative mind and witty intelligence when she needed them the most? What did she say to this man? Why did he make her feel so nervous, so insecure, so much like a green teenager?

He smiled lazily; her heart fluttered wildly. She absently wondered how any female executive could keep her mind on business with a gorgeous hunk like Lance Reynolds sitting across her desk. She abruptly asked, "What do you do for a living, Lance?"

He grinned mysteriously. He shrugged his massive shoulders and casually said, "Lots of things. I mainly work with some men in the oil business. Course most folks think I simply bum around most of the time. Why?" he asked, hoping his tone would prevent further questions at this early date.

She dared not tell him she had an overwhelming hunger to know everything about him. "I was just wondering if your trip into the Valley of Fire was on business or pleasure. Either one, it was most fortunate for me that you came along," she confessed, a smile tugging gently at the corners of her mouth.

He answered her question with a question, "Why were you out there alone? Sightseeing like me?" he deceptively queried to mislead her.

She cunningly avoided his probe, "For certain, that isn't a place to go alone or unprepared. Do you ride? Horses," she added with a laugh as his brows knit in confusion. "I raise Appaloosas on a ranch in Kentucky. You appear to be an outdoorsman from your tan and build," she explained her interest.

"You might say I've done my share of sitting in a saddle. Fact is, I own several golden racking horses. Have any of those?"

"No, only Appaloosas. Their colorings and intelligence fascinate me, not to mention their fierce loyalty to their owner. My father started the stables, and I caught the bug at ten. Do you live here in Vegas?" She returned to a personal subject.

He hesitated noticeably before answering her. She was slightly confused by the flicker of suspicion and annoyance in his blue eyes. "Visiting, I suppose. Did your husband stay behind in Kentucky?" he unexpectedly asked, his expression unreadable.

"My husband?" she repeated foolishly. "Who said I had a husband?" she inquired in a tone which unintentionally hinted at some deception in the making. She instantly chided herself for feeling like a teenager who was being approached for her first date by the boy who had been unanimously selected as "the answer to a maiden's prayer" for the fourth time.

"I naturally assumed you were married," he stated softly, watching her reaction closely from behind those entrancing blue eyes which like his poker face, revealed nothing. Why did he have this strange effect upon her? If he believed she was indeed married, then why was he here now, smiling and tempting her with such dangerous thoughts and feelings?

Suspicion flickered in her own gaze. "No, I'm not; and I never have been," she added quickly, in case he had a dislike or disrespect for divorcées, as many men did. "You?" she boldly returned his question.

"Me, what?" he parried her curiosity, smiling devilishly.

"Married," she replied, not backing down.

"Nope, and never have been either." For some reason, Brandy felt he was toying with her, teasing her in some curious manner. "How long have you been breeding horses alone?" he asked the suddenly wary woman.

"About eight or nine years, since I finished college. My parents were killed in a plane crash right after my high school graduation. The ranch belonged to my father, so I inherited it a little sooner than usual or desirable," she remarked, pain still evident after all that time. She became very quiet and pensive. Her gaze was clouded with reminiscent lights.

"What college?" he softly asked her, wanting to restore that natural glow and spontaneous smile. This female was a puzzle that had been nagging at him all day; he needed to solve it and get on with his business. Her clues had surprisingly set her age at about thirty-one.

"University of Georgia. Why?" Her gaze came back to his.

"Just curious. What major?" At her close scrutiny of his expression, he laughed genially and gingerly added, "Just wondered what a horse breeder studies in school."

She returned his contagious smile. "English major, Speech minor.... Of course the speech didn't help me much; I still get terrified every time there's more than five people in a group! I considered teaching Language and Literature in college, but I quickly rejected that idea. I just don't think I could abide students like me all day," she admitted with a merry twinkle in her green eyes.

He pursed up his lips and knit his brow in keen study of her. "Somehow I don't see you as the spinster school marm. Engaged?" he asked the stunned woman.

At a sudden loss as to his underlying tone and meaning, she simply shook her head. "Career woman, huh?" he jested, eyes glimmering mirthfully as if she were the butt of some unspoken joke.

"For now," she agreed; her smile had slowly vanished. She wondered if she was being too open or too forward with this stranger. She suddenly realized that most of this conversation had been about her; he was very skilled at keeping the spotlight off himself. She remained silent, letting him make the next move or comment.

He shoved himself from his negligent position and stood before her with feet planted apart and hands on hips, exuding an aura of insouciance and natural pride. He grinned broadly and headed for the door. He nonchalantly tossed a "See you later" over his shoulder, then vanished as mysteriously and suddenly as he had appeared.

The door closed. To Brandy, it was as if he had come on some fishing trip to catch something he had missed last night or this morning. He had cast out tempting bait and lengthy line several times, keenly analyzing his catch each time he slowly reeled in her answers and expressions. He suddenly seemed to have all of the information he wanted or needed. He had turned and swaggered out as if dismissing her from his mind the moment the door closed behind him. He hadn't seemed interested in light conversation or in getting better acquainted, only in filling in some blank or cloudy spaces. Very strange. . . .

Perhaps she should have told him about her writing career. She hastily decided she did not know him that well. She didn't want him to race out and to buy her last few novels just to study her further, to dissect her as most people felt they could do from a writer's works. Anyway, his manly image seemed disturbed by her "career woman" facet. It could make him feel threatened or intimidated if he knew she was a successful, famous, wealthy author. It would be best if they got better acquainted before he learned too much about her personal life; that is, if she ever saw him again. . . .

Adam Ross stopped by late that evening before leaving the hospital. He hand-delivered pink sweetheart roses and several magazines. He was exceptionally polite and genial. He chatted for twenty minutes, then smiled and bid her good night. After his departure, Brandy pondered his motives. She had been careful to be nice and friendly, but had not allowed an inch for misunderstanding her. Her reserve hadn't seemed to bother Adam, or to discourage his warm smiles, or to prevent his invitation to dinner after her release. When she stated she didn't think it proper to accept a date from her doctor, he had offered to remove himself from her case.

Taken off guard, she had said she would consider the invitation when she was feeling better. She actually hoped he would forget about it and her. She tossed upon her hospital bed for hours before falling asleep, fretting over the amorous Ross and tempting Reynolds. Did she dare pursue Lance Reynolds with carefree abandon?

It was evident the following morning that neither Adam Ross nor Lance Reynolds had forgotten about her. By lunch, Adam had visited her twice, revealing his best side. Even so Brandy found herself wishing he would ignore her. In spite of Adam's change of mood and tactics, she still disliked him.

Lance had stopped by briefly at ten o'clock, also to deliver some flowers: long-stemmed red roses. He had breezed into her room with his masterful air, inquired about her health, handed her the roses, smiled, and then breezed out—all in ten minutes!

Brandy fingered one of the roses, then held it to her nose to inhale its heady odor, a scent better than any bottled or sold at any price. She was contemplating two of his statements. Lance Reynolds was a mercurial and confusing man. Why had he been so concerned over her talk with the local police? Why did he insist on knowing if she had spoken with them yet? Was she mistaken, or had she sensed something odd in his expression and tone? Once he learned she hadn't seen the police yet, he actually appeared relieved. Why? If he wasn't interested in her, why the visits and flowers? Why had his parting words sounded like a final farewell? A curious pain needled her heart. If her concentration wasn't nil, she would work on the requested revisions for her latest book: oddly entitled *Valley of Fire*. Yet somehow she couldn't face working on her writing when the book featured a hero named Landis Rivera whose description matched Lance's.

Chapter Three

As Brandy frantically took in the colorful details of her recent accident and her shocking rescue by the stunning man who had visited her three times, her mouth fell open and her green eyes widened in astonishment and embarrassment. The talkative officer very vividly described the events of her misadventure. Her face altered between a bright red and a snow white as the incredible story unfolded.

Lance Reynolds had actually bound her hands like some captive and had then ridden her into civilization in a most humiliating position. No wonder he had looked so smug and amused; he had handled her like some sack of potatoes. She could mentally recreate the entire episode. Then, to come to her room and not even mention the manner of her rescue... How he must have enjoyed his little secret!

She had innocently assumed he had brought her here in his car, not tied to his sexy body like some war booty. No wonder their return trip had taken so long. Yet, she was perplexed by the officer's allusions to Lance's anger and resentment at being hindered so long. The officer came right out and said Lance was infuriated and embarrassed at his detainment; he even quoted his stinging comments about regretting her rescue! The officer was so intent upon lingering with her and with darkening the image of his flamboyant rival that he colored a few of his facts and greatly dwelt upon the harshness of others.

"Who is this Lance Reynolds?" she asked when she could force some words from her constricted throat, abruptly realizing how very little he had told her about himself.

"Don't rightly know much about him," the officer lied convincingly. "From what I gathered, he has some money and property around these parts."

Brandy's alert mind challenged Lance's earlier denial of residence here. She wondered why he had lied about such a minor thing. The man went on, "He was real moody; quite a hot temper. Real insolent and smart-mouthed! For a while there, I was afraid he was going to fight me and my partner. Had to pull my gun on 'im." He went on to reveal that Lance had been carrying a weapon.

Brandy could easily envision that proud man's reaction to such a degrading situation. She could imagine that powerful body taut with rage. She could also picture his jaw tight with rigid control, his white teeth clenched in suppressed fury, his blue eyes glacial and threatening. Her wayward thoughts returned to Officer Connelly's ramblings.

"He's got powerful connections though. Had to release him before we even reached the station! Didn't help any that his bike was demolished and stripped by vandals where we forced him to leave it behind. Whew, was he mad when I told him that news! Looks like somebody's gonna have to pay."

She couldn't imagine anyone forcing Lance Reynolds to do anything he didn't agree to. Still, she couldn't imagine such an intelligent man resisting the authorities. He had not even mentioned his motorcycle or its loss; why?

Baffled by these contradictions, she ventured shyly, "You say he was furious?" Was that why he wanted to know if she had spoken with the police yet?

"Like some caged tiger who hadn't been fed in days! Wouldn't want to be his enemy. No sirree," he stated emphatically.

"Is he married?" she asked to test Lance's honesty.

"Nope, but he's real big with the ladies from what I see and hear. Always around with some new or fancy bird on his arm."

"Are you positive we're discussing the same man? He came by here this morning. He was most polite and...kind," she hastily selected another word for charming. She did not mention the other visits.

Sensing the probable effect of Steven Winngate upon her, he scoffed, "He can be real kind and polite if he chooses. But I've heard tales about his ruthless ways in dealing with rivals or enemies, if you catch my drift. Nothing illegal, but mighty powerful," he quickly added when he noted her reaction, deciding he might be laying it on a little too thick. He was delighted this lovely creature didn't know Lance Reynolds was *the* Steven Winngate, but he wondered why Winngate was keeping it from her. However, he could not resist one last attempt to plant dislike and mistrust in her mind.

"Wonder why he came by here? From the way he acted and talked the other night, you're the last person he'd want to see again! Course you can't ever tell about men like that; always after some new filly. Did you offer him some reward for saving your life?" The tone of that question brought a peachy glow to her already rosy cheeks.

"No, Officer Connelly. I assumed he rescued me from the goodness of his heart...if he has one," she caustically added, suspecting Lance had been toying with her. Was this one of the flaws she had feared: masculine spite? She had innocently inconvenienced and embarrassed him, but did he need to punish her? He hadn't appeared the kind of man who would stoop to such childish methods. Perhaps he had changed his mind after meeting—really meeting—her.

The officer chuckled, vowing smugly, "Men like him never do, Miss Alexander." He waited for the intruding Dr. Ross to agree.

FOR THE NEXT TWO DAYS, Brandy anticipated another visit from the disarming Apollo. She wanted to hear his side of this curious situation. But he did not come again. Perhaps he had only been intrigued about the woman he had rescued. Perhaps he had been interested in some type of revenge or spite. Perhaps he was allowing her to simmer after making her vividly aware of his abundant male prowess. Perhaps after meeting her, he had been content to let her escape his charms or retaliation.

She gradually regained her strength and vitality. She took daily walks to aid her circulation. Too bad her walks were in the company of the besotted Dr. Ross. She forced herself to be cordial and grateful. It was unlike her to be rude or spiteful, but Ross certainly inspired those emotions within her.

In all fairness, she admitted that Ross was making an effort to control his temperament and affection, but she sensed his resentment toward her rebuffs. All she could do was get well and leave his domain. Her steady cooperation and natural resilience would make that possible in a few more days.

She was forced to politely endure another visit from Officer Connelly. She guessed that her dislike and mistrust of him were due to her preoccupation with Lance Reynolds and with Connelly's overly friendly manner. No matter, she thanked him for his visit and for the lovely bunch of flowers. When asked if she would see him when she left the hospital, she did a most uncommon thing; she lied to him. She told him she would be flying home to Kentucky on that same day. He sighed in disappointment as he announced that his present schedule might prevent him from seeing her before she left, as if she cared whether she saw him again.

She was delighted to hear that news, but concealed her relief. Why did these western men behave as if women were a rarity, as if each one was a challenge? Had the unusual circumstances of her accident and rescue intrigued them and inspired them to act in this curious manner? As if she owed each of them some reward? Brandy then annoyed Connelly with a question about Lance. "Where could I reach this Lance Reynolds? Can I find out what kind of motorcycle he lost?"

Connelly's eyes mirrored his feelings. "Why do you want to know that?" Besides, Reynolds was out of town on business.

"The man saved my life, and that help cost him his bike. I intend to show my appreciation by replacing it for him, the exact same kind if possible," she stated firmly, annoyed at feeling obligated to explain herself to anyone.

"No need to worry yourself, Kathy. His insurance will cover it. He's probably already gotten a new one. Besides, you thanked him already. That's enough gratitude for any man."

"Lance Reynolds isn't just any man," she vowed heatedly before thinking. Hoping to recover her error, she quickly added, "He's the man who saved my life! Like it or not, I feel I owe him more than a verbal thank you. Some impersonal reward which can be delivered by someone else . . . The bike is a perfect choice. I want to see to it before I return home to Kentucky."

Satisfied with her reasoning, he smiled and agreed. He promised to secure the information for her when he had it. They chatted a few more minutes before his departure.

When Nurse Kay Hart came to visit Brandy that afternoon, Brandy asked if she could pay her to do some shopping. She and Kay had struck up a friendship that first morning and they enjoyed each other's company and conversation. Wanting something special for her next meeting with Lance, she asked Kay to shop for a couple of feminine—but subtle—nightgown sets with matching slippers. She teased about needing something to brighten her spirits, but an alert Kay knew the motive behind her request. She giggled and agreed. After all, what female in her right mind would ignore a catch like Lance Reynolds?

That afternoon, Brandy made several calls to motorcycle dealers with the information which Officer Connelly had called in to her. She succeeded in locating a dealer who promised he could have her a Harley-Davidson FLT-80 Tour Classic bike which perfectly matched her specifications. She promptly agreed to his terms and price, including the one-week delivery date. She gave him the address supplied to her, then hung up the phone. One way or another, Mr. Reynolds would recall their mutual adventure and he would have no reason to resent her interference in his life.

Brandy was overjoyed with Kay's selections when she came by later that afternoon. "Kay, they're exquisite! I love this silvery gray one. It's so subtle yet sexy! It's gorgeous."

"I think the azure blue will look stunning with your coloring. That dusty rose one too. What's the fuss? Anything would look fantastic on you, Kathy! I wish I had your hair and eyes . . . and your tan . . . and your charm."

They laughed. "You're a dear to help me out like this."

"As I see it, a happy patient gets well much sooner than a miserable one. Besides, I loved every minute of it. I told them I was shopping for my honeymoon. You wouldn't believe the clothes in that shop, the prices either! I was glad to be using somebody else's money," she jested mirthfully.

When Brandy tried to give Kay one of the outfits as a gift, Kay exclaimed, "Oh, I couldn't possibly accept such an expensive gift! I was only helping out a new friend. Really, I couldn't," she vowed halfheartedly, her eyes caressing the satin softness of the tangerine set.

"You can, and you must. I would feel terrible about claiming your afternoon off if you refused it. Please, Kay."

When Kay realized she was serious and sincere, she smiled and accepted Brandy's generosity. She clutched the outfit to her bosom and danced around the room. "Never in my whole life have I owned such a costly, gorgeous outfit. Let's see . . . whom shall I test its magic on?"

They joined in girlish laughter and gaiety, agreeing to have lunch when Brandy was well. Soon Kay had to leave to prepare for her shift. Brandy hurriedly hung up the night-wear, already certain as to which one she would wear tonight. She was ecstatic to know this was Adam Ross's night off. He was making it more and more difficult for her to discourage him. At least twice a day he visited her and asked her out. She could hardly avoid him, but she wished she could. Perhaps he wouldn't ask her again, especially after her chilling refusal just before lunch today.

She pulled out the bronze briefcase which Officer Connelly had returned to her on his first visit. She opened it and began to make notes on her present novel. She was vexed to discover that she kept visualizing the alien spaceship captain as Lance Reynolds. She frowned as she read her fictional hero's description; it was Lance. Why did he keep haunting her mind, stifling her creative flow? Why hadn't he visited her again? Unable to concentrate very long, she tossed the pad into the case and snapped it shut. *Twilight* would have to be patient, unlike her.

Reservations flooded her mind; pursuing a man was new for her. What would he think if he arrived to find her clad in one of those sultry gowns? What if she had already given him the impression that she was too eager or too easy? What if he didn't want another female chasing after him? What if his other visits had only stemmed from kindness or curiosity?

Besides, why should a man like him be interested in her? She was pretty enough, but she sensed he could have his choice of the most beautiful and sophisticated women around. She was intelligent and well-mannered, but brains did not outweigh beauty and sex appeal. She was independent and confident, but men often felt hostile or turned-off by such qualities. What did she know about real love and romance?

Wholesome, bright, self-assured females lost the battles with frivolous, sexy, unbridled femmes-fatales. Successful women presented some kind of threat to men. To be accepted or talented in a man's field demanded firmness and aggressiveness, things which subtracted from femininity. Men still chose beautiful faces, sexy bodies, male-first attitudes, and near-empty heads!

God, how she had struggled to be taken seriously in her literary field. She had fought against the men who labeled her a "formula" writer or who referred to her talents as "limited to silly romances for bored housewives." It required a great deal to stifle the resentment which could interfere with her sunny attitude and ability. Strength and skill often labeled a woman as less than feminine. Such attitudes and difficulties made her glad she worked alone!

Alone... Maybe she spent too much time alone. When she wasn't touring for her latest book or visiting New York on business, she spent most of her time by herself. She often worked far into the wee hours of the morning, then slept until midday. She would go for weeks without seeing anyone other than the ranch hands and her housekeeper. She did ride a great deal; she loved the horses and often trained them. Did she enjoy being alone so much to cover her shyness and to protect her privacy? Was she becoming too captivated by her writing, by her fictional works? Was that why Lance Reynolds was so appealing to her, because he mirrored her perfect hero?

Yet, certain people were now intruding into her private domain and trying to force her to conform to their ideas and concepts. She fumed over how long it had taken her to firmly establish her talent and status, things they were trying to take away from her. She had proven she could write more than just a rosy romance; she had watched her mysteries and science-fiction novels climb to the heights of the bestseller lists: purchased and accepted by men as well as women! Surely she had proven herself.

But why then did they insist upon changes in the movie script for *Love's Cruel Arrows*? Why did they want to insert the very type of material which they falsely accused her of writing? *Arrows* had proven its literary quality. Why did they want to cut it to pieces and to infiltrate it with lurid details and vivid sex which she would innocently take the credit or guilt for writing? Why didn't they film it as written? With the drastic changes they wanted, it wouldn't be her story anymore. Why risk its dramatic demise? Should she reject the film offer? She didn't know.

But in all honesty, it was the vile story about her which was soon to appear in *Glitter Magazine* which riled and hurt her the most. Casey had been able to get her hands on the rough draft of that spicy, crude article. They had later met with the publisher and the writer; they had argued the scandalous, vulgar slant to the story. They had threatened them with a lawsuit, all to no avail. Brandy had offered to grant them an interview, including all the pictures they needed, if they would cancel the article which was scheduled for release in only two more months. That generous offer had been a terrible mistake, for it had been misconstrued as a desperate attempt to conceal the truth of Laura McGavin's fictitious story. Brandy had left their office in a near rage at such a gross misuse of their press. She deeply resented how that story would be widely circulated and innocently accepted as truth. The damage would be irreparable before the lawsuit could be written out. Such a malicious act! Such a misguided writer and cruel publisher! Somehow they must be stopped!

Until recently, Brandy had been so carefree, self-reliant, and happy. She had survived the battles to become a known writer. She had covered her loneliness by raising beautiful, intelligent horses. She had learned to bend with her demanding schedules and fame. She had made it on her own: she didn't owe anyone, except Casey, anything. She had worked long and hard for her success and happiness: things now threatened by uncontrollable forces.

It seemed as if some ominous clouds had moved over her tawny head. No matter where she turned, a new problem jumped up to slap her in the face. Her talent was being tampered with; her name was being smirched; her peace-of-mind was being torn asunder; her life had been carelessly endangered; she was being annoyed by two odious men. If that weren't enough trouble, now her very heart was being subjected to the whims and powerful allure of a bedeviling man she didn't even know and might never see again! Damn these feelings of indecisiveness and vulnerability!

She feared and despised this sudden loss of control and her diminishing self-confidence. She resented the idea of pursuing a man who obviously wasn't interested in her. Worst of all, she hated these feelings of weakness and dejection—both emotional and physical. She needed to get well and to return to those inviting, protective hills of Kentucky. No, she wanted more. . . .

That afternoon, Brandy received a special delivery letter from Casey. The moment of truth had arrived sooner than anticipated or desired. She read the contents a second time, then placed a call to her agent in New York. The answering machine was on, allowing her sixty seconds to give her decisions and messages after the mechanical "beep."

"Casey, Brandy. Accept *Arrow* terms. Make certain they list the scriptwriter's name in bold lettering and subtly splice in my name where least noticeable. I have no desire to assist with the movie rewrites; it's their baby if you agree to their terms. Be out soon."

She inhaled deeply, then redialed to finish her message before the tape halted again, speaking swiftly. "Doing fine. Work on *Twilight* going great, but slow. Try to halt that *Glitter* story by any means necessary or available. We might as well play dirty too! I'll do Tom's show in August. *Valley* revisions progressing. Deal for *Pendulum* super. Be in New York or at home in a week. Take care; you work too hard," she ended on a lighter note, knowing Casey would read her melancholy mood like an open page, hoping the tape was still receiving.

She hung up the phone and tried to forget her previous decisions. Thank goodness she had someone like Casey to handle such things for her. Before she could slip into a pensive mood, there was a knock upon her door. After she called out permission to enter, a laboratory technician came in.

"If you're ready, Miss Alexander, we'll do those other tests now. It'll take about two hours."

"A wheelchair? I can walk," she teased him.

"Hospital rules. Enjoy the ride," the freckle-faced youth advised in a boyish tone.

Ross came to her room while she was having her "sweating process," EEG, and EKG tests run. Realizing where she was, he sat down beside her bed to wait. His eyes touched on her briefcase. He grinned mischievously and picked it up, intrigued by a peak into her next novel and private life. He read her notes on the *Valley of Fire,* notes for a new novel by the famous Brandy Alexander. He could hardly trust his luck or his senses. In fact, he was surprised no one else had guessed her identity. After all, that lovely face and shapely body had graced many a television screen and magazine or newspaper article. He was perplexed by her desire to maintain her privacy. Evidently her modesty was phony, something she used to feign the innocent and softly seductive female.

He was irrationally offended by her secrecy and disdain. So, she was really here for research. Would any of them recognize themselves in this upcoming novel? He was anxious to learn more. He read her notes again, angered by the vivid description of her next hero. So, the sensuous romance writer was more interested in a wealthy playboy than in a doctor... He wondered if she planned to personally research those handwritten love scenes with the prototype for them. Childish spite filled Adam Ross. He was amused by the many problems which were roughly outlined in that long letter from her agent back East. Yet, he was envious of her success and popularity, the ease with which she earned a fortune and completely fooled people.

Obsessed with this tempting woman, he boldly searched her room. He knew the risk he was taking; but at that moment, he didn't care. He grinned as he fingered the luxurious gowns in her closet, guessing the purpose for them: to ensnare the Romeo who had rescued her. Or—he chuckled aloud—was she plotting more than her next book, perhaps the enchantment of Reynolds, her new hero? How would Reynolds feel about a guinea pig role? How would he react to being romantically exposed and exploited in her *Valley* book? Did he even know who she was?

Adam left her room to continue his rounds but only after trying to return everything to its proper place. He didn't want her to know he had gone through her things. He had already endangered his reputation and pride where Brandy was concerned. Once she was taught a lesson, he would dismiss her from his mind.

Ross had only gone a few feet when he encountered Lance on his way to visit Brandy. Ross glared at the huge bouquet of flowers in his powerful grip; he noted the playful smile which was tugging at the corners of Reynolds's lips. Did she want him? Was she only using him? No matter, the path for his long-awaited spite lay right before his eyes! If it wasn't for Reynolds, he would be recorded in her notes!

"Mr. Reynolds! What a surprise to see you again!" he stated as if totally flabbergasted by his presence there.

Lance's brows lifted quizzically. "How is Miss Alexander?"

"Oh, she's doing just fine. She'll be released in a few days. I know she's mighty anxious to get back to work, especially now that her research is finished. Sure was lucky to meet you," he remarked with some definite meaning which was unclear.

"Really?" came his lazy reply, mistaking his implication.

"Tell me, how does it feel to be the real-life model for a literary hero? She'd never see me as a new Rhett Butler," he muttered in feigned dejection, then turned to walk away.

"Exactly what does that mean?" Lance inquired, catching up with him in two, easy strides.

"Surely she's told you who she really is and why she was out there! I mean, I assumed you were cooperating with her research," he stammered effectively, faking embarrassment at his rival's ignorance.

"What research? I haven't the slightest notion what you're talking about. You are referring to Kathy Alexander?"

That name told Ross all he needed to know, that and Lance's behavior. "I have rounds. Forget what I said. I don't meddle in the affairs of other people. I thought you knew the truth."

"What I will forget is your reluctance to tell me what you're talking about, Ross," he stated in a tone which alerted Ross to his volatile force and impatience.

Nervous and undecided, Ross fidgeted as if debating some vital issue of national security; yet, it was too late to back down now. "If you insist, Mr. Reynolds. But I would appreciate it if you don't let on who told you about her. You can bet I've been treading lightly since I learned her identity! I'm not one to want to pick up the next bestseller and see myself exploited and exposed! I assumed you knew her," he stated foolishly.

Lance came to full alert with those clues. "What are you jabbering about, man? Who is she? What research? How could she exploit me?" The mere sound of that word savagely attacking him.

"She's the famous writer Brandy Alexander. You know, the one who writes all those juicy romances! Whew, the questions she's asked about you and that night you brought her here! What an imagination! She's had that young state patrolman in several times to fill in her gaps. She had him check out your bike, the style and such. She asked me hundreds of questions! She's using those details in a book entitled *Valley of Fire*. Looks like you'll appear as the mysterious, irresistible hero! I'd gladly trade places with you; that's what I call real research. . . ." he declared with a suggestive leer. "When she turns on her hypnotic charms, you won't stand a chance of saying no to her! Damn, what a lucky fool you are! While I was checking her over, I grabbed a peak at her notes; there's no doubt she's describing you and your little romantic escapade.''

He secretly glanced up at the moody, darkened scowl on Lance's face. "I don't understand why she keeps her name and job a secret. Course it might make people nervous or mad if they know she's only using them for research and ideas. She's going to appear on the *Tom Hadley Show* in August to talk about this trip and book. I'll be certain to catch it. Can you take it, a famous writer?''

Ross paused effectively before adding, "But I wouldn't want to be in her shoes when *Glitter* finishes with her next month. She's seething over that wicked exposé. She's determined to halt it.''

Knowing he had scored many points and fearing to overdo this perilous trick, Ross quickly left the pensive and scowling Lance standing in the middle of the hall, totally ignorant of the effect of his last statements. Wanting to witness the possible results of his cunning ruse, Ross hesitated just around the corner.

Ross observed the striking figure before his envious eyes. He wished he possessed the natural flair for impeccable, suave presentation which this lusty man portrayed without even trying. He glared at the man dressed in sensual earth-tones: the sandalwood, pleated, tapered slacks; the soft brown, revere-collared shirt; the buff-colored, single-breasted sport coat; and the deep brown Cabretta sheepskin side-zip boots. Ross wondered which of Lance's traits would surface to deal with this situation: bruised pride, vengeful wrath, or defensive desertion? Would Reynolds challenge and defend, attack and punish, ignore and tempt, or forgive and yield? Reynolds's pride was the key.

Lance's raven-black hair was casual and vital, ruffled from the wind and his Ferrari 308 GTS. Ross grinned satanically as he watched Lance angrily fling the fragrant flowers into a nearby trash container, then storm off down the hallway as he muttered curses to himself, something about not being able to trust any female.

"So much for you, my high and mighty Miss Alexander!" Ross sneered as he calmly strolled away, whistling jovially. On second thought, he retrieved the expensive flowers which Lance had discarded; no need to waste them, now that his competition had fled. He would unselfishly grant Brandy another chance to redeem herself, but only one more.

Chapter Four

The day came for Brandy's release. She donned a lilac dress with simple lines, belted with a deep purple sash. She allowed her hair to fall freely around her shoulders in natural waves; its shorter sides and top tossed in carefree, artistic abandonment. At times she could almost pass for a tawny-haired gypsy.

Brandy bid farewell to Kay and several others. She was disheartened by Lance's failure to show up again. She sadly concluded that Lance wasn't interested in her or he had too many women after him. Her pride was stung deeply by his treatment. Candidly, he did have reasons to dislike and resent her.

Brandy returned to her hotel. She was pleased and surprised to discover several vases of flowers in her room, sent from the hotel and from friends. She inhaled the sweet fragrance of the roses and studied the wild beauty of the waxy red Hawaiian passion flowers. She lifted the card from that arrangement and smiled as she read its message.

If there was ever a time when she needed to have dinner with a best friend, this was the night. She rang Nigel's room. "Hello, stranger. It's Brandy. Dinner sounds marvelous. How did you know I was here?"

"Casey phoned me when she heard I was doing a show out here. She suggested I look in on you. Said you were depressed. Now what does a beautiful, talented woman like you have to be depressed about?'' he teased lightly. ''Vegas no fun without me?''

''I'll tell you over a prime rib and a glass of wine,'' she parried.

''How about ten o'clock after the show?''

''How about if I tag along to see the show? I haven't seen you perform in such a long time. Any new songs? I loved *Roses at Midnight.* Did you write it?'' she chatted brightly, shoving her tension and memories aside for the time being.

''Did you write *Love's Cruel Arrows*?'' he mocked. Light laughter came over the phone. ''I'll pick you up about six. I only have the first show.''

''Marvelous, Nigel. See you then. Bye.''

Brandy fretted over her unforgettable encounter with Lance. If she had known of the trouble she caused him, she could have apologized.

Brandy selected one of her favorite gowns. The rusty tangerine was becoming with her green eyes, sun-kissed tan, and amber hair. Its fluffed top enhanced her bustline and small waist, while its semi-flared bottom gave a jaunty sway when she walked and flattered her hips. The spaghetti straps revealed just enough flesh to be subtly teasing without being daring, and showed off her silky, golden shoulders. She completed her compelling image with black patent evening sandals and a black beaded evening bag.

She placed a matching silk flower in her golden tresses and secured a gold open heart on a cable chain around her neck and gold heart studs in her pierced ears. She stepped back from the floor-length mirror to view the finished product. *Not bad,* she decided; then with a musical laugh, added, *Very nice indeed....*

The door buzzed. How she dearly loved these rooms with a door bell. She quickly raced to open it wide. She smiled, then hugged Nigel Davis. He was a man with a golden voice and a gifted hand for writing music. They had been close friends for several years, having met in New York at a party.

Tonight he looked so fresh and attractive in his black and gray flecked silk jacket, white ruffled shirt, black bow tie, and silver-gray slacks. His brown hair was a mass of small curls which always did as they wished. His hazel eyes glimmered with inner contentment and bubbly excitement. She hoped the right girl would soon come along to share this rare delight of a man.

They left for his engagement at a hotel on the fabulous Las Vegas Strip. She relished each song he sang and each joke he told. She desperately needed this relaxing distraction and warmth. After the show, they slipped out to dinner, surprised he had made reservations for a dinner show at another hotel on the Strip.

"Checking out the competition, Nigel?" she teased, her eyes sparkling like expensive emeralds.

"A circus act? Not hardly," he replied lightly. His face grew serious, as did his voice, "What's wrong, Brandy? That smile hasn't been real all night. This is Nigel, adopted brother; remember? Give," he ordered with a merry twinkle in his eyes. It brought an easy smile to her face, an honest one.

"Still recuperating from that accident," she said to excuse her somber mood. "It isn't every day one meets with the kind of fate one writes about. Facing real death can be most terrifying."

"How did you manage to keep it out of the papers?"

Astonished, she said, "I haven't given it much—" She halted in mid-sentence as her gaze touched upon a handsome man and a sultry female across the room. Nigel followed her wide-eyed gaze with its surfaced look of anguish. His brow knit in confusion. His eyes flickered from one table to the next, until it halted on her point of interest.

"You know Steven Winngate? Who's with him? Ah, Camille Blanchard," he declared knowingly, seemingly annoyed at her.

She traced Nigel's line of vision. Confused, she inquired, "Are you talking about the couple near the corner, the man in the sky blue jacket and the girl in the red gown?'' Was Lance already taken?

He laughed at the jealousy written within her emerald eyes. "Weren't you?" he countered, taking her cold hand and squeezing it affectionately. "I've told you all about Steven Winngate."

"Yes, but I thought his name was Lance Reynolds."

"He's been known to use that alias for privacy, but that's Steven Winngate, oil tycoon and multimillionaire, a totally self-made man. The female is Camille Blanchard; she's a world famous high-fashion model and aspiring actress, to hear her tell it. She's probably trying to convince him to finance her next commercial campaign."

Brandy recognized both names. Now she knew why that female was familiar; her face had graced many a magazine cover and commercial! Her every movement revealed her model's training: graceful, fluid, and meaningful. Her expression and behavior suggested possessiveness and familiarity with the man at her table.

No wonder he had found her dull and uninteresting; when compared to such a beauty and sophistication, she was just a plain Jane, a backward country girl.

As for Lance—no, Steven—she could easily accept his true identity. He exuded wealth, polish, and power. Yet, this knowledge was still mind-staggering and painful. The sky blue ultrasuede dinner jacket fit him like a cover of magnetic allure, an allure which pulled at her at any distance. Had manners or intrigue inspired his visits and flowers? Had he found her boring, not worth his time and attention? How could a man be so devastatingly handsome, so charming, and so captivating? Desire and anger washed over Brandy.

Brandy's brooding study and sad eyes alerted Nigel to a troubling problem. "Brandy, do you know Steve? You've never mentioned him."

"I thought I did, but not as Steven Winngate," she confessed quietly. "As incredible as it sounds, he's my rescuer from the desert.'' She sketched the details of that fateful night and their following visits to her trustworthy friend.

Nigel glanced over at Steven. ''I'll be damned! You're kidding me, aren't you? My old friend Steven rescued my little sister!'' he stressed, mischievous lights burning within his hazel eyes as he detected her attraction to her fellow adventurer.

''No, Nigel; Lance Reynolds rescued me, or so I was told. He lied, and they must have gone along with it. Surely they knew him. Amazing what money and power can accomplish, isn't it?'' she scoffed, feeling betrayed and duped by his unnecessary deception. He had only been making certain she did not know who he was, making sure she could not profit from his good deed.

She had not lied to him; she was Katherine Alexander. He, however, was not Lance Reynolds. He was one of the wealthiest men in the world! Did he think she would hotly pursue him? Did he think she would reward him in some improper way? Well, he had made a mistake where she was concerned! As for this female, she was not after Steven Winngate; she wanted Lance Reynolds, the man who had visited her in the hospital; but Lance did not exist.

Her gaze flickered back to the impressive, paralyzing man across the room. She assessed his companion, then scolded herself for her envious and harsh criticism. Her slinky, bold Chinese red silk gown was impossible to overlook. The red satin underskirt revealed a stunning figure which made Brandy squirm with a feeling of inferiority, until she decided she had no reason to be envious. Even in its barely decent state, the gown was perfect for her and she was perfect for it.

''Ravishing, isn't she?'' Nigel teased, his look mocking. ''Too bad her heart is as black as her hair. I hate to see Steven mixed up with a witch like her. He deserves better,'' he noted with sincerity. Nigel didn't add, *Steve can hardly tolerate her, even for business deals.*

"Do you know that woman, Steven? She's been gaping at us for ages," Camille purred, annoyed by Brandy's overt interest in her companion. She silently hoped it wasn't anyone special; she had enough trouble holding Steven's attention, when she could corner him.

Steven glanced up and looked around, "Who? Where?"

"Over there, the one with Nigel Davis, in that tacky orange dress!" she sneered coldly, her brown eyes lacking any warmth...as usual. What if Steven canceled this vital meeting? she fumed.

Steven's eyes scanned the room. They halted instantly when they touched upon the stunning profile of Brandy Alexander. His features turned to stone; his glacial blue eyes hardened and narrowed. He glared at her, hoping she might feel the force of his resentment at her deceit. There sat the conniving female who was trying to expose his privacy to the world, the brazen female who had risked her life to set up a phony accident and rescue just to meet him!

"Well, do you know her?" the petulant voice insisted.

"Brandy Alexander, the noted writer," came a terse reply.

She giggled, then taunted, "Don't tell me you're Colin Slade from her last novel! Yes, you fit the description perfectly... In fact, you could pass for every one of her heroes. Is she your last or next conquest?" she stated in a tone he found insulting, vain, and displeasing. Camille cursed this tempting man's disinterest in her.

"Drop it, Cam. I'm nobody's hero or guinea pig!" he forcefully vowed, his sea blue eyes as turbulent as the ocean before a violent storm.

Steven watched Nigel sign several autographs. He adamantly refused to look their way. Eventually he did; they were gone. "No doubt to do research," he muttered angrily to Camille's puzzlement. "Where are Jason's reports? Let's get busy. You positive you want this job?"

"IT WAS a wonderful evening, Nigel! I really needed it," Brandy remarked as he prepared to leave her room.

"Sorry about those A-hounds," he sweetly apologized.

"It comes with the territory. I don't mind. See you at the party, and thanks for the invitation. I plan to get lots of rest so I can dance until dawn," she teased him.

"Great! See you in my suite about ten on Saturday night after my show." He kissed the tip of her pert nose, then playfully pinched her chin.

"I'll be there," she agreed, happily. She wondered if he had invited his friend Steven Winngate, but dared not reveal her interest by asking him. If so, she would give him a view to recall in his old age! Hopefully he wouldn't bring Camille....

She was briefly tempted to invite another man, but couldn't think of anyone who might put Steven to shame in looks and virility. It was best to be Nigel's date, their handsome host. Besides, Steven probably didn't know they were like brother and sister. For the first time ever, Brandy was tempted to flaunt her fame and fortune, to show Steven she had nothing to gain from him. Nothing but Lance....

Brandy diligently worked on the *Twilight* manuscript. Having written much of it before arriving here, the rough draft was quickly finished. She mailed it special delivery to Casey to test her reaction to the unusual romantic slant. *Valley* revisions were kept on hold.

Elated with her progress and regained strength, she dressed in a carefree mood. For once, she had radically changed the physical appearance of her hero. This time, she called upon an amber-eyed alien with tawny locks to be her man of mettle and charisma. She would not permit anyone to draw a similarity between Steven and Varian Sarr; they would be like stygian night to golden day!

The dress which she had selected for this momentous occasion was a Gaylord original of rich emerald green satin; the bustline was cut low in a heart shape with the soft fabric joining the skirt near her sides at the waist. The top points of the heart were held by straps which criss-crossed in the middle of her back and then attached themselves to the very low-cut back. The A-line skirt enhanced her shapely silhouette and fluid grace. There was a heart-shaped emerald pendant, surrounded by numerous diamonds, at the hollow of her throat. Matching earrings dangled from her pierced ears. One solid jade band which was surrounded by two, single, twisted gold bands was worn upon the third finger of her left hand. Why not allude to some special mystery man back home? He had inquired about one!

Brandy had paid the hotel beautician triple her normal charge to do her hair up in cascading curls and romantic ringlets. The girl had artistically interwoven a string of mixed pearls and jade beads into the one circular braid which encased the striking style. Little curls dangled upon her neck and forehead and near her ears.

When all was completed, she critically viewed herself. At the girl's suggestion, she added another touch of forest green eye shadow to her lids and another light brushing of peach glow to her cheeks. While applying her heady Shalimar, she grinned playfully as she sprayed a touch upon her shapely ankles and upon her bare back. There was a conscious, dauntless determination not to give the beautiful Camille anything to overshadow tonight. Brandy fearlessly played up every charm she possessed.

Yet, the party began without Steven and Camille. Finally assuming they were either not invited or not coming, she relaxed and danced with several of Nigel's guests. But as she whirled around during her fourth dance, she came face to face with none other than Steven Winngate, grinning like the proverbial cat who had eaten the expensive and rare canary! Worse, she felt like that unfortunate bird!

She hesitated in surprise as their eyes met and briefly clashed in a cold war of wits and wills which she found baffling. To cover her reaction to him, she smiled seductively and turned back to her partner. But from that moment on, he was as good as the only man at the party! As fiercely as she struggled to ignore him, the more she became aware of his presence. He was utterly mind-consuming. His rich laughter would invade her alert ears; his smile would melt her coldness; his mellow voice would edge into her hearing and block out all others; his body would brush against hers and send helpless shudders over her. He was intimidating and arrogant, a despicable scoundrel.

Unable to adjust to this constant attack upon her senses, she finally stepped out onto the large stone terrace for a breath of fresh air to clear her head. She went to stand by the wall which surrounded the terrace. For the moment she ignored the buckets with small bushes and fragrant flowers. Money and fame had its advantages: lofty penthouses with privacy and lovely views, for example. She let her eyes roam the colorful, almost frenzied display of countless lights and signs along the Las Vegas strip. It was such a contrast to the nearby barren desert, just as this glittering life was a bold contrast to her quiet one back in Kentucky.

A deep, husky voice inquired from behind her, "How are you feeling tonight, Brandy? For certain, you look radiant and beautiful. Lovely view, isn't it, Brandy?" He waited patiently, and impatiently.

She wisely ignored the emphasis he placed upon her name and the fact he used it twice with that sullen inflection. She absently wondered how long he had known her name. Perhaps that had been the reason for his second visit that day: waiting for her confession. She did not ask him. She turned slowly to look up into his antagonistic features. "I'm just fine, Mr. Winngate. And you?" she politely inquired, placing the same emphasis upon his real name while fighting the powerful urge to plead for a rational explanation to his prior deceit and his coldness. Of course, Nigel told him, and now he was offended!

Catching the use of his real name, he grinned mirthfully. But then, she had known it all along. This cunning feline foolishly assumed he would not learn the truth about her and her so-called accident. "It seems we both have a curi-

ous penchant for assumed names. Since we have each discovered the truth, we need not stand upon formalities and
pretense," he stated mysteriously.

"Absolutely not, Steven. But Lance Reynolds is such a
beautiful, strong name; do you mind if I continue to call you
by it?" she sweetly inquired just to annoy him. It did not
seem to bother him at all; in fact, it amused him. His sapphire eyes sparkled with devilment.

To test his cunning and intelligence against hers, he replied, "Certainly not, Kathy," skeptically slurring her first
name.

"Just to set the record straight, Lance, Katherine is my
real name, and I do go by Kathy." Her eyes glittered with a
small victory. He grinned and nodded to indicate acceptance of a mild defeat.

Score one point for her, he playfully mused. "How did
you come by a provocative name like Brandy Alexander? Is
it just your pen name?"

She laughed at some private joke, then said, "Believe it
or not, it was my mother's favorite drink. She thought it a
lovely and unusual name, so I was labeled with it. I suppose I was extremely fortunate that small children didn't
know where it came from; I was spared from endless teasing and name-calling. You know that old maxim, 'Where
ignorance is bliss.'" She allowed her tone to give it a dou-
ble meaning which he alertly caught. "Katherine Brandy
Alexander at your service, *Sir Lance*lot. Nigel's told me a
great deal about you."

He couldn't suppress a humorous chuckle at her choice of
images of him, nor at her emphasis upon the "Lance"
within it. "Yes, it is; isn't it? Nigel tells me you'll be ap-
pearing on the *Tom Hadley Show* in August. Congratulations. That's a nice feather in a female writer's cap." There
was a hidden inflection to his tone which Brandy couldn't
decipher, but he had gained her full attention with his careless slip.

Knowing he had just lied to her again, she studied him for a moment. Nigel did not know about the Hadley show; no one did, or so she thought. "Is there some special topic for the interview?" he went on, noting the strange look which flooded her sea-green eyes. Did she always research her sexy tales in real life? What was she to Nigel?

"Yes, there is. I just sold the movie rights to one of my novels. Tom wants to discuss the rags-to-riches theory," she lied very noticeably, wanting his reaction to her blatant dishonesty in response to his previous deception. Both knew she was baiting him, but he skillfully avoided it.

"Congratulations again. Seems you're heading for the top of another field. Any snares along the way?" he probed, hinting at some dark secret within his possession. "Life in a glass bowl can be perilous and costly, can't it? Fishbowls are so fragile and tempting; they can include mighty expensive species. Nigel's also told me a great deal about you. I didn't realize I was saving the life of a famous lady."

Her eyes slowly moved up and down his towering frame. Encased in the ivory suit, he easily presented the image of the legendary White Knight. His white façade was broken only by his black bow tie and the black-rimmed diamond studs on the front of his ruffled shirt. She absently wondered why his formal attire made him appear a romantic pirate rather than an elegantly dressed gentleman. She also wondered why his gaze was so hard to resist and why it was so impossible not to stare at him. This vital man was a novel experience, and Brandy didn't know how to deal with it. His seductive voice was like honey, flowing over her and oozing into her pores and making her thoughts too sticky to separate and view clearly.

"Absolutely true, Lance. I've encountered many of those snares and expenses lately." Her eyes became unreadable, even though fused with his. Why was he so inquisitive, so subtly hostile and sarcastic?

"Such as?" he boldly inquired as he picked at an imaginary speck of lint upon the lapel of his off-white silk, single-breasted jacket.

"I doubt you would find my life or problems interesting, Lance." She decided to deny him an answer for the moment.

Hearty laughter rumbled within his chest and his eyes captured playful lights. "In view of our little adventure together, I would call your life anything but dull and safe, Brandy. Do you always get into so much trouble when you work?" he nonchalantly delivered his probing question. His gaze traveled over her face with measured slowness, bringing a flush to her cheeks and an increase to her respiration.

Brandy concluded Lance Reynolds was playing games with her again. If only she knew the rules and prizes . . . He was purposely attempting to unnerve her, and he was succeeding. To dispel the stimulating aura which had surrounded them, she laughed saucily and declared, "Very rarely. But I'll have to change my M.O., if a Sir Lancelot will be around to defend me each time. It isn't often a writer gets to—" Hearing her ridiculous confession coming forth, she halted.

"That a writer gets to do what?" he seized her accidental slip. Live out one of her fantasies? Meet one of her illusive heroes? he mentally speculated with rising intrigue. She was positively an interesting and exciting female, and very different from the ones he knew. But she was good at her craft: matching words and wits as a skilled politician.

Brandy laughed mirthfully. "Have a real-life daring adventure," she murmured, as if telling a private joke. "I'm grateful to you for saving my life; I know it was troublesome," she added to astonish him.

"Do you believe in old sayings?" he inquired, eyes glowing with mischief. When her eyes clouded with confusion, he clarified, "The kind which spilled forth from the mouths of wise old men?"

"I suppose so; why?" She fell into his silver-lined trap.

He stepped forward and captured her face between his hands. "Then, you belong to me now; save a life and it's yours," he dropped his bombshell, searing his burning lips over her parted ones.

Caught by surprise and trapped within his strong embrace, Brandy swayed against his hard frame and surrendered to the intoxicating kiss which was flavored with Scotch. She had dreamed of this moment since meeting him. His kiss was a provocative mixture of savagery and gentleness. Wild and wonderful emotions surged through her.

Her arms eased around his waist beneath his dinner jacket and wandered up the muscled back. Steven's mouth greedily devoured the sweet abandonment of hers. He hadn't planned on this and it stunned him. His arms tightened around Brandy, almost fiercely and painfully. His lips became insistent, demanding, ravishing.

It was clear to Brandy, even in her dreamy world, that Lance Reynolds was a skilled lover. He possessed a magic which was perilous and winning. She vaguely realized she was losing control of her emotions, but it didn't seem to matter to her. This man had haunted her night and day, and she needed to understand why. As his lips leisurely moved over her cheek to press a kiss on her ear, she quivered and sighed. She pressed closely against his taut body, drawing fuel from it to feed her insatiable fire.

Without warning, Steven went rigid and released her, so abruptly that she nearly fell backwards. He tilted his head to study her, observing the passion-glazed eyes and undeniable surrender emblazoned within them. Instead of being pleased with his success, a look of anger and resentment stamped itself upon his handsome features. He berated his stupidity; the game was no longer a game, at least to him. He wished he didn't know the reason behind her tempting allure and eagerness. Did this baffling creature hold nothing precious and sacred: not her life, her honor, her body? How far would she go to get what she wanted? He would comply, if it wouldn't extract a costly price from him. Oddly, he felt it would. He defensively backed down.

"You're playing with fire, Brandy," he warned bitterly. "I have a reputation for shattering fishbowls and devouring little goldfish. Isn't there something more important on your mind tonight than me? What can I do to help?" he asked tenderly, anticipating a stirring bargain. No matter who or what she was, he wanted her, but without deceptions. He was determined to burn off the playing field and work with the charred remains. Whatever her motives, he was certain she had found him just as disturbing and appealing. She looked like an innocent angel, but she didn't kiss or work like one!

Soft emerald eyes met entreating sapphire ones. Her tone was like a silky caress as she replied, "Other than annoying changes in my book for the movie script and a slanderous story which will soon be released by *Glitter Magazine*, nothing of real importance. There's no way you can help with those battles, my dashing knight," she cheerfully informed him, yearning for the return of his arms and lips.

He chuckled, the mocking sound of it failing to warn Brandy of his quest. "So, *Glitter*'s after you? You best run and hide, Brandy; they go for blood. Or so I'm told," he playfully warned. "Any truth to the story, or just spicy gossip?"

"I'm sure a man in your position has run up against this kind of situation before, a fictitious story which might be accepted by a trusting or naive public. How did you handle it? Is there any way to stop them?" she inquired seriously, hoping he could suggest a victorious fight.

Her comments seemed to have some special, enlightening effect upon him. He gazed down at her, assuming he now had his answer for their initial meeting. "Truthfully?" he asked in that stirring accent which reminded her of a Welshman.

"What else but the truth, Lance?" she softly replied, her breathing altering as she gazed up into his face, her hand reaching up to caress his tight jawline. She wondered at his change in mood; he actually appeared deeply troubled and clearly annoyed.

"Do what I did," he advised, coldly ignoring the look of vulnerability and honesty within those green pools. He captured the warm hand which was burning his face, then methodically kissed the tip of each finger. When his tongue drew moist circles in the palm of her hand, she trembled and inhaled. Such a talented actress!

"What, pray tell, was that?" she asked indulgently, feeling he was playing with her in some inexplicable manner. Her other hand went up to steady her balance against his chest, noting the thudding of his heart. He was so distracting and encompassing.

Steven hesitated as he observed her. Her eyes were like a lush, green forest which invited him to boldly trespass and to physically enjoy the scenery. There was no mistaking the look within those green depths. He understood why she had sought him out at such an expense, or so he painfully concluded. This game wasn't getting anywhere; in fact, it was costly. It was time to call her bluff. "There's one way to control the media. Buy them out; I own *Glitter Magazine*," he calmly stated, assuming she already knew he was the owner.

She simply stared at him in total disbelief and shock. He should have guessed from her reaction that she had not known that fact. "You? You own it?" There was no mistaking the triumphant smirk in his eyes or curled upon those sensuous lips.

Brandy's mouth fell open in astonishment when he tauntingly accused, "You see, Miss Alexander, I know everything. I know why you were so desperate to meet me. Though I must admit, your method was highly dangerous for both of us. Your time-consuming rescue nearly blew a half million dollar deal. I also know why you're playing the willing temptress tonight. Your performance is brilliant, but a waste of our time. I don't interfere with business at *Glitter*."

"You believe I planned all of this?" she demanded. When he nodded and grinned mockingly, she visibly balled her fist to keep from slapping his smug face, digging her nails into her palms. So, her rescuer would soon become her executioner.... Her eyes went as cold and forbidding as the Arctic Ocean in the dead of winter. "I see," she sneered contemptuously, barely able to restrain her anguish at this tormenting revelation. Why hadn't Nigel told her?

Brandy knew she was playing out of her league; this man was a master of this sport, this cruel emotional game. Even if he had reason to suspect some mischief on her part or to resent her intrusion into his business affairs, his vicious sport was undeserved; it was beneath him. She had been accurate the other night; Lance Reynolds didn't exist, only the malicious and devious Steven Winngate.

There was a mental tinkling of fragile glass as he shattered her dreamy illusion about him. "Why did you even bother to save my life out there when you plan to destroy it soon?" she heatedly accused. "I've never met a man like you, Steven Winngate, and I pray I never do again. You should go into teaching; you're quite an education."

"The act's over, Brandy; you can drop the pretense," he suggested, trying to ignore the expression on her face, one which strangely pulled on cords of remorse. He waited for her to explain, to ask for forgiveness, to admit it was no longer a game between them. They were no longer the strangers who had begun this ruse.

Brandy's eyes trailed over him from head to foot; she wanted to make certain she never forgot this treacherous man. Something in his strained expression caused her to say, "You're right, Steven; the game is over. But I don't think either of us came out a winner." With that statement, Brandy turned and walked away without offering an explanation; she didn't feel as if he deserved one. He had been making a fool of her. For the first time in her life, Brandy had offered her body and soul to a man; his incisive rejection wounded her deeply.

Steven watched her graceful departure, the proud tilt to her head. He cursed his blunder. Why hadn't he forced a confession from her? Why hadn't he allowed space for a truce? He prayed he wasn't wrong about her.... Either she was wily and brazen, or honest.

Brandy's mind was whirling with the events which stormed her senses as she sought out Nigel. Wild speculations flooded her spongy mind, to be absorbed there, to saturate it with pain and doubts. Had Steven known about the article before or after her rescue? Had his visits to the hospital been exploratory missions, missions to test her, missions to uncover more dirt to fling at her? No doubt she would read a terribly wicked account of their joint adventure. Had he been carrying a camera on that fateful day? Her imagination was running wild again. She was certain of it when she asked herself if the accident could have been a setup.

Her eyes searched the crowded room for Nigel, locating him near the bar. She headed to meet him. "I have to leave, Nigel. See you in New York in a few weeks. Thanks for everything."

"What happened?" Nigel demanded, aware she was distraught, close to tears. He also knew who had been on the terrace with her.

"I can't stay in the same room with a beast who's trying to smear my reputation. If I don't get out of here, I'll probably claw his eyes out. Why didn't you tell me he owns *Glitter*?"

Confused and concerned, Nigel argued, "You can't just run out like this, Brandy. Tell me what he did," he coaxed insistently.

"Back home in Kentucky the only worry I have is what to eat for breakfast. Out here in the real world, it's whether to battle this dragon or the next. This isn't for me, Nigel. I'm going home."

Nigel followed her to the door. She grabbed her lace wrap and kissed his cheek. ''I'll be fine,'' she told him, but her expression belied her brave words. She hugged him and thanked him again. ''Please don't invite us to the same party again.''

Nigel caught her elbow to halt her departure. ''Give, Brandy.''

''Another time. Please,'' she murmured in a strained voice.

He kissed her forehead and released his grip. He opened the door and she was gone. Nigel turned and glared at the man who was poised lazily in the doorway to the terrace, intently witnessing the scene between him and Brandy. The annoyed man headed in Steven's direction.

''Let's talk, Steve. You and I have something to settle,'' he stated sternly, then walked outside. It didn't matter that he and Steve had been friends for years, friends since one of Steve's investment companies had backed his career. Nigel had told Brandy about Steven Winngate, but they had never met, until recently. Somehow his two friends had never been in the same place at the same time. Oddly, Nigel had been planning to introduce them tonight. They seemed so perfectly suited to each other; evidently he was vastly mistaken. Did Steve actually own that rag? Did Steve know what they were planning for Brandy? Perhaps he didn't know Steve at all....

Steven glanced at the door where Brandy had disappeared moments ago. If he didn't know any better, he would think she saw him as the black villain of all time. He pensively rubbed his clean-shaven jawline, then went to join the furious Nigel.

As Steven approached the stalking man, he was reminded of a caged panther who was eyeing his prey, preparing to spring for the attack. ''What the hell did you say or do to Brandy?'' Nigel snarled, teeth bared in unleashed fury. ''Damn it, Steve! She's like my own sister!''

Chapter Five

Brandy sighed heavily as she leaned back in her desk chair. It was good to be home and to be engrossed in writing. To her, nothing felt better or worse than completing a novel; it meant saying hello to new characters and good-bye to beloved personalities who had lived with her for months. The revisions for *Valley of Fire* were finished. She finally comprehended why that work had been difficult; *Valley*'s hero and Lance could be twins, or the same man! She painfully admitted what the new novel *Twilight* had brought into her life; and what it had taken from it, from her.

She had not seen or heard from Steven Winngate since the party in Nigel's suite three weeks ago. She had returned to her hotel room, packed frantically, then caught a flight home. She had fled to safety and to defensive solitude, hoping to forget his magnetic pull upon her ravaged heart. Yet, the passage of time and the distance between them had not helped her. His face and memory still haunted her.

She packed her suitcase and her briefcase. She caught the early flight to New York City, the revised manuscript in her possession. Within a few hours, Brandy was seated in Casey's ultramodern office on Park Avenue. As she patiently waited for Casey to skim the final draft, she sipped the cream sherry which Casey had poured for her. She absently toyed with the numerous, permanent pleats of her tomato-red linen skirt. She ran her slender fingers down the broad lapels of her stark white linen blazer, then checked the placement of the red silk tuft in the slash over her left breast.

At last, Casey glanced up at her and grinned broadly. "You've done it again, Brandy; it's terrific! Just wait until Webster reads this! I can just imagine Jeffery Kearns playing the lead role in the movie version," she said dreamily, then laughed.

"What's next? What about the story on the Viking prince? You could use a long and romantic vacation in the Scandinavian countries. You might locate an amber-eyed, blond hunk," the sunny female teased her favorite client. "Devon loved the draft of *Twilight*," she added.

Brandy smiled at her overt attempt to lighten her somber mood. "For your information, Agent, my next story will be set on the Great Bear Lake, in the heart of the Northwest Territories. I'll be leaving after I complete *Twilight*. My guide just happens to be a giant blond, but he's not golden eyed. Plus, he's very happily married. He's taking his wife along for protection."

They both laughed. "What about coming to a party with me tonight? It'll be at Shelly's penthouse. Besides, Nigel's in town and wants to see you. He's been worried about you since Vegas."

Brandy stiffened. She wanted to decline, but changed her mind. She had been rude to Nigel in Vegas, running out on him like that. If only Lance/Steven hadn't stunned her with the news of his ownership of the magazine which was seeking to malign her.

"Sounds like fun; I'll be there," she answered swiftly. She could not continually retreat from reality. Why should she permit that arrogant tyrant to rule her life? To make her miserable? After all, she reluctantly admitted he had reason to mistrust her.

"Do us both a favor, Brandy; scan the script for *Arrows* this afternoon. Calvin handled it beautifully. The changes are just fine. It might work wonders on that sour attitude."

"All right, Casey. Will he be there tonight?"

"I think so. There's someone else you should meet. He could possibly help us with this *Glitter* problem," she hinted wistfully.

"Who? How?" she hastily responded to that good news.

"Wait and see.... Be on your best behaviour and wear a gorgeous gown." After lunch, they parted company until later.

THE DOOR WAS OPENED to Shelly's luxurious, lofty apartment. Brandy was shown inside by a butler in a scarlet jacket and black pants. She handed him her lacy shawl, then walked into the large open area, hesitating just inside the archway. Her eyes leisurely scanned the large, crowded room which suddenly made her feel like that small-town girl once more. The elegant decor was almost intimidating and overpowering.

She desperately needed and wanted her self-assurance and vivacity returned to her. New York City and London, Kentucky seemed aeons apart. Sighting several friends and acquaintances, she smiled warmly and slightly relaxed her tense body. Maybe she wasn't so out of place after all.

A feeling of resignation washed over her taut body, relaxing it. What did she have to worry about now? The movie script was terrific; her deadline had been met; her next book wasn't due for ten months. She had worked hard lately, and she deserved some excitement and happiness. All in all, things seemed to be on an even keel. Brandy impulsively decided to stay in New York for a few days: to shop, to see plays, to visit friends, to find the sparkle she had lost somewhere, long before Vegas and Lance, and his wild suspicions and betrayal.

"Well, well," a masculine voice crooned softly in her left ear. "Who do we have here; surely not another lovely damsel in distress?" he playfully taunted, wondering how she would greet him.

Brandy wished the floor would open up and swallow her. She would never forget that heart-stopping, lazy drawl. She stiffened her back and called upon all of her hidden reserves to help her survive this perilous moment. She forced a radiant smile to her soft lips and turned to confront him, using every feminine wile she possessed or had used in her novels. She felt challenged to prove this man wrong about her.

"Lance," she murmured softly, as if delighted to see him. "My distressing days are in the past. As you can see, I'm just fine. Since we obviously share so many mutual friends, it's amazing we've never met before. Strange, isn't it? I didn't expect to see you again. If you'll pardon the rush, I have to greet someone," she excused herself.

Before Steven could reply, she waltzed away and slipped into the crowd. As he watched her nearly float away from him, he was surprised she continued to ignore and to avoid him. If she was planning to use him to squelch that story, she was playing it mighty cool! Was that her ploy: entice him to chase an elusive butterfly? To feign indifference to him to spark his intrigue?

Steven was still smarting from that severe tongue-lashing Nigel Davis had given him in Vegas! Since then, he had read the notorious article which had her so distressed. He didn't normally show any interest in his publishing business; not until it had become a very personal matter, or when he had purchased it to get them off his back. What had she been after in Vegas? Inspiration for *Valley* or destruction of the *Glitter* story? How could she instigate and live out her fantasies, then appear so natural, so pure, so softly bewitching, so artless? Why and how could she exploit such private moments and innocent people?

Strange she hadn't claimed innocence or abuse. Was she so naive or vain that she assumed meeting her or supposedly saving her life would alter his judgment about printing that rather nasty story about her private life? But then again, what famous woman wouldn't fight a story which alluded to her sexual preference for women over men? She did live alone, and she was unattached. But that didn't mean she hated men, or was overly affectionate to women. The reporter had been cunning with her words: a clear insinuation without stating facts. What would Brandy's adoring public think about her then? Recalling Brandy's fiery passion, he felt the implications were false.

All evening Brandy could feel the warmth and power of Steven's gaze as it followed her around. He was deliberately trying to ruin her and it amused him to watch her squirm. If only he hadn't been the one to rescue her that fateful day! Of all people to come here tonight! Why were they suddenly being thrown together all the time? She determined she would not leave this party because of the ruthless, domineering Steven Winngate! Not even that sultry Camille in her sexy—almost wickedly indecent—yellow gown would be permitted to harass her with those glacial sneers in her direction. How could he possibly believe she was guilty of such vile charges?

Brandy glanced down at her own gown and critically studied her appearance tonight. Made from black peau de soie, it fell to an angle which left one shoulder totally bare, while the other one was only slightly hidden by a large, ruffled shoulder knot. The dress then flowed to the floor with a provocative slash from the hem to midway between her shapely knees and thighs, revealing beautiful legs in lacy black evening hose. The dress and its color were perfect for her, simple and elegant at the same time. Yet, she failed to realize the full impact of her beauty and allure, things Steven was all too conscious of in this enchanting creature.

As the demanding evening progressed the angrier she became. Why not speak to him about that vile story? Why not try to make him understand her side? Why not prove to him she was a real woman, not some....? Why not prove she could be just as supercilious as he was? Fiery lights danced wickedly and bravely in the emerald depths of her eyes. She would at least show him one thing: She was a woman, a *real* woman.

"Lance?" she called to him from behind. "Could we share a dance and a few words? There's something I want you to know."

Caught unaware, he whirled and stared down into her intoxicating smile. His blood warmed at the seductive look written there. Her eyes reminded him of expensive, beautiful emeralds. He smiled, thinking the game would be met and won this very night. Perhaps he could get her off his mind then! Like a pesky mosquito, her memory had constantly attacked him since their last encounter.

Without a word, he reached for her and pulled her into his possessive embrace. They danced around the floor, unaware of the presence of others. He whirled her onto the terrace beneath the moonlight. A cool breeze ruffled her long hair. They danced until the music ended. Still, he did not release her.

Her heart drummed madly with the danger of this farce. Her respiration quickened. Her gaze fused with his. He watched the moonlight play with her eyes. She could not look away or pull free; she was paralyzed, hypnotized. "I wanted to...." She couldn't remember what she wanted to discuss with him!

It seemed aeons before he slowly pulled her closer and closer until their bodies were touching from shoulder to foot. The heat and contact between them were like an electrical jolt of high voltage. Their lips met, then clung to the other's. His mouth branded her with his mark of ownership. Denied passions tore at their reason, blinding them to all except this fierce need for each other.

Time ceased for Brandy. For the first time in her life, she was the heroine in an unwritten novel. She was feeling those same ecstatic emotions she had described many times, but never experienced. Before her was the man of her dreams, as if created by her own pen. In the heat of the moment, his cruelties and doubts were forgotten.

It was reality; yet, it was a dream. She swayed against his hard body; she totally surrendered her lips and will to him.

No one had ever kissed her this way. One was slow and de-
liberate; another, passionate and demanding. One kiss fused
into another, then another, and another until she was
breathless and quivering.

His fingers slid over her bare arms and shoulders, causing her to tremble against him. His lips seared a fiery trail
across her face, her throat, and her golden shoulders. His
embrace was fierce and possessive yet gentle and persuasive. She felt drugged by his intoxicating aura, his hungry
lips, his tender touch, his warm breath in her ear, his all-
consuming maleness, his dangerous proximity.

"Damn you," he cursed softly and huskily into her ear.
"You've been driving me mad for weeks. I want you,
Brandy; hell, I need you," he confessed, closing his mouth
over hers.

"Steven, I'm so sorry about our misunderstanding," she
whispered against his lips. "Honestly, I didn't plan any of
it," she was compelled to reveal to him. Brandy made a terrible error when she entreated, "Please don't print that
story, Lance; it isn't true. I can prove it," she vowed, but
didn't mean to prove it in the manner he surmised. She
didn't even realize she was calling him by two names, or the
damage her innocent plea had caused.

He leaned back and cupped her face between his large
hands. His gaze probed those lucid, emerald depths for
some clue to her heated response to him. Her hands slid
under his jacket and she caressed the firm muscles on his
chest. His face lowered and his mouth claimed hers once
more. She lost herself within his powerful magic. Nothing
existed except them and this moment. Nothing and no one
until a cutting voice sarcastically sneered, "You were right,
Steven, love; she would do anything to halt that story. Such
a vivid imagination, Brandy! If this is part of your job, I
would do research for you any day...."

Brandy jerked away from him. The look of humiliation
and betrayal in her eyes seared into his brain. "The joke's
over, Mr. Winngate. Print your malicious article. But I

swear to you I'll sue you for every cent you have. You aren't
the only one with money and fame. I will see you in Hell
before I allow you to blacken my name with those vicious
lies. He's all yours, Camille; you two deserve each other!"
She left them standing there, exchanging shocked looks after her biting insult. This battle was childish and ridiculous!

The remainder of that evening was a painful blur for
Brandy. Yet she bravely refused to leave and to grant either
of them another victory at her expense.

Two days later, Steven watched the *Tom Hadley Show*
with intense interest. She did not mention him or the Valley
of Fire incident the first time! She appeared totally relaxed
and genial during the lengthy interview. The woman he
watched on his color set was the same one he had met that
first morning after her accident. Damn if she wasn't a
blasted enigma!

THE PREMIERE for *Midnight Melody* was held while she was
still in town. Steven glanced up to see Brandy on the arm of
the scriptwriter for her latest bestseller. He had made a point
of learning all he could about her since that night at Shelly's. He couldn't keep his eyes off her. Unaware of his presence, she was completely at ease, utterly charming to those
around her, a breath of fresh air for any red-blooded man.
Novel pangs of jealousy gnawed at him.

She looked like a floating angel in that dress of white silk
chiffon with its muted splashes of soft blue, green, and
purple . . . or perhaps a fragile butterfly who was too easily
eluding his captive net!

That gown was perfectly suited for her delicate personality. Steven grinned as his keen gaze passed over the bewitching female who was driving him wild with desire. The
neckline was low and square with small half-cap sleeves. The
area between her bosom and waist was strikingly encased by
numerous tight folds of unstitched, diagonal pleats, making her waist seem smaller than Scarlett O'Hara's.

The full, flowing skirt was diaphanous gossamer over creamy satin. The delicately transparent overskirt was imbued with soft shades of cerulean blue, forest green, and soft purple. Her golden tresses were secured into an abundance of leaf curls and grecian ringlets. Sprigs of baby's breath and short lengths of white ribbon were cunningly placed here and there among her curls. Her cosmetics created a look of fresh and powerful allure. It was abundantly clear Brandy recognized her best points and enhanced them subtly and artfully. Yet, she didn't appear a female overly concerned with her looks or with using them on unsuspecting men; she appeared to accept her attractive allure naturally.

"We might be up there next year, Brandy," Calvin declared optimistically to his ravishing companion. "When *Arrows* is released, you'll become a household name, have a gala premiere of your own."

She smiled and jested, "I'm already a household name, but I dare not say it out loud for fear of offending someone."

"You are too beautiful and cunning, Brandy. The stars will soon bow down to you," he stated romantically, playing with a tawny curl, soaking up the warmth of her radiant smile.

"Those in the heavens or those on the silver screen?" she wittily returned. "What movie did you create that marvelous line for?" she teased him. Calvin laughed.

The night was long, demanding, and glorious. After the showing, they headed to a dinner party at the Connecticut home of Daniel Darcy, the noted movie producer who had purchased the rights to her novel, as well as the one Calvin was working on at present.

Brandy's eyes glittered with excitement and pleasure. She had instantly accepted Calvin's invitation to accompany him tonight. So many things were looking up for her lately: the movie script—thanks to Calvin—had not slaughtered *Arrows; Glitter* had mysteriously withheld that vicious story for future publication; and she was finally beginning to re-gain some of her old sparkle and self-reliance. No doubt that story would appear simultaneously with the debut of the *Arrows* movie. No matter, she had been granted a short reprieve. . . .

Just like the many glasses of champagne which floated around the room on silver trays above the heads of scarlet-jacketed servants, her laughter was bubbly and clear. Brandy had never seen such an array of beautiful, expensive gowns and jewels. She had never experienced a flight of fantasy into the world of the super-rich or the super-powers of the entertainment field. The food was delectable; the decora-tions were unbelievable; the music was stirring; and the aura was magical and contagious. Perhaps she should feel intim-idated or awed by such a blatant show of wealth, fame, and power. But she was far too ecstatic and enlivened to care.

Brandy slowly and cautiously sipped her third glass of heady champagne, for her nose was tingling a warning to be careful of its potency. Dinner had already been served in several locations in the stately mansion and around the pic-turesque pool. She had eaten on the terrace which over-looked a lake where the full moon was skillfully swimming. In great demand, Calvin was constantly detained by others.

Brandy had danced with countless men, some friends and others acquaintances. There were so many people present that she had not seen all of them. Catching her breath on the terrace, she now wished she could stroll down to the wa-ter's edge and intoxicate herself with that stunning view at close range.

"Always the scenery buff, Brandy? Or is this only a rest from all your many admirers?"

She jumped, then relaxed herself. She turned and looked up at him. "Have you suddenly become my shadow, Lance Reynolds? Every time I go out, I see you. Why is it we're constantly running into each other these days? We never did before. Don't you ever work or travel? And I was having such a marvelous time tonight,'' she scoffed irritably, hinting that he would now spoil it.

His darkened gaze passed appreciatively over her entire body. "I'm much too large to be your shadow, Brandy love. Not that I would object to standing that close to you at times. As for work, I do that every day; I did travel here to New York," he teased lazily.

She unknowingly rubbed her tingling nose with her fingers, bringing a grin to his sensual mouth. "I suppose you're right," she reluctantly admitted, ignoring his veiled compliment.

"You look utterly breathtaking this evening. But then, you always do." His gaze leisurely traveled the translucent, flowing lines of her gown. He reached out and lifted the heart-shaped diamond pendant from her throat and studied it. "Do all these hearts come from countless admirers?" Damn, could he be wrong about this woman?

She cocked her head sideways and looked up at him. "My, aren't we the gallant gentleman this evening! Have you doused your fiery flames for tonight, Sir Dragon?" she softly cooed, alarmed more by the real fires which leaped uncontrollably at his nearness and manly odor.

"I will, if you'll sheathe those sharp claws, my little golden Kat. I only wanted to thank you for replacing my bike. It wasn't necessary; my insurance covered the loss," he murmured, his fingers toying with a golden curl and sprig of tiny white flowers. "I meant to thank you the last time we met, but it slipped my mind."

"I always pay my debts, Lance. Officer Connelly was kind enough to secure the correct model and specifications for me; I trust they delivered the right one? It should have perfectly matched the bike which was stripped. It was only right that I should replace it for you. Surely my life is worth a measly FLT-80 Harley-Davidson motorcycle? Replacing it seemed the best way to reward your chivalry since I so obviously detained and humiliated you that fateful night, or so I was told. Shall we call it even and avoid each other from now on?''

She started to walk away, needing to leave his masterful aura and disturbing touch. Perplexed by these curious facts, he seized her arm in a firm, but painless, grip. She glared at his hold upon her arm first, then up at him. "Release me this instant, Steven! There's no way I'll let you set me up like that again. This cold war between us has gone far enough. It's apparent we can't be friends, or even civil to each other. That was the lowest thing anyone has ever done to me," she hotly accused. "I wish I knew why you despise me so much."

"For one thing, I didn't mean for Camille to disturb us. Another thing, I have some questions for you. You said you asked Officer Connelly to get that information about my bike for you. Was replacing it the only reason for checking it out?" His tone was mocking. Now that he was on to her game, was she merely altering her tactics?

"Why else would I want such information?" she questioned, sensing a point to his demanding query. She was weary of fencing in the dark with this insufferable and disarming rogue.

"Why else indeed? Did you know I was the owner of *Glitter* before I told you?" he probed, imprisoning her gaze.

"What difference does your ownership make? I've already been to see your editor, your publisher, and that vicious reporter Laura McGavin. I offered to let them come to Kentucky to research a true story about me, including all the pictures they want to take! But they're no more interested in the real facts, which are far less colorful and earthshaking, than you are. It doesn't make any difference if that story is utterly false. You don't even care if I sue. You know it could take years to prove my innocence; by that time, terrible damage will be done to my name and reputation. I might be vain, Steven, but a person's name is her most precious possession. I swear to you I'll go down fighting you every inch of the way! What have I done to earn this hostility? Kindly remove your hands!"

"In a moment," he calmly stated as he tried to analyze this new information. "Why didn't you mention your recent accident and your new book on Tom's show?"

Startled, she faced him fully. This was the second time he had mentioned the show in that strange tone. "Are you kidding? We were both extremely lucky the news wires didn't get wind of that accident. I can just imagine how it would have been exploited clear across the United States: 'Wealthy Oil Tycoon Rescues Romance Writer in Distress!' They would have had a field day with our personal lives. Surely you aren't planning to add it to that vile story you're already holding?" she asked in vivid dismay.

"Certainly not! It cost me a blue penny to squelch it that same night," he said, letting her in on the reason why it had not hit print.

"You?" she stammered. Her head was spinning with crazy ideas. Before she could thank him, he made it impossible.

"As you said, my private life is nobody's business, including yours, my infamous writer. Have you completed the novel you went to Nevada to research? Let's see... *Valley of Fire*, wasn't it?"

She gaped at him. How did he know so much about her affairs? She didn't correct his error about *Valley*. She parried his question with an insult, "You lied when you said Nigel told you about that interview. I had just been asked to do it that same week; nobody knew about it. How you found out about it, I'll never know! Do you have other spies like your Laura McGavin? If so, I surely hope their reports are more accurate and civil than hers. As for *Valley*, I turned it in when I arrived here... not that it's any of your business!"

"You've already finished it and turned it in?" he stormed at her as if she had just hurled a deadly spear at him which he was trying to fend off with the mere force of his voice and anger.

Alarmed by his inexplicable reaction to that news, she tried to pull free of him. His eyes had gradually darkened with a violent storm brewing deep within him. He seized her wrists, one in each hand, and unknowingly tightened his grip until she cried out in pain. He instantly lightened it, but did not let her go. His strength and mood were potent. He retreated into pensive thought.

She glanced over his magnetic image. He was wearing a dark blue suit with flecks of brown and light blue interwoven into the expensive material. His cream shirt was custom cut, molding to his torso. His dark brown tie was Italian silk with designer initials near the bottom. She irrationally wondered why he wasn't in a tuxedo or evening attire. Yet, he overshadowed all men present with his elegance.

"That's too bad, Brandy; I had planned to trade that manuscript for the *Glitter* story. I've already told them to hold it until I give the okay for its release. If we could have made a deal, I would have canceled it altogether," he stated regretfully, shockingly.

"That's why it hasn't been printed yet! Why didn't you call me? What do you want with a draft of *Valley*?" Why did this mysterious and moody creature demand a manuscript written and sold last winter?

His smile was deadly and sensual. "For my private collection. It holds special meaning for me," he said, shrugging his shoulders.

Brandy was astounded and bewildered. "Is that what it's all about, Steven? My weird accident? Your vile story? Your surveillance? Your harassment? Your eccentric whims? You want a souvenir of your rescue, a treasure of mine? If I had known you wanted it that badly, I would have given you the script rather than a new bike. It's too late now; Webster has it. It's scheduled for release within two months."

"Then, we've both wasted our time and energies. Get it back, Brandy, and I'll kill the story on you," he offered once again.

"It's too late, Steven. They're up to galleys now."

"Yes, it is...." He released her so suddenly that she swayed. She grabbed at the lapels of his jacket. "Just to clear the air, you don't know why I really want it. Your charges against me aren't true."

Instinctively his arms reached out to catch her. She looked up at him. "I should write a story about you, Steven. I could entitle it *Devil Incognito*. You're perfect for that role!"

"You flatter me, Brandy. Two books about me?" he growled mysteriously. She had plotted, written, and already sold their escapade!

"Two books? About you? What are you talking about?" she asked confusedly.

"You're saying I and our adventure aren't featured in your last book? Not a single reader will see me as the hero?" he snarled.

"I must admit you fit the image of most romantic heroes, but not mine. Varian Saar is amber-eyed and blond-haired. Unless you plan to change the color of your eyes and hair, I'll have to disappoint you."

He openly gaped at her. "You didn't describe me?"

"Don't be absurd! I made certain there was no resemblance," she rashly confessed, then wanted to bite her careless tongue.

"What about his character? Will I recognize myself there?" he continued, unaware they were discussing two different works.

She taunted, "Perhaps. You are a throwback from that type of man and age. Is that why you wanted the manuscript? I could offer you the next one," she mockingly ventured.

Her words amazed him. When he did not release her, she sneered, "I thought you were finished with me! I can't give it to you, and it isn't about you or us. What more do you want?''

''Research, Brandy love... Research for *Devil Incognito*,'' he murmured huskily. His embrace tightened. He watched panic fill her lucid, wide eyes. His lips came down upon hers in a demanding, bruising kiss. His mouth forced hers apart. Instantly, the kiss softened and seared her mind. It ordered her to respond; it stripped away all resistance. She trembled in his warm embrace.

She desperately wanted to resist him and the powerful invasion of her senses. She could not. She swayed against him. She failed to note his release of her arms or to notice how they had helplessly slipped around his narrow waist. There was no end to that kiss or a beginning to the next one; they all mingled into one endless kiss which tore away her will and reality.

Soft, romantic music came from somewhere far away. She shuddered as his lips blazed a fiery path across her cheeks and inflamed her senses as he softly whispered into her eager ear. As his lips leisurely traveled her throat and shoulders, her head fell backwards and a soft moan escaped her throat. His mouth nipped at her golden shoulders and at her dainty earlobes, sending chills over her weakened body.

She murmured his name time and time again. She was like putty in the hands of a master artist. She had no will of her own or any ability to control herself or him. For the first time in her life, she wanted a man completely and instantly.

Shrill laughter invaded her dream world, rudely jerking her back to reality. There was a drunken couple racing towards the lake, laughing and shouting loudly. Her senses slowly returned. His gaze glued to the fires of passion within her emerald eyes. They slowly drifted to the rapid rise and fall of her bosom. He noted the helpless tremblings of her slender body as she fought to regain some measure of control over her unleashed emotions, yet not seeming to know how. At his close scrutiny, her face flamed red in shame and resentment.

She panted sharply, "You've made your point, Mephi-stopheles! This book should interest you far more than the other one."

He chuckled in pleasure at his distressing effect upon her, for no one could claim she was not interested in men.... "If I could help you write it..."

"You arrogant, hateful devil! You're the last man to in-trigue me in that way," she hotly declared, her impassioned aura loudly belying her words. "Where do you get such crazy ideas?"

"Something tells me that isn't quite true, Brandy. I won-der what it could be that makes me think you're being dis-honest," he casually remarked, rubbing his smooth jawline with his left hand. "Let's see.... You spurn my advances; you resist my touch and kisses; I have no effect on you at all. Tell me, love, is it too difficult or impossible to prove that story a lie? You could very easily do so, couldn't you?" he challenged, eager for this new role.

She swallowed hard. "You can't be suggesting what I think you are! No trade, Winngate!" she nearly shouted at him, her pulse racing wildly at such an intoxicating ar-rangement.

"Is it impossible, Brandy love? You've written such a scene many times: handsome, ruthless lover seduces the in-nocent, vulnerable heroine.... Cue me with the proper lines and actions to terminate this scene exactly where we both want it to end. Unless I'm badly mistaken, you're just as attracted to me as I am to you. Isn't that right?" If she wanted accurate research, he would gladly oblige her.

She flushed a deep scarlet before she could conceal her face by lowering her head. His amused laughter sliced her ravaged heart without mercy. "Well, well. How does it feel to be caught in your own trap, love? To be researched in-stead of to research? You make a lovely specimen under glass, Brandy. You realize I have the power and means to break it or to polish it? Admit it: You want me as much as I want you." She had instigated their encounter; why was she being so coy and reluctant now that he was baited and hooked?

She didn't verbally answer him, but her reaction spoke loudly. Terrified by the truth of his words and tormented by his virulent spite, she murmured, "I can't offer you *Valley* or my services, Steven. I'll see you in court," she vowed and hurried off before he could stop her.

He sighed heavily. Too many facts didn't add up right. In addition, others were being logically explained or being reduced to false impressions. She had done nothing to directly offend him or to publicly exploit him. Why was Brandy such a heady challenge, one he couldn't master, one which infused him with determination, one which could conquer him if he allowed it, one which scared the hell out of him?

When Steven returned to the ballroom, he was astonished to see her calmly dancing with Nigel Davis. In her agitated state of mind, he had assumed she would quickly vanish once again. He headed for the totally unpredictable female. Camille, clad in her Egyptian style gown, tried to halt his steady progress and to prevent his clear intention, but he simply moved her aside. His eyes never left Brandy's golden mane and ivory gown as he moved across the floor like some graceful, black panther intently stalking his vulnerable prey.

He tapped Nigel upon the shoulder and smoothly slid between them before either of them could argue. He whirled her away from the shocked singer. When she threatened to stomp his foot or to slap his smug face, he flashed her an engaging grin and warned her of the terrible scene it would make: a scandal for the morning papers to report.

Trapped within the warm and protective confines of his arms, she could only obey his whims. Her small hand was icy cold within his large warm one. He laid his taut jawline against her temple. He held her tightly and securely, denying her the chance to steal away during one of their turns. She mischievously decided to turn on the charm and throw him off-balance. This conceited ass needed a stunning lesson!

"Your hands are mighty soft for a horse breeder," he murmured. He inhaled a fragrance which sent his mind to reeling and to planning.

"The miracles of expensive hand creams and trusty helpers," she replied sweetly, deciding two could play at his mocking game. She boldly caressed his sun-bronzed cheek with one of those soft hands. Flames danced within his fiery blue eyes. His hold upon her tightened. She moistened her dry lips in a most inviting and flirtatious manner.

"Don't tempt the devil to claim his due in public," he warned in a husky tone. His lips pressed a light kiss on her forehead before he returned his jaw to her fragrant temple. "You smell delicious."

"What is your due, Sir Lucifer? Wasn't the new motorcycle sufficient reward for my life?" she asked in a voice of soft velvet.

He looked down at her. "I think not, Brandy. Like your namesake, you promise fire and enjoyment to someone who can afford your expensive and rare brand. You'd be good on a cold winter's night or when the body and spirit were lagging. Can you intoxicate a man beyond his control?" His tone was such that she trembled. He grinned.

"Can you afford my price and effect, Sir Demon? As for intoxicating a man beyond control, evidently you're immune to my potency. What about my other name, Kat? Shall I claw out your black heart, Sir Demon? Shall I shred your handsome face and deny you your magic and charm? Shall I become just as cunning and destructive as the devil himself? I've tried to make amends for causing you such trouble, but you clearly dislike and repel me. Which facet do you prefer: warm, golden Brandy or precarious tawny Kat?" she purred, thrilled by the astonishment on his face.

"Being a connoisseur, why can't I sample both?"

Their eyes forged in fiery speculation. "I've already supplied you with one daring adventure; care to risk or claim another?" he hinted.

Brandy saw Camille heading in their direction, eyes blazing with anger and embarrassment at being ignored by her envious date. Brandy smiled mischievously, then offered, "Whichever you're due, Lance. Later though. Your Camille is on the warpath, my love."

There was some meaning behind her choice of names and the silky way she had spoken it. Their eyes fused in mutual study. Camille seized his arm and softly spewed forth her displeasure with them, reminding him in no uncertain terms that he was her date. Her furious gaze challenged Brandy to deny her prior claim on Steven.

Recalling how this vile woman had degraded her not so very long ago, a reckless Brandy sent him a dazzling, apologetic smile. Her hand went up to leisurely fondle his chest as she seductively murmured, "Halftime, my dashing knight. The game plan calls for a defensive withdrawal to form a new strategy...." She turned and glided away from him, unaware of the effect of her words and mood upon him.

Brandy grinned happily, thinking she had finally gotten in the last point in their game of wits. At the archway to the next room, she paused and glanced back into the room. Her smile faded instantly as she observed the retreating backs of Steven and that spiteful Camille as they headed for the moonlit, rose-lined terrace. His back to Brandy, she could not know of the black fury which was furrowing his handsome features at the dauntless and unwanted interference by the spoiled woman upon his arm. Another game lost....

Brandy was mistaken if she believed Steven wouldn't take the bait she had brazenly offered him. After the party, she returned to her hotel suite and took a long, relaxing bath. Deciding to make some notes on the sights and feelings of this special night, she slipped into a silky caftan and sat down at the table. She glanced towards her door when someone knocked on it. She wondered who would come calling at two in the morning; probably the wrong room. She tried to ignore it, but the persistent person wouldn't leave.

Chapter Six

Brandy anxiously called out, "Who's there?"

She was stunned when a mellow voice announced, "It's me, Steven. I need to talk with you."

"Do you know what time it is? What do you want?" she asked frostily.

"It's three o'clock, but I have to settle something tonight," he pressed, leaning against the door. "May I come in?"

"You and I have nothing to say, Mr. Winngate. Besides, it's late," she responded, knowing she didn't dare confront him again tonight.

"I'm not leaving until we talk, Brandy, face to face," he warned stubbornly, persistently.

"No. You've made yourself perfectly clear; so have I," she refused apprehensively. Why wouldn't he leave her alone?

"If you want, I can get awfully loud. We don't want a scene, do we?" he challenged ominously.

Brandy opened the door a crack. "What is it?" she demanded.

"Obviously we've had a terrible misunderstanding, Brandy. I think it's time we cleared up some matters between us," he insisted, pushing the door open and walking inside.

Brandy whirled to look at him. The self-assured man strolled over to the window and stared outside, calmly waiting for her to join him. "Just what do you want?" she asked, the door still open as if she feared to close it, to seal them in a world of intimidating privacy.

"First, we need to discuss the *Glitter* article," he began, turning to watch her. "Then us."

That remark seized her attention. Had he changed his mind? Had she judged him too quickly and too harshly? She sighed wearily and closed the door. She came forward, halting a few feet from him, eyeing him skeptically. "What about the article?"

"Nigel tells me I've misjudged you. Is that true?" he almost demanded, stunning her with the insinuation in his voice. His gaze drilled into hers, as if to forcefully open it to his scrutiny.

"What difference does that make?" she asked, confused and intrigued. She had a fairly accurate picture of his opinion of her.

"It makes a hell of a difference to me!" he thundered into the quiet room. He shoved the tumbling lock off his forehead, his eyes daring her to lie.

"Yes, you have. You've done nothing but embarrass me and deceive me. I didn't know your real name; and I didn't know about your connection with *Glitter*. I have no intentions of exploiting you in any form or fashion, professionally or personally. What other charges are leveled against me?" she sarcastically snapped, ready and eager to open this can of worms and empty it on the table.

"Why did you conceal your identity? Why intentionally mislead me?" he accused, his towering frame taut with some unknown emotion. "Were you afraid I'd make demands on you for saving your lovely neck?"

"I didn't mislead you; I am Kathy Alexander. If anyone lied, it was you!" she said, distressed by this crazy scene. "Did you set up that accident so you could *rescue* me?" she purred. "I'd think you were saturated with females!"

"Did I what?" he asked incredulously. "Are you nuts, woman?"

"It's awfully strange that you, of all men, would be the one to save my life," she hinted meaningfully.

"That was my exact thought," he retorted, coming to stand within inches of her. "I've endured some wild accidental meetings, but yours tops them all. Were you hoping I'd halt the article if you enchanted me? Do you always go to such lengths for accurate research?"

Her eyes grew wide with unleashed anger. "You can't honestly think I arranged that accident to meet you!" she fired in disbelief.

"Didn't you?" he challenged, a bedeviling grin capturing his mouth and eyes.

"Don't be insane!" she shouted at him. "I wouldn't risk my life for anything. How could I possibly know you would happen along?"

"Not even to meet the man who held the power to save your reputation and career?" he added, watching her closely.

"I do want that article halted, but not at any cost. Besides, I didn't know you owned *Glitter;* I didn't know who you were until Nigel told me at Lido's!" she stressed. "Just what are you after? More dirt to include? Damn you, it was an accident, nothing more. If you dare use it for sensational publicity, I'll sue you for every dime you have," she warned. "Did you have a camera that day?"

He realized she was serious, serious and worried. "You really didn't know who I was, did you?" he pressed, convinced.

"I swear it," she stated, eyes clouded with nervous tears.

"Then why didn't you tell me who you were?" he returned to his prior question. "You must admit I had reason to be suspicious."

"You know why. For the same reason you fiercely guard your name and identity. I have enough problems with men because of my romance writing; I don't like to give strangers any ideas. I don't care how it looks or what you think. I don't want anything from you, Lance," she vowed, but her eyes told a different story.

"Don't you, Brandy?" he asked, closing the short distance between them. When she started to retreat, he caught her shoulders and halted her. "I'd have to be a damn fool not to realize what's happening between us. What I don't understand is why we keep fighting it. You see it too. You know why we're both being so damn defensive, don't you?" His head lowered and his mouth closed over hers.

The kiss shattered her anger and resistance. He pulled her into his arms and held her tightly. Her senses began to spin wildly, for she had never been kissed in such an all-consuming manner before. His mouth was demanding and stimulating. The gently exploratory kiss deepened to one of urgent need. Brandy trembled within his possessive embrace; her arms eased around his waist. She responded passionately to the hunger of his mouth and to the yearnings which plagued her body.

After several kisses which vanquished her will, Steven leaned back and gazed down into those limpid pools of green. "I want you, Brandy, and I'm tired of fighting it," he murmured hoarsely, the intense need in his voice matching the desire written in his eyes. "Ever since that morning in your hospital room, I haven't been able to concentrate on anything but you. For some insane reason, we keep cutting each other to ribbons. I've been rude and mean; I'm sorry. I was wrong, Brandy, terribly wrong," he confessed. "Forgive me?"

Brandy couldn't pull her eyes from his or think clearly. She was past fighting this overwhelming attraction between them, as was Steven. So many emotions were demanding to be freed, so much of the unknown struggling to be explored and understood. She couldn't think of any reason to refuse what they both wanted and needed—each other. She didn't speak, but Steven comprehended her willingness and eagerness. His lips captured hers once more and he lifted her and carried her to the bed. Brandy didn't refuse or argue.

Fires of passion burned brightly and dangerously as Steven assailed her senses with staggering kisses. When he eased the caftan off her shoulder and allowed his tongue to circle a taut peak, she shuddered and moaned. As his fiery lips left one to torment the other, Brandy thought she would go mad with overpowering need for him.

As Steven continued his tantalizing journey over her body with seeking lips and probing hands, she thrilled to the wonder of his expertise. Insecurity flooded her. Steven was accustomed to women who were well-versed in seduction. She didn't even know what to say or how to behave.

When she tried to pull away, Steven gazed down at her frightened face. "What's wrong, love?" he asked tenderly, hoarsely.

"I—" she began and halted. She weakly went on, "We can't, Lance. We just met."

"It's too late to stop now, Brandy," he informed her, his eyes melting into hers, comprehending the war between desire and panic.

Brandy knew he was right. "But—" she began once more.

"But what, Brandy?" he asked, his gaze imploring and gentle. He dropped little kisses over her eyes, then claimed her ears. His hands enticed her mind to forget all else except him, which she did. "You want me," he stated, rather than asked.

She met his entreating gaze and whispered, "Yes, I want you, Steven." She couldn't deny it or fight it any longer; emotions as old as time itself would brand her a liar and a fool if she tried. Whatever the cost, she must have the man who brought her dreams to vivid life.

When Steven slackened his pace to undress them, he was keenly aware of the flush upon her cheeks and the way she avoided his eyes. Suddenly her hesitation and fear struck home; would this be her first time? How was that possible?

Steven wondered how he should handle this dangerous situation, if his assumption was correct. There was a warning bell sounding loudly within his head. "Have you ever made love to a man before?" he asked unexpectedly.

"What?" she stammered in confusion, her cheeks burning.

"You heard me, Brandy," he stated sternly.

"No," the shaky voice answered so softly that he just barely heard her shocking admission. "Does that matter?" she asked naively.

She was yielding to him what she had refused all other men. The weight of that responsibility stormed his warring senses. If she was willing to surrender to him, what did that mean? The answer to that question disturbed him greatly. Brandy wasn't like the other women he had known and taken lightly. She was different, special. Could he bind her to him by taking her today, for surely he would? Did he want to? He was a carefree bachelor. He could take women and leave them, without guilt or commitments. But Brandy— could he take her and leave her? Yet, could he take her and keep her? Something about this female troubled him. Damn, he wanted her; but he would be damned for certain if he took her! Brandy was the type to expect some commitment in return....

"Steven?" she entreated. "Does it matter that I've never...I mean, I know you're used to women who know what to say and do in situations like this. I..." She faltered and fell silent.

"Do you realize what you're doing?" he asked, almost wishing she would change her mind, praying she wouldn't.

"No," she admitted with a nervous laugh. "But I assume you do."

He chuckled. "Frankly, I've never been with any woman on her first time. I've heard it can be...uncomfortable. I wouldn't want to hurt you, Brandy, or spoil such a moment for you."

She eyed him closely. He was actually worried about disappointing her. That show of insecurity and concern warmed her very soul. She smiled, then laced her fingers through his sable hair and pulled his head down to fuse their lips. When the kiss ended, she gazed up into his eyes and murmured, "I want you, Steven, more than I've wanted anything in my life. Love me," she pleaded softly, without reservation or modesty.

"Are you sure, Brandy?" he forced her to admit.

"Yes. You've tempted me and tormented me for ages. I want you," she stated with determination and confidence.

He was assured she knew what she was doing, but did he? No matter, he couldn't refuse either of them. His mouth claimed hers. As a talented musician, he played on the strings of her body, creating a heady melody, music which was mesmerizing and stirring.

Deft hands tantalized and stimulated her pliant body, admiring her beauty and softness. He seductively ravished her lips and breasts, inspiring soft moans and eager responses. His hand slid over her flat stomach to explore a tawny forest and torment her senses. When he felt she was ready to challenge and conquer the unknown, he moved above her, gliding between her welcoming thighs.

He hoped it was true that one persistent thrust was best for her. He positioned himself and as tenderly as possible entered her receptive body. She stiffened briefly and inhaled sharply, then relaxed. He moved slowly and carefully, intensely aware of the throbbing within him, an aching need which selfishly demanded instant relief.

After a few moments, he leaned back and asked, "Are you all right, Brandy?"

She smiled and nodded. He grinned happily and captured her parted lips with his. The tension and pleasure increased. He was hard pressed to control himself, but managed to do so. He didn't realize she was so close to ecstasy until her grip tightened around him and she kissed him feverishly. His rhythm increased as he forced her over the edge of reality and completion, then hastily joined her on the downward spiral they had just conquered.

He continued to spread kisses over her face and lips until his thudding heart slowed to normal, then pulled her tightly against his sated body. He chuckled when she laughed and stated, "I was right; you are very talented in this area, Steven."

"I take it I didn't disappoint you," he teased, stroking the warm flesh on her back, nuzzling against her fragrant hair.

She leaned her head back and bravely met his contented gaze. "If anything, Mr. Winngate, you utterly amazed me. I know this sounds like a line from one of my books, but I didn't know it could be like this. To quote one of my heroines, 'You are magnificent, utterly irresistible.' Now I understand why you're in such demand," she joked lightly, feeling relaxed and enchanted.

"I'd like to be in demand by you, if that's possible," he hinted slyly, flashing her a beguiling grin, pleased that her innocence was real.

"Why?" she foolishly asked. "I'm not your usual type."

"That's my point; you're refreshing and exciting, Brandy. There's something special about you. You're so many things rolled into one neat package. You're as complex as you are simple. You're as carefree as you are reserved. You're fragile and strong. You're a damn contradiction, woman," he concluded with a frustrated laugh.

"A mystery to hold your interest, Mr. Winngate?" she playfully teased, caressing his cheek, then running her finger over his lips. "I'm really a very plain and uncomplicated person."

"There's nothing plain, or simple, or uncomplicated about you, Brandy," he debated. "I think I'll enjoy unraveling you."

"I'm a challenge, is that it?" she retorted, gently tugging a lock of ebony hair.

"Damn right, you are," he came back instantly.

"Good. Then you won't be bored too soon."

"Bored?" he echoed mockingly. "If you have as many secrets and facets as your countless heroines, I'll never discover the real you."

That statement hit Brandy like ice water in the face. She tensed. "You've read my books?" she asked guardedly.

"All of them, some twice. You're damn good; did I forget to tell you that? You know what I found intriguing?" he inquired.

"What?" she responded warily, dreading his reply.

"Writers always claim they aren't their characters, but you can't. The more I get to know you, the more qualities and traits I see you sharing with them. Fess up, Brandy; there's a part of you in each one," he declared, mischievously.

"I suppose writers do give traits to their characters which they like or possess. Which of my heroines tempts you the most? Which would you like me to be for you?" she asked, her tone angry and sullen.

Steven realized he had struck a raw nerve. He was doing what she hated men to do, placing her in a fictional role. "I didn't mean it like that, Brandy. I was referring to traits like shyness, sensitivity, innocence, honesty... If I offended you or upset you, I'm sorry. I wasn't analyzing you through your works."

She stared at him. "I suppose I do give them qualities I wish I had. I would love to be carefree and daring sometimes. I'd like to be confident in situations like this one. You know something weird and incredible? You're the first real man I've ever met. And yet, you're so much like my creations that it scares the hell out of me."

"There's one big difference, Brandy; I'm real and they're not. Is that why you've been fighting this attraction between us? Are you afraid I'll behave like they do, or do you fear I won't? What do you want from me, Brandy?" he asked, a look of utter seriousness on his face.

"Only you, Lance, just as you are," she replied candidly.

"I'm not Lance, Brandy," he stated meaningfully.

"Aren't you?" she debated, wondering at his underlying point.

"Lance is a fictional creation, just like your heroes. I'm Steven, nothing more or less."

"I feel as if I walked into a theater in the middle of a mystery movie. I don't understand. Who are you, Steven?"

"Only a man, Brandy, a red-blooded, real man."

Her confusion increased. "You're not just a man, Steven."

A curious sadness filled his eyes. "That's the problem, Brandy; you see me as more, and I'm not. I'm not even sure you're separating fantasy and reality. I'm not your hero, Brandy."

"I didn't say you were," she vowed in exasperation. "I know the difference between fiction and reality."

"Do you? Our meeting could have come off the pages of one of your books. You've already said I was just like your creations."

Brandy couldn't argue that last point, but she knew she could never make him understand. Maybe she was experiencing some magical mixture of both worlds. But it wasn't of her doing. She tried to lighten the gravity of their mood. She laughed and teased, "Your wild imagination beats even mine, Steven. I take it you've never met a writer before? Sure, we draw from our own experience and knowledge. But there is a definite line between reality and fantasy, one I recognize and respect. I'm not trying to place you in any role. I like you just as you are. I don't understand your concerns."

Steven had to unmask one point which plagued him. "Your stories always end happily ever after. What do you expect from me after this?" he asked, sweeping his hand over their still entwined bodies.

"Now I understand," she stated thoughtfully. "You're afraid I'll misread your intentions? You're worried I might make demands on your time and energies, expect some commitment from you?" She wisely didn't add, *Just like a hero, always defensive when he comes to protecting his freedom.* Brandy almost felt as if she had lived this scene many times before. *Think,* she warned herself. *Think before you screw up!* In light of his worries, she scolded herself for speaking like an historical heroine half the time; but it came so naturally for a Southern girl, especially a romance writer.

She reached up to caress his cheek. "I realize this is something new for me, Steven, but I don't expect anything from you. You wanted me, and I wanted you. You didn't seduce me or ravish me. I'm a grown woman, and this isn't the middle ages. I can't help it if I see you as a very special and unusual man. I don't mean to intimidate or unsettle you. I won't pressure you or hotly pursue you. For one thing, I don't have the time. When I get home, I'll be confined to my office until my next book's finished. Rest assured, we won't even be accidentally running into each other anytime soon. If you want to see me again, I'm willing. If not..." She left that sentence hanging.

"Look, Brandy, I know I've been obnoxious to you since we met. But I've explained my reasons and apologized. Maybe I am too damn cynical, but I believe what you said. We could have avoided some of our mix-ups if we'd dared to speak honestly. Stupid ego-trips!"

"I said I understood why you treated me so badly. Our meeting was a crazy coincidence, nothing more. Why can't we forget it? Why not relax and enjoy this truce? It could be ages before we see each other again," she announced to calm his worries.

"I thought you came to New York frequently on business," he said.

"I do, on occasion. But I doubt we'll be here the same time."

"What about when you sue me for libel?" he asked solemnly.

"When I what?" she inquired in astonishment.

"I can't halt the article, Brandy. I make it a policy not to interfere in businesses I own and don't personally run," he tested her.

"You mean you won't even try to prevent it from being published? It's your company! What about tonight?" she cried at him. "You can make love to me, then destroy me? What kind of man are you?"

"I can only promise to intervene, Brandy, but not override their decision. The story obviously isn't true; you proved that."

"Proved it?" she sneered at the sound of the implication. "I wasn't trying to prove anything! My God, is sex always this demanding and complicated? No wonder I haven't gotten tangled up with a man before! You're all selfish idiots! Damn you, Steven Winngate!" Brandy sat up in the bed and pulled the sheet up to cover her breasts. "Just get the hell out of my room and life! Your head's too screwed up to see anything! If anyone's functioning in a fantasy world, it's you!"

"Me?" he stormed back at her.

"Yes, you. You don't even know what real emotions are. You're so hung up on thinking everybody wants something from you. You're selfish and egotistical. You've proven you're irresistible. I'm no threat to your precious freedom! I don't crave your name, or your money, or your lofty status; I have more than enough of my own. I don't even care about that stupid article anymore! If anyone doubts me, I can certainly prove them wrong!"

"You wouldn't dare!" he snarled angrily, her meaning clear.

"Try me," she challenged. "I'll make you and your sleazy magazine look like fools!"

He glared at her. "If you dare start acting like a slut to discredit that story, I'll..."

"You'll what, Mr. Winngate?" she taunted.

"I'll become more like one of your ruthless heroes than you can even imagine. I told you I'd try to crush the story."

"You've certainly been paid a high price for your assistance. That is what you think, isn't it? Is that why you came here tonight? To see if I would bribe you? To see if I was immune? Well you're sadly mistaken; I slept with you for one reason only. I wanted you."

Her fury astounded him. "No, Brandy, I didn't come for any of those reasons. Why are we attacking each other again? This is crazy!"

"No, Steven, this is reality," she scoffed. "If I tried to explain, you wouldn't understand. Let's just leave it at that—we're both different and we find that trait intimidating in each other. We both want something we don't understand. It frightens us to find another person so tempting and pleasing, and we fiercely rebel against that confusing fear and against changes which the other implies. We don't want to let go, but we're afraid to demand or to even want more."

"Maybe you're right, Brandy, maybe we are a threat to each other. You tempt me to outrageous lengths. I came because I wanted you, for no other reason. Other than to make peace. When will you be leaving? I seem to keep saying and doing the wrong things with you."

"In a few days." She couldn't ask, *Why?*

He stood up and dressed. For once, Steven didn't know what to say. Multimillion dollar deals were less complicated than this situation. He pulled out the insurance check and handed it to her. "This is yours; the insurance company paid for the bike."

Brandy accepted the check and smiled. "Take care of yourself, Steven. Next time, let someone else rescue me."

"I hope there won't be a next time, Brandy. Promise you'll be more careful in the future? You aren't sorry about tonight, are you?"

Their gazes met and searched, each seeking an answer to what was going wrong again, why it was so hard to accept this gift from Fate.

Brandy realized Steven was overly concerned about his attraction to her. He was trying to view her as a novelty, a challenge to his ego, a debt she owed him, a passing fancy. Sadly, there was nothing she could do but let him work out his problems.

"You're quite a woman, Brandy," he whispered against her lips, then kissed her soundly. He held her tightly for a moment.

"Thanks. I have no regrets, Steven. Good night."

"Good-bye, Brandy." He slowly walked to the door and hesitated before leaving. Then he was gone.

Brandy snuggled into her cozy bed. "And you're quite a man, Lance Reynolds," she murmured, "one that I don't plan to lose so easily."

If Brandy had ever known in her life what she wanted, it was Steven Winngate. She warned herself to step lightly; he was running scared. She looked at the check, one from his personal account. She smiled and shredded it. "It was worth every cent...."

Chapter Seven

Brandy opened the buff-colored envelope which had been delivered by the bell captain. She focused weary eyes upon the stunning message which was written in bold, beautiful script:

"If you're serious about that new story and pictures for *Glitter,* meet me for lunch in the hotel restaurant at one o'clock. Accept my new terms, and the McGavin story will be permanently shelved or handed over to you. If you reject this generous offer, I can only assume the truth doesn't really interest you."

Naturally it was signed by Steven Winngate. She handed the summons to Casey, whose eyes also widened in astonishment. Casey glanced over at the mutinous look on Brandy's face. "Are you going to meet him and hear him out?" she asked anxiously. "How did you like him the other night? Obviously you impressed him."

"It's pure and simple blackmail, Casey. I shouldn't trust him for an instant!" Yet, her green eyes narrowed in feminine mischief and gleamed in anticipation. "What should I wear, Casey? I left my Joan of Arc outfit back home." Even though Casey was a liberated free spirit, Brandy couldn't confess the events of their night to her.

"Why not dazzle him, Brandy? From what I witnessed, he's teetering on the edge of defeat now; knock him over.

That story can do a lot of damage to you. Its demise is worth a little flirtation.''

Flirtation, she mentally scoffed. ''Me, bewitch Steven Winngate? He can have his choice of women; why would he be interested in me? Camille Blanchard is his type, not plain Brandy Alexander.'' Why had he waited for days before sending for her? What did this quicksilver man have in mind for them?

''You, plain? Never! If I read him right, I know why he's constantly trailing you. His types are all alike: rich, powerful, spoiled. But add handsome and virile to that list, and he's dynamite. Trouble is, he's used to getting anyone and anything he desires. He's surrounded by beautiful, sophisticated bores! He's probably tired of fighting off such types all the time. No doubt, you're a provocative challenge to his ego.''

Casey laughed, then pointedly asked, ''What kind of woman would such a man find intriguing, different, compelling? Someone who's fresh and natural, but polished and charming; innocent and yet sensual; helpless and yet strong; witty, honest, and vital; a challenge to his hunter instincts but not his bachelorhood; someone to offer but not to take....'' She paused dramatically before continuing.

''Nothing is more exciting or tempting than a woman who cannot be captivated, or seduced, or dazzled without a stimulating hunt. He made a public play for you the other night, but you sweetly spurned him. You've resisted and parried his magical attacks. You're his one defeat, the forbidden fruit, the golden apple at the tree top.''

''Should I be taking notes for my next romance novel?'' Brandy joked, wondering what Casey would think if she knew the truth. ''He literally terrifies me, Casey. I'm no match for a man with his skill and experience. He could eat me alive! If he suspected I was leading him on....'' She shuddered to think of that black temper aimed at her, or his powerful magnetism captivating her, again.

"I'm not suggesting an affair with him. Just make friends. Who knows, maybe he does have a heart or a conscience after all. If he gets to know you, he couldn't possibly print that vile story. He could be offering you an olive branch; if you're smart, you'll snatch it before he withdraws it," she advised seriously.

"What if he only feels I owe him something for saving my life out there? That's certainly the way he's been acting." That silly remark hit a strong chord. What if it was true? How would Steven act after their night together? There was only one way to find out....

At one o'clock sharp, Brandy approached the maitre d' of the restaurant. She gave him her name, which instantly brought recognition. She followed him to a table in the corner, one in the dim shadows. Perhaps it was the heavy crimson drapes and matching carpet which devoured the light and made it appear evening.

Steven rose to greet her. His admiring gaze passed over her white linen suit and her hunter green blouse with its bold splotches of snow white. The cut of her suit was simple, yet flattering. He realized a previously ignored fact: She could fit perfectly into any setting or circumstance. Her walk and movements were fluid and graceful; she possessed a natural ease which hinted of an inner vivacity and enjoyment of life. Strange, but he noticed something new each time they met.

She smiled warily as she was seated. The headwaiter was instantly at their table to take their cocktail order. Needing to keep a clear head, she hesitated briefly before ordering a glass of white wine. He grinned knowingly as he ordered a Chivas on the rocks.

"You asked to see me, Steven," she stated, coming directly to the point in a tone which was clear and formal. How did one act with one's reluctant lover, or more accurately a one-night stand?

"Surely business can wait for a while, Miss Alexander." He also assumed that mocking formal tone, a compelling grin dancing across his face and settling within those peaceful sea-blue depths. "It's been a hectic morning. Do you mind if I relax and clear my wits before we discuss our business?"

"As you wish," she politely agreed, unable to relax with those striking eyes focused on her and memories from that passion-filled night flickering dangerously and boldly before her mind's eye. How could he sit there so calmly? No tender greeting?

Their drinks arrived, briefly halting any further comments. Brandy thanked the waiter as he placed a red napkin on the table before her, then set a crystal wine glass filled with golden liquid on top of it. Steven never took his gaze from her the entire time they were being served. She shifted uneasily in the velvet chair.

His black suit had tiny white pinstripes running through it. His white shirt was monogrammed on the cuff peeking out beyond his sleeve. His black tie was secured into a neat knot.

Even when she glanced around the room to see if anyone familiar was present, she could still feel the heat and contact of those searing blue eyes. Evidently he was determined to use their potency to make her notice him. Casey could be right: He was unaccustomed to encountering resistance of any kind. What better way to entice such a man than to feign mild interest or to reveal only polite tolerance of him? Or should she reveal her attraction?

Her liquid green gaze came back to his face when he softly stated, "You look lovely, Brandy; or shall I call you Kathy today?"

"Whichever you prefer, Steven. As I told you, both names are mine. My close friends call me Brandy, as did my family. I've discovered it best to use Katherine around strangers. I'm certain you've also discovered the privacy and serenity which Lance Reynolds affords you. Kathy does it for me. Kathy doesn't intimidate or sway the feelings of other people. Kathy can be herself when Brandy can't. Brandy must conform to certain expectations and rules

which Kathy does not. When I'm lucky, I can be both.'' Her
reserve and explanation appeared to amuse him.

She laughed. ''Surely it's much the same for Steven and
Lance? Lance isn't plagued with the public and business
demands which constantly face Steven Winngate. Money,
fame, and success have certain responsibilities and rewards
which Steven and Brandy must adhere to; Kathy and Lance
are free spirits who can do and say what they please.
Right?'' Why did he keep staring at her, surveying her like
a new piece of property?

He chuckled. ''Absolutely correct, Kathy. May I treat her
to lunch instead of the intelligent, businesslike Brandy?''

She caught herself before retorting, *If Lance is doing the
treating.* He alertly perceived her hesitation. ''Kathy is a
private person, Steven; and this is a business luncheon. If
your new angle is to dissect either or both of them, it won't
be at this lunch. Besides, the card summoned Brandy to
lunch,'' she coyly reminded him, stressing the words *summoned* and *dissect* as she gazed into his eyes, hoping to disarm and to confuse him as much as he did her.

''But they're one and the same person, aren't they?'' he
teased, cunning lights filling his keen eyes, pearl white teeth
standing out amidst enchanting bronze features. He lifted
his squat glass to sip his aged Scotch, his eyes laughing over
the rim.

''Are Lance and Steven one and the same man?'' she
parried his gentle thrust. ''I think not. I have the distinct
impression I met Lance Reynolds that first time; since then
I've been presented with Steven Winngate. Isn't that true,
Steven?'' She stressed his real name, since he had doubted
her knowledge and acceptance of reality.

Speaking of accurate dissection! He was disquieted by
hers. No one knew the real man; yet, this near stranger was
doing a superb job of reading his innermost character and
nature as if she had written it herself! More research....
Perhaps they were both on a fact-finding mission. He had
surely underestimated her charm, persistence, and cunning

intelligence. Perhaps she was the one making the rules and subtly calling the shots by pretending to let him. Was it a mistake to reassess her and their relationship? After what happened between them the other night, how could she sit there so cool and calm? She hadn't even attempted to get in touch with him. Maybe her curiosity was sated.

"Isn't that true, Lance?" she asked again when he continued his pensive, intense study of her. Should she clarify the *Valley* issue before attacking the *Glitter* fiasco?

At that name, he smiled and nodded. "I had briefly forgotten your profession and many skills, Brandy. Witty remarks...psychological, personality analysis...cunning conversation... Does that brain of yours work all the time?" he accused in a tone which was almost insulting and defensive.

She stiffened very noticeably. "Only when it's forced to do so, Steven. Contrary to common belief, writers do not continually analyze every person or situation they meet. Hopefully I never put anything into writing which might embarrass or offend anyone I know. I write fiction and fantasy, Steven; I leave reality to better qualified writers or to those with social or vindictive axes to grind! I write to entertain, nothing more. I promise you I'm off-duty right now."

She stared at him, daring him to interrupt her before she had her complete say. "That same biased opinion is the very reason I keep my name and profession a secret from strangers. As soon as the world *writer* is spoken, people change. They think I'm mentally taking notes for a new novel. That encounter becomes a phony pretense to influence or impress me in one way or another. Then, there are the men! It's a toss-up between trying to figure out which one of my heroines is the real me or which of my heroes they need to fake in order to capture my attention," she snapped at him.

Her hand trembled as she lifted her glass and foolishly downed its entire contents. Her eyes watered and she coughed. "Bravo, Miss Alexander! Are those the opinions of Brandy or Kathy? Have I received a justly earned scolding?"

"Both, Steven. All you need to do is scan your own thoughts and feelings about me, or writers in general; isn't that what people think and feel? Isn't that what you insinuated the other night? Now do you see why I conceal myself in Kathy? I want people to know and to like me, not *the* Brandy Alexander. And I want to meet them as they truly are, not as they pretend to be. Is that such a terrible deception? After all, I am Katherine Alexander," she said, reminding him of his blatant lie while hers was merely a half-truth.

He smiled mysteriously as he reasoned upon her attempt to disarm him with that crafty scheme of hers. Was she underestimating his cunning and perception, or was she insulting his intelligence? Misunderstood, put-upon writer? Claiming to be sweet and sensitive Kathy except when working? *No way, Brandy love. You're far more than even you imagine.*

"I asked you here for a specific purpose, Brandy. After we eat, I'll outline what I have in mind." Curious undercurrents swirled beneath his ocean-blue eyes.

"I would prefer to know now, if you don't mind. Lunch will taste better if I know how you intend to settle our differences of opinion. What terms do you have in mind?" she anxiously pressed.

"As you wish," he jested. "You claim Laura's story is false and malicious. You also insinuated I don't know the real Brandy or Kathy. If the story and my impression of you are inaccurate, there's only one way to prove otherwise. If you succeed, I'll print the new version which you supply."

Confusion joined suspicion within her gaze. "Let me get this straight; you want me to prove who and what I am in order to cancel that fictitious story in your possession?"

"That's about the size of it. If McGavin hasn't captured the real you, then introduce her to me. Show us the real woman; let us write about her. You know what stuff the readers want: likes, dislikes, habits, personality. Where do you go? How do you act? How did you succeed? How do you work? Where do you get your ideas? How do you live? I won't print anything you feel is offensive or embarrassing. If you wish, you can edit the story yourself. You can also select the photos to be used, within reason. I want shots from all angles and from varying locations. The writer and photographer will, shall I politely say, live and breathe with you for two weeks—here and in your beloved Kentucky. Give me a real story about a real woman. Show me Kathy and Brandy." He waited for her reaction.

"You want someone to escort me around here, then fly home with me to do a full story and layout there? You said nothing offensive or embarrassing; yet, you want to strip away all my secrets and invade my private life. That's a contradiction, Steven! I'm not some bug under a public microscope. I can agree to certain things within reason, but having Laura McGavin as my shadow for weeks is out of the question. Besides, you already know the story is a pack of lies, from personal experience I might add. No deal," she stated emphatically, speculating on his wild idea.

"I didn't have her in mind for this new assignment. I doubt she could be impartial or fair since I questioned her last story on you," he stated calmly, opening his golden trapdoor. "You didn't want me to explain how I know the story is false?"

"Who do you have in mind?" she asked, naively falling into it.

"Lance Reynolds," he smoothly and unexpectedly replied, secretly shutting it before she could escape in panicky fear. "Who better than the man who already knows the truth, who's biased in your favor? I've missed you." He chuckled when she blushed.

"Is this some joke? Or perhaps a cunning attempt to add some juicy tidbits to that tale?" she asked, struggling to free herself.

"I can assure you I'm a qualified photographer. I know what angle I want, so who better than me to shoot it? As for the story, all I need is a collection of facts and interesting information to hand over to a qualified writer. Or you can do the story for me. There's no better way to control what the public will get."

"You honestly want us to work together on a new story? No tricks?" She ceased to resist his enticing captivity.

"People call me ruthless and heartless, Brandy; but I'm also honest and stubborn. I don't want to crucify anyone, especially not a beautiful woman whom I personally find fascinating. But I can't halt that story if you fail to supply me with another one. Two weeks of working together, no tricks. Agreed? Am I invited to your scenic ranch in Kentucky?" he tempted her in a husky voice. "It could be lots of fun, quite educational for both of us," he hinted roguishly.

Alone? Brandy contemplated that exciting, but precarious, idea. She pondered his motives for this curious situation. She was besieged with doubts and fears. If he had missed her, why hadn't he called? Yet, they wouldn't be alone. She had workers and a protective housekeeper. She smiled as she recalled Nigel's imminent visit. Since they both knew him, Nigel was the perfect answer to her dilemma. She would be in a position to prove the story wrong and to get better acquainted with Steven. Perhaps something could develop between them.... But why did she feel she was being maneuvered into this situation? Blackmailed was more like it! Suddenly, she wasn't certain she could trust this man. If all he wanted was a brief affair, this subterfuge wasn't necessary, and he knew it. Should she ask Nigel to visit later?

"You're on, Steven. Place the old story in your safe. When you return with a truthful one, you'll burn the old one for me? Promise?" She paused at the escape hatch.

Unaware she was waiting for an answer, he remained silent and alert. "I demand your solemn word, Steven. Swear

that old story will not be used if I agree to do this new one—
with you."

"You have my word. Do we begin our research tonight?"

She reasoned over some problem for a moment. "I'm
having dinner with some friends. Would you like to come
along?"

"What time and where?" he asked casually, mentally
dropping the prison door key into his pocket, until he freed
her, if ever.

"My room at seven thirty. As for our working together,
we have to clear up some matters first. No more deceptions, and fights. No more bloody games. Agreed? This is
a business deal, right?"

She met his devilish gaze. "No friendship or pleasure?"
he teased wickedly, searing her with the flames in his smoldering eyes.

"Friendship sounds terrific to me, and I hope we'll enjoy
our mutual business." Should she tell him Nigel would be
there? No...

"You lost my meaning, Brandy," he softly chided her.

"No, I didn't, Steven. I read you loud and clear. If memory serves me correctly, I didn't reject you last time and I
haven't pressured you since. I told you I wouldn't," she reminded him.

"Would you object if this visit is more than business?"
he inquired, watching her expression closely.

"Would you?" she parried. "I've made it this far without using my feminine charms and wiles in such a manner;
and I don't intend to change my methods to influence you.
Whatever happened or happens between us in private has
nothing to do with our business deal. If that's clear and ac-
ceptable, I'll be returning home Wednesday. Allow me a few
more days to get things settled and prepared, then come
down anytime. Do you fish or hunt?" She caught him off
guard with that last question.

"Both. Why?" he asked curiously.

"There's a lovely pond filled with delicious catfish on the edge of my ranch. It might prove relaxing and exciting. I also have a skeet range. Naturally there are horses for riding. There's a swimming pool, lake, and tennis courts. Pack your luggage accordingly. I think I'll give a real Southern barbecue one night. We might as well have some fun and relaxation while we work. I would suggest jeans and boots; country life is very casual. Oh, yes, I also have a couple of Yamaha motorcycles if you know how to ride one," she teased him, relaxing more each minute.

He chuckled. "Do you?"

"Let's just say the last time I attempted to jump a bank, my side was sore and blue for weeks where the handle bar smacked me when I fell. I think horses are much safer and more dependable. I keep the bikes for friends who either don't like horses or who are afraid of them. Bring lots of film; the scenery's beautiful. Any other questions or terms? It's best if we understand each other right up front."

"None. As for your rules, they aren't necessary. I'll be on my best behavior." He grinned and winked at her.

"Does *I* refer to Steven or to Lance?" she jested, as if it made some vital difference to her. "You did say the reporter would be Lance Reynolds; is there some particular reason?" Although they were joking around, there was an odd strain between them. Brandy wondered if it had anything to do with their sexual relationship.

"Who's invited?" he probed with undisguised curiosity.

"Since you're one and the same man, I can hardly include one without the other," she artfully avoided his snare.

"A new deal: How about we be ourselves for a change?" he offered a tempting solution. "If you're afraid of being alone with me, Brandy, you can relax; even I can behave when absolutely necessary. Truce?" he asked, extending his hand to her to seal their pact.

Why not play this game for a while, she recklessly decided. What did she have to lose? She slipped her hand into his and murmured, "Truce, Steven."

"Now, how about we forget this *Glitter* mess and simply enjoy our lunch, and each other?" he suggested.

"Sounds marvelous to me," she quickly and cheerfully agreed.

There was one other matter she wanted to clear up, but didn't want to bring it up just yet: *Valley*, and his inexplicable obsession with it. She didn't know how he had learned of its existence or why he desperately wanted it. She hadn't been researching *Valley* in Vegas; she had been working on *Twilight over Venus*. *Valley* had been written and sold last winter....

There was a slight tensing in the man sitting across from her as he leaned forward and lent her his full attention. When Steven unknowingly clenched his teeth and narrowed his eyes, she keenly observed his baffling reactions. "Is something bothering you, Brandy?" he pressed, his voice tightly controlled.

Brandy exhaled softly as she focused her cloudy gaze on him. Did she dare ask him why he was so intrigued by a contemporary romance which takes place on a tropical island following a volcanic eruption, not in the Valley of Fire? It sounded like a crazy coincidence, but it was true. The hero wasn't modeled after him, and the story wasn't about their perilous meeting. Perhaps it was best to forget her wild speculations. If she tried to explain, he might think she was being guiltily defensive. She decided to wait until Steven related the importance of that story to him, if he hadn't forgotten about it.

She smiled and replied optimistically, "What could possibly be wrong? You've just made me an offer I can't refuse, a trial by a jury of one. Now, how about that lunch you promised me. I'm ravenous."

His laughing gaze met hers. Had he really expected her to refuse his offer? He only hoped she wouldn't discover why he had suggested it. How would she react if she learned there was no new story in the making? It was amazing what a little investigative research and greased palms could uncover! "What would you like to eat?"

"You order; surprise me. I need to make a quick phone call."

"They'll bring a phone to our table if you'd like," he politely offered.

"No thanks. The call is personal. I'll return shortly. By the way, I hate blue cheese dressing and oysters," she tossed over her shoulder as she waltzed away.

He chuckled to himself in rapidly rising spirits, wishing his contact at Webster Books hadn't supplied him with the very evidence he had hoped wouldn't surface, the description of her next hero: Landis Rivera from *Valley*. Lance Reynolds and Landis Rivera . . . Valley of Fire and *Valley of Fire* . . . This deceitful truce promised to be an intoxicating and enlightening challenge, and he thrived on conquering the impossible. . . .

Steven's eyes clouded with a sad reluctance. He berated himself for having her investigated. Some things were best left unmasked. He should have known this woman was too good to be true. Could he change her, or had she already changed since meeting him? Could he pull her from her fantasy world into the real one, his world? He was convinced the *Glitter* mix-up wasn't intentional on her part. But to willfully use him as a research project? Then again, it could be unconscious absorption. Perhaps she wasn't even totally honest with herself. He wanted her, and he was determined to prove to her that he was a real man, not one of her heroes come to life, even if he did seemingly match her images.

Steven had given Brandy countless hours of deep thought, as well as numerous hours of conversation with the detective he'd hired. He feared she was drawn to his romantic and dashing image, rather her creative image of him. He didn't want her to be influenced by the way in which they had first met. He had to make certain Brandy wasn't living out a fantasy, that she truly wanted him. He wanted Brandy to share his life. Somehow, he had to work things out between them. It would be hard work, but he was accustomed to difficult and demanding tasks, especially when the stakes were so high and priceless.

Steven had gone from wildcatting on other men's oil rigs to owning his own slew of wells and businesses: refineries, gas stations, a computer firm, an electronics firm, and even foreign oil leases and a tanking business. He had lucked up, if he could call it that, when his partner had died shortly before their first oil well burst a seam. Since both had been heavily insured to protect their holdings, Steven had come away from his first strike an extremely wealthy man. Every time another oil well came in, he reinvested the money or purchased another business. He owned so many now that holding companies and corporations had entered the picture. He possessed more investments and stocks than he could keep track of. But that was the mark of a truly wealthy man, to be unaware of how much he owned or was worth. He had been labeled the "man with the Midas Touch," which was fortunately true. Whatever he touched, especially in oil, always succeeded. He was tough and resilient; he was relentless and cunning. Things hadn't come easy for him, but it surely looked that way.

He had been cynical and carefree towards women, until Brandy entered his life. Steven felt she had surrendered her body to him, but nothing more. She appeared physically attracted to him, but she didn't seem interested in establishing a deeper relationship. Was she playing with him, as he had done endless times with females? Was she afraid she couldn't become more than a passing fancy to him? Damn, he was confused and frustrated. He needed some answers; he needed and wanted this vital creature who caused his blood to sing and burn. He had always been able to analyze any situation, to master it, to remove all obstacles, to buy or take what he wanted. Brandy made him feel vulnerable, helpless, downright nervous. He had read her books; maybe Brandy knew him too well. He had felt stripped naked, for she had frequently described him to a T. It was as if she had been reading his mind or observing him for years, as if she knew him better than he knew himself, or as well. Her insights and perceptions troubled him. If only she hadn't cheapened their relationship by using it in *Valley*. He had to get a look at that manuscript! Surely there was a copy at her home. . . .

Steven leaned back in his chair, stretching out his long legs while he waited for her return. He wondered what else the detective's report would reveal. He would have it in his hands within days, before he headed for Kentucky. He sipped the Scotch and plotted. He had hired the best workers and executives he could locate for his many companies and corporations; they could function without his eagle eye for a few weeks. Life wasn't one endless circle of meetings, deals, wealth, power, and social obligations. He was successful, the master of his fate. Now, he had everything except for that special someone to share it with. . . .

Chapter Eight

Brandy had waited until the powder room was empty before placing a call to her agent, who must be sweating out this unexpected meeting. "Casey, Winngate's deal includes a story and photos in Kentucky. Winngate says if I'll let him do another story, he'll burn the old one. I'm scared stiff, but I'm going to bluff it out. Besides, I'll have protection from the big, bad wolf. Nigel's already made plans to visit me at the same time."

Brandy listened to Casey's reaction and comments, then chatted for a few more minutes. "I'll bring him along as my escort tonight." She waited for that news to settle in. "Of course he agreed. I'll talk to you later. My lunch is on the way." Brandy still couldn't reveal this offer included more than business, that she was in love with this unpredictable and mysterious man. Yet, Brandy had a nagging sensation there was some critical point which she couldn't put her finger on....

When she returned to the table, Steven arose once again to politely seat her. "I was afraid you'd deserted me," he murmured into her ear as he pushed her chair up to the table.

She glanced up at him and cooed, "Not before lunch; I'm dying to see what delectable surprise you ordered for me."

Their eyes met and fused. He leaned forward as if to kiss her right there in public; she did not move away. A curious look swept over his face as he drew back and stood up to the full height of his towering frame. She faced the table once more, feeling strangely denied of something special.

He returned to his chair. "Get your call through?"

For some unknown reason, she replied honestly, "Yes, I thought it might ease Casey's mind if I let her know I hadn't been consumed by the dragon's fire. I hope it was all right to let her in on our deal? She was pleased to hear we're collaborating on a new story. Needless to say, a percentage of a ruined, has-been writer doesn't amount to much," she jested.

Her tone and look became serious as she stated, "I really do appreciate your kindness and generosity, Lance. I know you aren't obligated in any way to do another story. Just to show how grateful I am, I'll do my best to provide you with a good one. Plus a marvelous vacation," she added with a bright smile.

His eyes flickered with mischief as he lazily drawled, "I plan to soak up every ounce of Southern hospitality I can find. Your lunch is here," he said to alert her to the approaching waiter.

She observed him closely as the waiter removed the cork from the green bottle of Johannesburg Riesling and handed it to him. He carefully checked the number of linear markings and the texture of it. He sniffed it three times, then placed it on the table. He nodded for the waiter to pour a small amount into his glass. He lifted it, holding it by the flat base, and swirled the contents in a counterclockwise direction. He held the glass at a slanted angle to check its hue. He inhaled its delicate bouquet, noting the scent of dried apricots. He smiled and took a few small sips, letting it linger in his mouth and then ease down his throat. He smiled his acceptance, and the waiter filled their glasses.

After the waiter's departure, Brandy playfully declared, "You can order for me anytime, La—Steven. You'll have to bear with me, Steven; since I first met you as Lance Reynolds it's hard to call you Steven. This looks scrumptious. Do I look like a lobster person?''

"You look like a person who loves anything... but oysters and blue cheese dressing. What else do you dislike?" he probed as he cut off a piece of succulent lobster.

"Men who are far too attractive and charming for their own good. Men who have everything. Men who blackmail women into obeying their enticing whims. Men who stare at women with entrancing blue eyes which makes eating and relaxing impossible," she teased happily, nipping at his ego and confidence. His eyes twinkled in hearty amusement and undisguised appreciation.

"In conclusion, you dislike me; is that it?" he taunted devilishly, a sensual smile caressing his lips. "At least that's how it appears every time we meet," he remarked casually, then roguishly added, "Except for our last encounter. Did I change your mind about me, or did I paint myself into a corner?"

"Was I describing you?" she mockingly questioned, warming but not responding to his last words. "On the contrary, Steven; I find you utterly fascinating and irresistibly charming. I've never met anyone like you before. You're confident, bright, witty, well-mannered, suave... and valiant," she surprised him with her bold flattery and bold look of admiration. "And most enjoyable company..."

At a loss to comprehend the meaning behind her unexpected confession or to fully accept the blaze with her sparkling eyes, he inquired, "In what sense do you use *valiant*? Brave and daring, or intrepid and gallant?"

"Yes," she succinctly replied, placing a morsel of freshly baked bread in her mouth. She slowly sipped the tasty wine.

"Yes to which meaning?" he stressed for clarity.

"To all of them of course. From my viewpoint, there's no lack of confidence within you."

"In short, you think me overbearing and conceited?"

She mused on that question for a minute. "Conceited, no. Arrogant, not really. You strike me more as a very self-assured, contented person. Although you're vividly aware of your wealth, power, and good looks, you accept them with ease and pride. You wear success exceptionally well, Steven," she astonished him further. "I envy that ability. Does it come with the territory? Or were you always like this?"

"I thought it was the man's place to flatter and to compliment the lady, not the other way around," he chided huskily.

"I never flatter, Steven. If I can't speak the truth, I remain silent. What's wrong with a well-deserved compliment from a lady to a gentleman? Besides, if you didn't want to know the answers to those questions, you shouldn't have asked them," she cheerfully rebuked him.

"Where does it say only men can speak their minds? Women have opinions and should be allowed to state them freely. I merely stated my opinion; no flattery or compliment was intended. If you want to analyze me, doesn't that include my feelings and thoughts? What better place to begin a truce or friendship than with the truth about my temporary boss? What do you want to know about me?"

"Everything. That way, I can select the proper angle for the story. I want to know you as well as you know yourself."

"Everything? That's a simple order; I can accomplish our trade before this lunch is over. There isn't much to learn. I'm just me. When I'm not writing, or rewriting, or proofing galleys, I work on the ranch. Believe it or not, I clean the stables; I ride and train horses. I'm not too good at some chores and I dislike them; but I do cook and clean house and go shopping, when I can't get around them. I read a great deal for pleasure and for my work. For exercise, I take long walks and I play tennis with my ball-machine. I'm usually in jeans and barefoot. I sleep late and work late, a staunch night owl; I'm practically in a daze until after lunch and several cups of black coffee. Spring and fall are my favorite seasons. Red and green are my favorite colors. I like to eat on the floor in front of the fireplace in the winter or on my screen porch during other seasons. You already know about my college years. I started writing professionally during my junior year. I write in any genre that I like, or that sells," she added with a musical laugh. "You know—give the public what it wants?

"Most of the time I do all of my work, but I do occasionally use a part-time typist when my deadlines overlap. When I began writing, I was blissfully ignorant. I assumed writers wrote; I didn't know about galleys, revisions, promo tours, and reader mail. They can play havoc with a fantastic schedule when they conflict. I do my own research; I visit locations whenever possible. I love old western movies, plus most science-fiction films. While growing up, I was a terrible tomboy. I still have a tendency to be one every so often. What else do you want to know?"

"How about your social life? Who's in it? Where do you go? What do you do? Readers love those topics."

Between bites and sips, she related the answers she assumed he was after. "First, I'm sort of a loner. I used to be very shy, but I've worked on improving it. Traveling and promoting my books have worked wonders for me. I lean more to a few good friends rather than a lot of lukewarm ones. I spend a lot of time on my ranch, working or writing. I travel mostly for researching a new book or for publicity tours. In all honesty, I do like fancy occasions, but only in small doses: That's what makes such things and events special. As for the big *who*, there isn't one right now."

"Why are you still single?" he attacked a question which held special interest for him. Brandy, however, took his mocking inquisitiveness in light of the lewd article which she was trying to discount. He noted the raw nerve which he had rubbed.

Her eyes chilled; her smile faded. She inhaled deeply and slowly several times as she sought to master her anger and resentment at his bold intrusion into the most private area of her life. If she refused to give some logical answer, it might encourage him to think the worst; yet, he should know the truth by now. Even though he was the first man in her life, surely he didn't doubt her? She gazed into his vivid blue eyes for a few moments, then cunningly parried, "Probably for the same reasons you're still a carefree, happy bachelor."

"Such as?" he challenged her witty answer, not to be denied this vital information.

"Is it necessary to expose my personal life this fully?"

"I'm not going to print everything we discuss, Brandy; that was a question from me to you. I need to understand who you are, and where you're coming from, and where you're heading. Has there ever been anyone special in your life?"

"All right, Steven. Off the record, from me to you, I'm not married yet, and never have been, because I haven't found the right man to suit me or to fit into my life-style," she answered bluntly.

"Surely there's some man alive worthy of you?" he jested.

"It isn't that. Considering how I work, he would have to be very understanding and compatible. He would have to be totally confident in his own right, a man who wouldn't feel threatened by my success and wealth, a man who didn't demand I become his shadow, his possession, his extension. I have to be me; I have to write. I've watched the effects of marriage and children on other female writers. I'm selfish; I couldn't place everyone and everything above my needs. Creative flow and deadlines don't recognize family demands. I've seen it create terrible problems and bitterness; I've met women who were given a choice between writing and their marriages. Frankly, I can't imagine changing myself and my inner clock to suit another person, or persons.

See? It's really very simple, just personal. The insinuations in Laura's story are lies; but you already know that,'' she helplessly added.

"I believe you. You're waiting and searching for the kind of man you just described? Surely you've met countless men?"

"I'm not searching, Steven, and I'm not waiting with bated breath. As romantics claim, he simply enters your life at some unexpected moment and sweeps you off your feet. Love is said to be charted and ruled by destiny. Fated lovers? Romeo and Juliet...Cleopatra and Mark Antony...David and Bath-sheba...Scarlett and Rhett...Wallis Simpson and King Edward...Superman and Lois Lane..."

They both laughed. "What's been wrong with all of those you've met so far? You must be very selective," he teased, leaning forward and propping his chin on his folded elbow, absently rubbing his forefinger over his lips.

"Probably the same flaws you discovered in all of those women which you cast aside," she tried her same ruse once more.

"This story is about you, not me. You said earlier that women should have the freedom to express their views and opinions on any subject," he jested with a devilish twinkle in his mocking blue eyes.

"I didn't mean it to sound like that, Steven. Let's see now, what have my choices been so far? There's the spoiled, selfish brat type; he's usually a little boy who hasn't grown up yet, or a weakling who feels threatened by a woman with my personality or success, or a bully who wants to rule my life as if he owned it and me. Then, there are the phonies who are either after *the* Brandy Alexander who is supposedly the real-life model for one of my heroines or who constantly pretends he is what he is not. Then, there are the fortune hunters who want to cash in on my fame and success. There's the man who still believes his wife should be meek, silent, and servile. There's the man who feels I should give up everything, including my writing and traveling for him...settle down, have babies, and wait upon him hand and foot. There are those macho men who feel threatened by my confidence or aggression, those who resent me and my success. There are those who dislike my style of life and would insist on changing it and me. That should pretty well sum up the countless choices I've been given so far. Frankly, I've met few real men who possess the strength, pride, confidence, and personality which could—" she laughed as she dramatically paused before finishing "—sweep me off my feet."

"In short, you really dislike men in general," he concluded aloud, just to vex her into revealing more information.

"Heavens no! I normally get along better with most men than with most women. I was referring to the romantic angle which you were inquiring about: possible suitors. Most men are charming and interesting; they're thoughtful and chivalrous. A friendship with a male doesn't involve that fierce, feminine competition which you frequently find in relationships with other females. If a man accepts you as an equal, the friendship can be rich and stimulating, as with me and Nigel. Both parties can learn and profit from a mixed relationship like that. With men, the conversation can be witty and interesting; you can discuss more than children, shopping, clothes, new hairstyles, makeup, and other necessary trivia. See?"

At his skeptical expression, she added, "Of course, few men will permit such an amicable arrangement. They seem to have difficulty seeing past a shapely body or pretty face. Others let their fear of being mocked by other men stand in their way. Then, others still feel the woman's place is in the home. I think if a man is strong and confident in his masculine role, he won't feel threatened or resentful towards modern women," she stated smugly.

"Doesn't such aggression and assertiveness take away from your femininity and warmth? Don't you find it boring or costly to be friends and equals with men?"

"You're a better judge of my femininity and warmth. I hope I'm not damaged by my personality. Most of the time, I try very hard to conceal such opinions because they seem to offend both men and women. I prefer to be myself. I only bare my claws when I'm forced to defend myself or my rights as a person. I can only hope that doesn't make me appear mannish or hostile. I'm a woman, and I love being a woman. But I also want to be successful, which sometimes forces me to be aggressive or assertive. Why is that so different from a man wanting to be or to do the best he can in his chosen field? Actually, I think women feel more resentful and hostile at being forced to become that way in order to accomplish their hopes and dreams. Why should it be a man's world? Why should we be denied the same pleasures, rewards, or sacrifices which your sex enjoys simply because we're women? Am I any less talented than I would be had I been born a man? Are you any more intelligent than you would be had you been born a girl?"

He chuckled at that frightful thought. "Naturally there're many differences between us. Physical strength, for one thing. We aren't equal in lots of ways; I don't want that to ever change. Yet, there are lines drawn in certain areas which need to be erased...or adjusted. In all honesty I do sometimes become cold and haughty. When a man refuses to be discouraged, I behave that way. Like with that asinine and conceited Dr. Ross in Vegas; you remember him, don't you? He practically tossed you out of my room that first morning. He asked me out at least six times each day. In such cases, they become the hostile ones! I've been called many names which I won't repeat to anyone. I suppose I have the most trouble with being likened to my heroines. People force a conflict between my wanting to be myself and their demands of what I should be."

At his intense, silent study of her, she began to shift nervously beneath his intoxicating stare. She challenged, "Don't you find many of those same things true in your life? And you don't have the additional problem of being a female. You can do what you please, where you please, how you please, and when you please; you aren't judged less of a man because of such decisions or actions. Isn't wanting and needing to be yourself at times the reason for Lance Reynolds's existence? I simply want to be me," she declared softly and honestly.

He smiled mysteriously, but simply shrugged his shoulders in feigned indecisiveness or nonchalance. She boldly locked gazes with him and resolved to have some answers. "From what I perceive, Steven, you're from the old school of thought which still confines a woman to the home with her respectful tongue and meekly obedient manner. You dislike career women, don't you? How do they threaten or harm your masculinity? Does it antagonize you when one isn't awed into silence or mesmerized into hot pursuit? Tell me, how lacking is my warmth and femininity because of my personality and position?" she dared him to answer. "How do I repulse or offend you?"

He threw back his dark head and flashed her a seductive smile as lusty chuckles escaped his throat and broad chest. "Why would a beautiful woman like you want to compete in a man's world? You couldn't find happiness with a good husband and a houseful of children? Why not?" he asked, ignoring her previous questions, as if he hadn't even listened to her explanations.

"I didn't mean to insinuate I don't want a husband or some children. I just haven't found the right man to share that much of myself with. Marriage is very serious and special; it should last for the remainder of your life. Such a joint venture requires work, patience, and the right two people. Most of all, I feel it requires a lot of love, trust, and unselfishness. When I do locate such an irresistible man, I'd be willing to marry him in the flicker of an eye," she confessed without a modest blush.

"What about your beloved career?" he probed.

"I would still be a writer."

"Why?" he asked seriously, leaning forward to catch each word and to study her tone of voice and facial expression.

"Because of what it does for me as a person. I'm happier; I'm a more interesting person, more well-rounded. Surely a happier, more vital woman makes a better wife and mother? I would want to discuss more than my children, home, husband, and chores. I would want to visit more places than the PTA, pediatricians, grocery stores, other bored housewives for coffee, and all those other necessary tasks which mothers and wives must perform. I want to see other places, do exciting things, meet interesting people. I want to be respected and accepted for who I am, not for whom I'm married to or whose mother I am. I want and need my life to be rich, full, and settled before I attempt to control the lives of others. That's a big responsibility, a frightening one. I have to be Brandy before I can successfully become Mrs. So-and-So. Besides, writing is like a smoldering fire inside; if I didn't control its power and size by letting off flames with each book, I would be consumed and destroyed. I wouldn't be worth a damn to anyone, including myself."

"You're very perceptive and intelligent, Brandy; a lot smarter and more sensitive than I gave you credit for. You have far more depth and angles than I realized. That is, if you're being honest and sincere.... Have you ever been in love with any man or tempted to marry one?"

Brandy flushed a deep red and hastily lowered her long, lush lashes to conceal her vivid emotions. As she obviously hesitated, he remarked, "Was he married? Or did you sacrifice him for your beloved career?"

Her startled eyes jerked up to meet his fathomless ones. She panted indignantly, "No! I would never put myself in such a humiliating position. And no, I haven't received an irresistible proposal yet."

"But you have been flooded with offers?" he taunted almost cruelly, jealousy gnawing viciously within him.

"That wasn't your question. No proposal is tempting if it doesn't come from a man you love," she replied, slowly and coldly enunciating each word.

If she hadn't been so unsettled and angered, she could have read the naked look upon his face which clearly exposed his pleasure and astonishment. "Would you marry a man who fits your demands and description?"

"Love isn't something to be turned on and off like a faucet, Steven. Either you feel it or you don't. If we loved each other and were compatible, of course, I'd marry him."

"What if your dream man wanted a perfect wife, but not a career woman?"

Brandy tried to puzzle out this riddle. She was irrationally vexed with the persistence of this handsome man before her who was the answer to his own question.

Ignoring his loaded question, she went back to another point. "Since we'll be spending so much time together, it would be more relaxing and enjoyable if I knew more about you. Introduce me to the real Steven Winngate," she softly coaxed. "How old are you, Steven?"

"I'm thirty-seven years old. As for your other demand, I would prefer for you to draw your own deductions and conclusions about me. I dislike prejudice and foregone conclusions. You can get to know the real me while I study the real you, if you're interested. That way, our findings will be based upon facts, not fantasies, or gossip."

She sweetly argued against his logic. "That's impossible. While you remain a total mystery to me, you're well acquainted with my life. That puts me at a definite disadvantage. How can I get to know you if you constantly refuse me any information or answers? As for being interested, of course I am; you saved my life and now you're saving my reputation and happiness. You've accomplished an awful lot for such a young man, especially since Nigel's already told me you didn't inherit your status and wealth. I'm very heavily indebted to you for both rescues. But what I know about you could easily be contained within one long sentence.''

He laughed and denied her dramatic words. "I only know what you've told me and I've perceived. As for what the story for *Glitter* claimed, we both know it's a complete fabrication."

"I was referring to your claims of 'prejudice and foregone conclusions,' Steven. From your past actions, I'm forced to believe you're already biased against me," she stated as she sipped the tiny glass of Courvoisier cognac.

"Perhaps I was in the beginning," he admitted to her surprise. "Yet, I promise you an open mind and genuine sincerity during these next two weeks. You've just explained your views on men. As for Laura's other deductions, I know you well enough to deny them. I'll admit I did come on to you rather strongly. Can you blame me? You're a very attractive, intelligent, exciting, and charming female. One thing is crystal clear; I've only seen the tip of the iceberg where Brandy Alexander is concerned."

She smiled, her eyes glowing with pleasure and gratitude. "That suggestive statement could be said about you, Steven. Except," she added with a sly smile, "I doubt I've even viewed your complete tip as yet. You appear to be just as private and selective as you claim I am. I'm looking forward to discovering the elusive Steven Winngate."

"In such light, this trade of information should prove to be a most intriguing and interesting vacation." His eyes eased over her in a manner which said he knew what lay beneath those clothes and air. His gaze was appreciative and stirring.

"I fully agree, Steven. Who knows, you might—"

Her sentence was rudely cut in half by a venomous voice from behind her. She did not have to turn to see who was gracefully poised there. The annoyed lights which glittered within Brandy's darkened gaze told Steven of her inner feelings where Camille was concerned. And he couldn't blame her one bit.

Lunch had been over for a long time. They had been chatting with such concentration and enjoyment, they had failed to note the swift and lengthy passage of time. It had reached the cocktail hour, that time when Steven had absently invited the sultry model to join him for a drink. He had not expected his luncheon with Brandy to be so intriguing and fulfilling. Yet, he did not reveal his aggravation and disappointment to either female. He smiled provocatively as he arose to seat Camille. "Have a seat, Cam. Brandy and I were just finishing our meeting."

Brandy could not decide what angered her the most: that warm glow in Steven's eyes, or the surly contempt in Camille's tone and expression, or her own singed pride and painful dismissal. Clearly this was not an accidental meeting, not from their remarks to each other! She inwardly fumed at this disruption by a rival. She scolded herself for feeling imperfect and inadequate when in such close proximity with this particular woman. Surely their many differences would stand out to Steven. Brandy didn't realize how accurate she was, not that she could easily win a competition with this woman.

As those two exchanged polite banter and social amenities, Brandy quickly reassessed this hostile beauty. She looked about twenty-two. She was a slinky five-feet-nine inches tall. Her perfect weight enhanced her with a svelte, stunning figure. Camille was dark and sultry with her coal-black hair, dusky complexion, and velvety brown eyes which were nearly black. She knew how to dress, walk, talk, and move. She had a sophistication and wily knowledge which Brandy could not help but envy. Yet, her savoir-faire was not innate; it had been carefully learned and was used to the fullest upon her victims, male and female.

Brandy wondered how men could ignore such vanity and coldness from a woman, no matter how beautiful and sexy. Why did they exchange warmth, spontaneity, and intelligence for such a perfectly groomed, falsely charming, and haughty woman upon their arms? Women like Camille demanded attention from other men and envy from women. She was a perfect companion for an important evening.

Yet, the Camilles of the world brazenly stole other women's confidence and rightful attention. They possessed the unfair knack of making other females feel inferior, drab, or homely. They seemed to give off a cold-blooded, arrogant aura. They felt no qualms about humiliating or belittling other women. They felt no misgivings about using men for any purpose which suited them. Following her assessment of Camille, Brandy felt lighthearted and confident. She was delighted she wasn't like Camille, and she never wanted to be.

Brandy stood up. She smiled at the striking female clad in a dusty rose dress of the softest, clingiest material ever developed for the fashion industry. Camille did not return the affable offering. Instead, storms of disdain and fury flickered warnings of encroachment and animosity within her narrowed eyes. Brandy grinned as a funny thought came to mind: Tell her it causes wrinkles to scowl like that!

Camille tossed her head as she dismissed Brandy. She addressed her words and attention to Steven alone, making her feelings about both of them as vivid as her mauve lipstick. Her sultry voice crooned petulantly, "Sorry to make you wait so long, darling. I hope you weren't too bored and impatient," she stated, making her insult to Brandy clear.

"Not at all," Steven cordially stated. "I had some business to discuss with Miss Alexander," he declared formally. "We were having a most pleasant interlude. In fact, we completely lost track of time."

Business! Interlude! "If that's all, Mr. Winngate, I'll leave you two alone. I'll see you about seven in my room," she added, just to annoy that hateful snit. "Oh, yes, it's casual dress."

Camille's eyes shot fiery daggers at the audacious girl before them. "Steven, love, are you forgetting our engagement with the Zartoffs this evening? We did promise to escort them around town tonight." Camille intentionally didn't reveal it was a business obligation, just like this meeting. Damn Steven and his constant rejections!

Steven reasoned for a time, trying to decide which date to break. He wished Brandy hadn't mentioned their plans before he could find some logical and polite way of canceling those with Camille and the Zartoffs, part-owners of the company which would soon handle the cosmetics firm he had just purchased. If he had known Camille and her modeling would be included in that deal, he wouldn't have entered what was claimed an easy way to earn a fortune, which he didn't need, only the challenge of something new and different. He recalled how one of his past investments into movies had thrown him and Camille together. Since that day, she had stuck to him like a leech. At times, she had presented him with an excellent date for special occasions, but she was wearing thin. One set of arrangements had been made first. To cancel them now would give both women the wrong idea; or worse, the right one!

Infuriated by his entrapped position and annoyed with Brandy for causing it, he smiled ruefully at her and drawled, "She's right, Miss Alexander. I should have recalled those plans before setting up our business meeting for this evening. I'm afraid we'll have to complete it some other time. How long will you be in town?" he asked, trying to sound casual while his gut was tying itself in knots.

Business again! Brandy wisely concealed her outrage and anguish from this antagonistic female who was grinning triumphantly and maliciously at her. She also hid her pain and disappointment from the man who obviously wanted to conceal their relationship from his lady friend. Not a single trace of their previously shared warmth, openness, and compatibility remained in his aura. He revealed nothing more than politeness and formality. She chided herself for mistakenly reading more into their new relationship than he had intended or presented. So be it.

Hurt, but still proud, she graciously stated, "I'll be flying home tomorrow, Steven. Just phone Casey for another appointment; she handles my schedule. Good-bye, Miss Blanchard, Steven.''

Brandy left the table and gracefully made her way to the door. His eyes never left her retreating back until she had closed the door behind her. Not once had she lost her poise, temper, or manners; nor had she looked back a single time while departing. He had hoped to see her again before she left town.

Seething with jealousy, Camille bored her eyes into the unfamiliar and disturbing look within his mellow, hungry gaze which was brought about by the enchanting writer who had just left them. What did this carefree man see in that uptight little priss? Camille wanted what Steven Winngate had to offer, all of it. She raged at his stinging insults and rejections.

The instant Brandy was gone, Steven's furious gaze settled on Camille. ''If you ever do anything like that again, Miss Blanchard, consider yourself washed up with any of my companies. You and I have a business arrangement, nothing more. I don't like you insinuating that there's more between us. Frankly, if you weren't doing the ad campaign for my new firm, we wouldn't even see each other again. Now, if you have the marketing report from Jason, I suggest you pull it out and let's get this matter settled quickly. After we wine and dine the Zartoffs, I expect you to be on the next plane back to California. Tell Jason to send his next report by someone else. Understood?''

BRANDY RETURNED to her room. Determined to let the chips fall where they may, she placed a call to Casey. A sudden feeling of homesickness and a desperate need for solitude possessed her. She informed Casey of her intention to catch a plane back to Kentucky as soon as possible. She sent her regrets to the others. When Casey questioned her about her hasty departure and her date with Steven tonight, she laughed bitterly and glossed over the details of their lunch.

Knowing her well, Casey guessed she was becoming too emotionally involved with Steven Winngate.

"The deal called for a story on location in Kentucky. He broke our date for tonight. Let him do the pursuing and asking next time! If he's serious and sincere, he knows where to find me. Besides, I really want to go home for a while. I'll be back soon; I have that publicity tour to do, remember?"

Casey wondered if she should relate her suspicions about this man to her friend and client. She had received an alarming phone call right after Brandy's. After which, she had done some checking around; she didn't like what she had discovered.

"What's up, Casey?" Brandy asked curiously into the silence.

Why would Steven Winngate offer Webster Books a million dollars for Brandy's latest book? Why had Jensen's Bookstore also phoned to get a complete list of her books, the publishers, and dates of release? A man named Lance Reynolds was offering whatever amount it required to buy a copy of each one, even those out of print. Casey knew who Lance Reynolds was. She had phoned *Glitter* and been snottily informed the story and layout on Brandy were ready and waiting for publication, this week. If that wasn't enough, a little man in a brown suit was checking her out around town, probably a private detective. The little sneak was trying to get copies of every interview and television show she'd done. What devious scheme did Steven Winngate have in mind? When Casey genially asked for Brandy's opinion, she listened intently to the answer.

"All he said was he wanted to know me as well as I know myself. If he carries out his plan in motion, he certainly will," she declared saucily.

It didn't make sense. If he'd checked her out, why this deceptive offer? Maybe it was just an eccentric whim. "Is that all there is to it, Brandy?" she inquired gravely.

"Steven doesn't strike me as impulsive. He plans every move he makes. I think he's convinced I didn't set up our first meeting to prevent the *Glitter* story; maybe I'm wrong. I just don't understand what he wants from me."

"Perhaps you've bruised his ego with your rejection," Casey ventured.

"That's impossible! After the party, we—" She lit up like a Christmas tree with red lights and halted, delighted Casey couldn't see her face.

The perceptive Casey didn't have to view her guilt; Brandy's voice shouted it. Casey's mouth fell open and she stared at her phone. "You and Winngate? You have a relationship going with him?"

"I mean . . . Steven and I . . ." Brandy couldn't find the proper words to extricate herself. "Not exactly," Brandy replied. "What the hell, Casey!" she exploded in exasperation. "We're not kids. I slept with him once, the night of the party. I'd met him five or six times before that. Lunch was the first time I've seen him since that night. He'd have to be blind not to see how I feel about him."

"Then why is he trying to—" Casey halted and began to giggle.

"What's so funny?" Brandy demanded softly.

"Don't you see, Brandy? You've got him hook, line, and sinker; and he's scared. He isn't trying to harm you; he just wants to know if you're good enough for Steven Winngate." Casey's mind was spinning with speculations. Landis in *Valley* was like him; he could afford to purchase his whims, and his whim was to own that love story. "He simply wants to know everything there is about you before making a commitment. My Lord, Brandy, he's probably in love with you. That's his motive; he wants time alone to woo you," she teased. "Are you sure you want Nigel around?"

"What if you're wrong, Casey?" she asked fearfully. "Besides, Nigel was invited first. I can't call him and tell him he's not welcome now. It should work out fine; he and Steven are friends."

"Bet you I'm not wrong," Casey stated confidently. "Give him some rope and time, Brandy; he'll either hog-tie you or hang himself."

By six thirty, Brandy was packed and on a plane, to some measure of safety from the hypnotic effect of Steven Winngate, to some protective distance where she could intelligently analyze these conflicting emotions which she could not control or understand. If only love and romance were the way she wrote about them....

She wanted Lance Reynolds, but did he exist? She wanted to enchant and to win Steven, but he was a hard nut to crack. Without asking or trying, he could get his wishes. When their paths crossed again, she could not permit him to walk upon her susceptible heart with those cleat-bottomed shoes. She had foolishly lowered her guard and revealed too many secrets to that disarming, magnetic man. She must have appeared silly, naive, amusing, and idealistic to him. No doubt he had enjoyed playing with her, mocking her naiveté and romantic notions about life and love.

But she would show him. She would be just as stubborn and wily as he was, just as casual. She fumed at her foolishness, her inexperience. But if this was just another game, she was no match for his skills and prowess.

Chapter Nine

Golden sunlight played upon Brandy's tawny hair and skin. Her green eyes glowed with renewed vitality and zest. Laughter was uncontrollably torn from her parted lips and sent to float upon the breeze which fanned her silky mane out behind her. The sky was azure and clear; the air was fresh and invigorating. The recent rains had left the trees and grasses a lush, verdant hue. Colorful wildflowers scattered themselves across the landscape with striking splendor.

For six days and nights she had battled her unrequited love and powerful desire for Lance Reynolds. He had not even bothered to call her since her return home, if he even knew about it! Perhaps he had changed his mind about doing another story; perhaps the lunch and offer had been some mischievous joke on her. Perhaps he had only been attempting to prove she was just as susceptible to him as most women were; perhaps he had wanted to disprove her indifference and resistance. She must never let him discover the truth. She must never become the toy or sole possession of such a selfish, complex man!

On the morning of the seventh day, she had forcefully rebuked herself; she had given long and deep study to her feelings and situation. She must halt this destructive and demanding mood of self-pity and rejection. She could not forever moon over a man who had no use or affection for her, one who cruelly tantalized her. She must get over him, forget him completely! As he had obviously forgotten her.

The best medicine to heal a broken heart was concentration on some other matter, something mind-consuming and important. She would take care of some matters here at the ranch, rest for a while, fulfill her tour obligations, then head off to the Northwest to research her next novel, just as planned before he stepped into her life that morning at the Las Vegas hospital.

Their meeting in the Valley of Fire appeared symbolic to her. The flames in his smoldering sapphire eyes could melt her soul. Her life's valley had been tranquil very seldom since knowing him. To be trapped in his strong arms was like being imprisoned in a furnace, one which refined her love and passion, one which forged a stronger bond to him. Each time she invaded his blazing valley, wildfires attacked her body and threatened to consume her. His touch singed her as a brand of ownership. He was her valley of fire....

If she could control it at all, she should make certain their paths never crossed again. She would not chase a dream, no matter how much she wanted to.

Encouragement and assistance had arrived two days past. Just before dinner on the fourth day, Nigel had arrived for his visit. They had laughed and talked far into the night. He was good for her morale. He made no demands on her. They were as kindred spirits. Both had realized long ago they would be close friends, confidants, solaces, and companions... but never lovers or spouses.

Nigel was easygoing, natural, genuine, and affectionate. They frequently helped each other through rough or trying times, with a companion for a trip or certain event, with the warmth and closeness of an innocent love. If there was trouble, he was around to see her past it. If she was sad or disheartened, he was there to encourage or enliven her. At times she wished he were her real brother, for he suited and performed that role perfectly and continuously.

Nigel had slept late this morning. Brandy had risen early to ride Wildfire, as was her daily custom when home, when not writing late. Wildfire was a huge, powerful Appaloosa whose intelligence and loyalty made him dear to her heart. His hide was off white, with gray and black splotches dashed upon his flanks; his head and neck were heavily gray and white. His flowing mane and tail were dark gray, his legs solid white.

She moved across the open pasture with life-giving energy entering her body and mind. She never felt freer or happier than when she was sitting on Wildfire's broad back with his hooves barely touching the ground as they raced across the grassy terrain. Clad in cutoff jeans whose color had long since faded to a sky blue and in a cotton shirt which was made from red bandana material and tied in a snug knot just beneath her firm breasts, she appeared a carefree wood nymph to the stormy blue eyes which heatedly traced her aimless ramblings.

Her slender fingers were tightly intertwined in the flowing gray mane of the massive beast. Her bare legs and feet were tucked around the wide breadth of the animal's stomach. Steven couldn't help but wonder how she held on without the benefit of a bridle or the security of a saddle. He was alarmed and frightened by the speed of their abandoned race with the wind. Yet, she appeared to be one with the horse. Their joint movements were as graceful and poetic as the swaying of those wildflowers beneath them.

To any observant eyes or alert ear she was totally relaxed and vividly exuberant. Her laughter was like the soft babble of a mountain stream; her aura could rival the wind for its freedom and restlessness. Steven absently wondered if this could be the same helpless girl he had rescued from death in the Valley of Fire, or the same ravishing female he had met again on several social occasions since that fateful day, or the same enchanting woman he had treated to lunch that day before she left town without so much as a phone call or a polite good-bye! She had not even bothered to leave

him a message about her hasty departure or their business
deal to salvage her name. Had she forgotten all they had
shared that one night in her hotel room?

Had she hoped he wouldn't show up here after all? Had
she thought he was joking? Had she been angered by his
broken date? Or was she only trying to learn if he would
pursue her?

As she paused to allow her horse to catch his wind, she
leaned forward and hugged his neck with affection and admiration. She lovingly stroked his head and neck and spoke
words which Steven could not hear from that lengthy distance. He smiled secretly as he lifted the camera which was
suspended around his neck. He focused the telephoto lens
and brought her image into perfect view. He took numerous shots without her knowledge. Both his heart and his
loins leaped hungrily at the sight she presented. His task
would be tough, as easy as seizing the wind or capturing mist
or chasing a fleeing shadow.

As Brandy finally headed towards the nearby stables,
Steven centered upon her rapidly altering facial expressions
which spoke of her various inner moods. One of his favorite shots was the one which revealed her first, unanticipated
sighting of him. Utter shock was written upon her lovely,
fresh face. If he cared to do so, he could easily win a photography contest with that gem of a snapshot!

Brandy halted abruptly and stared at the man's form
which was partially visible through the split-rail fence. Although his face was concealed by his hands and his camera,
she knew whom that virile frame and arrogant stance belonged to! Knowing he was no doubt focused upon her face,
she hastily lowered her head. Her flowing mane hid her face
until she could bring her scattered emotions into some kind
of safe confinement. She feared his lens might reveal the
heavy drumming of her heart as she sought to control this
unleashed hunger and excitement which helplessly surged
through her body and mind at the mere sight of his close
proximity.

If his intention was to startle her into revealing his true effect upon her, he was a great success! She breathed deeply in an attempt to slow her racing heart and to cool her molten blood. She failed to note the look of anger and resentment which filled his features at the sighting of her supposed irritation at his sudden arrival at her ranch.

If she thought he would not keep their enticing appointment, she could only blame herself. Just as she was sadly mistaken if she believed she could long deny him his wishes and desires. Before he left this lovely ranch, she would no longer be an enigma; she would no longer be an obsession; she would no longer be untouched by his magnetism. If there was one thing he knew for a fact, it was his effect upon women: They had certainly proven it enough times. Brandy Alexander would never qualify for "the one who got away!" If her disinterest wasn't a farce, she still would be unable to battle him and come out the winner. Perhaps that was the heart of his obsession: Could he win this rare woman?

He scoffed at his foolish feelings. He hadn't met a woman who could tempt him to give up his freedom until Brandy. He hadn't found anyone to suit him or his life-style until Brandy. Yet, this golden girl—woman—encompassed all he wanted and needed to make such a drastic change in his life....

Staring his possible defeat in the face, Steven couldn't honestly decide if he wanted to risk a rejection. A curious resentment and novel hesitation filled him, resentment at her possible rejection, a hesitation to challenge the unknown future. She had been perceptive and accurate with her statements that day at lunch: Love and marriage were a big sacrifice and responsibility. Was she just as scared and hesitant as he was? He did not realize these moody, stormy lights were vivid within his blue eyes as she slowly walked her horse over to where he was nonchalantly leaning against the white fence.

Steven reflected on their passion-filled night together. Did she regret her submission? Had he physically hurt her? Was she frightened by her feelings for him? Had sex perhaps disappointed her? If only he knew her thoughts and feelings....

"Steven, this is a surprise," she remarked in a formal tone. "Since I hadn't heard from either you or Casey, I assumed you had decided against coming. Please excuse my lack of hospitality and sloppy appearance. You should have called me; I would have picked you up at the airport. If you'll wait for me on the porch, I'll shower and dress. Have you eaten yet?"

"No, ma'am," he lazily drawled. "The early flight didn't serve breakfast this morning. I thought it was best to rent a car, in case I have to rush back for business reasons. I've got a merger going out West; I'll need to keep a check on it. I must apologize for the mix-up; I suppose my secretary forgot to send you a telegram. If I'm intruding..." He halted as he allowed his words to speak for themselves.

"Certainly not. I'll have Mary bring you some coffee while I make myself more presentable for company." She visibly relaxed as she smiled at him, intrigued by his arrival and enticing persistence, confident on her home turf.

He flashed her an easy smile which made her breath catch in her chest. His eyes leisurely roamed over her entire body from tawny head to bare feet. "I see nothing wrong with the way you're dressed right now," he murmured in a mellow tone, eyes dancing playfully over her provocative appearance once more.

She flushed a deep red. She wondered why he had the easy ability to make her feel totally within his power and at an utter loss as to how to handle herself or the situation. She stammered, "You're too kind and polite. I'll meet you in twenty minutes. Make yourself at home, look around if you wish."

She turned and raced away in a flurry of flying grass shoots and thundering hooves before he could comment upon her looks and company again. He chuckled as he tried to decide if she was embarrassed or simply unnerved. He headed towards the stables instead of for the house as gently ordered. He patiently waited by the gate while she softly issued orders for her beloved mount's rubdown. It was clear from her request that she normally did that chore herself. That unexpected discovery pleased him.

While she spoke with her ranch foreman, Steven glanced around at the tranquil sights before him. Somehow he had expected to find a rambling, two-story, white country house with a long porch and several white rocking chairs surrounded by massive magnolias and lofty pines...or perhaps a huge mansion along the Southern plantation lines. He had certainly not expected an angled L-shaped, two-story house whose rustic exterior was a mixture of redwood and dark brown rock. Both the redwood and the exterior trim were painted a creamy light yellow.

The massive oaks and the slender willows wed the house to its site, making it appear a cunning combination of past and present architecture. Its three porches gave it an air of casual, comfortable living. He had been given a partial view of its interior when he had first arrived.

Her cheery housekeeper had answered his ring at a mid-level entry which immediately led in two directions. One could go upstairs to the formal living areas, dining room, kitchen, bedrooms, and a large porch which was connected to the glassed living room and ran the full length of its thirty-five feet. The view from any of those rooms was magnificent. Or one could go downstairs to a large recreation area, two guest rooms, several other rooms with specified duties, a two-car garage, and another concreted area which matched the position and length of the upstairs porch.

Mary had shown him to one of those downstairs guest rooms which was decorated in a definite masculine flair. When he had told her he needed to speak with Brandy as soon as possible, she had guided him out of the lower level, past a sunken stoned porch, up a few steps, and onto a back patio which encased a swimming pool. She had pointed out the stables not far away and had told him to ask for her there. She had smiled and returned to the house through a screened porch—no doubt where Brandy did a great deal of her writing, considering the lovely view and the sound of the horses and the gurgling brook with its stoned waterfall.

He had leisurely strolled past the inviting pool and the pool house. He had taken in the sights as he walked along: the nearby tennis court, the stream with its manmade cascade, the storage buildings in perfect condition, miles of split-rail fencing around lush green pastures with colorful wildflowers and tall trees which stood like dauntless sentinels, and several stables whose state of excellent repair revealed constant care and alert attention. The composite setting gave off a picturesque, serene storybook look and inspired a homey feeling.

When Brandy joined him and they headed back toward her home, Steven was aware of her nervous, hesitant air. She seemed distant and preoccupied. She abruptly exclaimed, "If you were taking pictures back there, I would appreciate it if you wouldn't use them in your magazine."

He looked down at her, unable to read her strange look from the downcast angle of her head and eyes. "Those were strictly for my private collection: vacation memories," he teased her. "No need to inflame the minds and hearts of countless men who haven't a chance of pursuing a dreamgirl. We'll take some shots for the magazine later."

His tone suddenly became pensive and rueful, as did his expression. If things were going to proceed as hoped, they would need an understanding and a truce. "Sorry about that little misunderstanding at the restaurant in New York. We were getting along so well, I completely forgot about Camille and our dinner."

She halted and glanced up at him, pondering his words and their underlying meaning. "That would be most insulting to any female, Steven. Do you always treat your ladies so casually, or is Miss Blanchard close enough to be taken for granted?''

He winced and murmured, ''Ouch! I hope my manners aren't that lacking or that bad. I blamed it on the enchanting company I was in. As for Camille, there's nothing personal between us. I'm doing some business with the Zartoffs, and I'd promised to show them around town. It's a cosmetics firm, and Camille's the model for the ad campaign. She's developed this annoying habit of hand-delivering the reports and photos; she thinks she can persuade me to go along with her concepts, rather than the photographer's. You left before I could see you again,'' he softly accused her of running out on him.

His unnecessary explanation pleased her, relieved her. She laughed softly. ''If you'll take a good look around you, I think you'll see why I was so anxious to get home. I have two more lengthy trips coming up fairly soon; I wanted to spend as much time as possible here. Plus, there were some ranch matters which I had to take care of before running off again,'' she stated calmly to conceal the real reason for her sudden departure. She wasn't exactly lying, just stretching the truth.

Feeling he was turning that powerful charm on her once more, her guard was quickly rising to protect her vulnerable heart from another attack and defeat. She cautioned herself to defensive distance from him while he was in residence, unless he made the first overture. She could not forget or forgive his quicksilver moods and behavior. After Camille's arrival, she might well have been a stranger, or mere business matter as he had indicated.

Brandy left Steven having coffee on the porch while she went to shower and change. She was briefly tempted to put on a frilly sundress, but dismissed that idea as being too obvious. She pulled on a pair of her best Levi's and an aqua chambray shirt. She brushed her long hair until it displayed vitality and fullness, then applied just enough makeup to enhance her looks without being bold or noticeable. She splashed on fragrant Ciara, then rejoined Steven.

Shortly, Brandy and Steven were served a delicious breakfast. Alertly noting the softened lights in Brandy's eyes as she asked for breakfast to be made, Mary had tried to provide the best early morning meal she had ever cooked or served. Having known and worked years for Brandy, Mary Carter felt no qualms over this man's visit, even though Mary's hours were eight to four daily, except on Sundays or special days. Mary smiled and left them alone to eat and chat.

Steven had removed the casual jacket to his western suit and had negligently tossed it over the back of an empty chair. He had undone several of the upper buttons on his tan shirt with its contrasting designs of rich bronze to match his jacket and pants. His feet were neatly encased in brown Nocona boots. He courteously seated Brandy before claiming his own place directly across the table from her.

They ate in near silence, each trying to outwait the other to begin this conversation and to reveal the coming mood for their arrangement. The meal ended and coffee was served for a last time. Steven leaned back in his chair. He inhaled deeply and smiled mysteriously. His gaze lazily passed over the view which surrounded him. It was so peaceful and relaxing here. It was a perfect setting for the girl seated before him. She appeared so at ease, so natural, so genial.

Blue eyes came to rest on the emerald ones which were astutely studying him as he studied the scenery and girl before him.

"You're right, Brandy; it would be most difficult to trade all of this for big city life. Why do you?" he asked, opening their conversation.

"Honestly?" she teased lightly as she sipped her tepid coffee.

He stood up and walked over to a large post. He negligently leaned his husky, tall frame against it. He glanced back at her and smiled. "Naturally," was all he replied.

"Off the record," she began in a silky, jesting tone, "I leave only to remind myself of who I am and of what I have here. Then, there are business matters and tours to take care of. I also have to research certain types of novels; it's easier to write about locations after you've seen them. I've also found that people are more willing and eager to enlighten you on certain topics if you visit, rather than write or phone. But I think the main reason is to prevent myself from growing complacent and boring. Other people, places, and events stimulate me; they teach me things. That keeps me from being dull and stagnant."

"Such as?" he probed without taking his eyes from her face.

She came over to stand against the next post. "What goes on away from the security and solitude of this place—how people and places are changing with the times. To stimulate my mind and my imagination, to see and to learn new things. I suppose I'm inwardly afraid I might become a narrow-minded, boring, ignorant, country girl if I remain secluded here all the time. Plus, I need to see friends."

"You mean to analyze people and situations to use in a new novel…research, isn't it?" he inquired in a tone which she found confusing and almost resentful.

She sighed heavily and shook her head. "I thought I had made myself clear the last time you hinted at such a despicable thing. For the last time, Steven, I do not use my friends or mere acquaintances as guinea pigs or role models. I'm talking about living history, or past history, or locations, or certain jobs and events. I'm not denying that some things or some people make an impression on my unconscious mind, but I do not intentionally dissect or exploit the personality or life of anyone."

As soon as the pages were ready for *Valley,* he would know whether or not she was telling the truth. He baffled her further by smiling broadly.

"What does that sneaky smile mean, Steven?"

"Oh, I was just thinking about something," he hinted.

She waited for him to continue. When he did not, she asked curiously, "Thinking about what?"

He chuckled at her vivid interest. "Nothing that would interest you, Miss Alexander." Before she could insist upon some logical answer, Mary called him to the phone in the living room.

"I hope you don't mind if I left your number with my service; I have several important business deals in the making."

"Of course not," she sweetly replied, grinning saucily.

"You don't care if someone discovers I'm spending a few weeks here with you?" he taunted roguishly. "Mary isn't a live-in, you know."

She boldly parried, "What better way to discount your initial story than to entertain you at my secluded ranch. Knowing you, who would dare believe it was merely business? Besides, we are adults." Before those words had left her mouth, she flushed a crimson red.

As he chuckled in unsuppressed pleasure and merriment, he teased, "What better way indeed! Now I know why you tricked me into coming here." His hand reached out to caress her cheek. He failed to note her tremors as he fought to conceal his own. Damn, she was beautiful and alluring! Nights alone will be awfully tempting.

Her gaze fused with his as she sexily whispered, "But I didn't, Steven. You heartlessly blackmailed me into allowing you to come here and to charm me into a truthful story for that malicious paper-rag of yours. You can hardly blame me if I would rather enjoy your surreptitious visit than constantly resist it. How can a poor, defenseless female battle such persistence and power?" she taunted.

"If my hold over you is that powerful and frightening, I should have demanded more than a mere story from you," he genially countered as he headed into the house.

"Perhaps you should have," she murmured softly.

He whirled to face her; his expression was deadly serious as he firmly demanded, "What did you say?"

His strange tone and piercing gaze warned her to secrecy. "I said, perhaps you should take your call; someone is impatiently waiting on the other end," she lied with a mysterious smile.

He stared at her for a few moments, knowing that was not what she said, wishing he could be certain if he had heard her correctly. He shrugged and went to answer the phone.

A short time later, a masculine voice asked, "Is that who I think it is, the man on the phone? He did show up?"

"Good morning, Nigel," she murmured with a dreamy look still filling her eyes. "Yep, that's him all right. You do recall the main purpose of his visit, don't you?" she whispered into his ear as she affectionately embraced him, then laid her face against his cotton shirt and linked her arms around his waist.

Nigel shook his head as he laughed. He hugged her tightly to his firm body and rested his face atop her silky head. "What would I ever do without you, Brandy love?" He stated with a rueful chuckle, "Sorry I slept so late...."

Before she could reply, a frigid voice stated formally, "I hope I'm not intruding, Miss Alexander?"

Brandy stiffened, then forcefully relaxed herself. Why should he make her feel ill at ease in her own home! She looked up into Nigel's grinning face and smiled lovingly. "Not at all, Steven. You already know Nigel, I believe," she remarked with a hint of subtle amusement in her voice. "I hope you don't mind, Steven; Nigel was invited first. He loves to crash here and relax, plus write great songs."

Nigel turned to face the stern, shocked look in Steven's eyes. "Sure we know each other, Brandy love. Good to see you again, Steve. Brandy says you're going to do a new story about her. Or rather, correct a malicious one." He commented with relief, "I'm glad. There wasn't any truth to that other one."

"You look surprised, Nigel. After all, you're the one who told me I was completely wrong about her. I just never realized why you were so positive and well-informed. If I had known you were going to be here, I would have brought me a companion along to make a foursome. In fact, that was a very annoyed Camille on the line just now. She was insisting on joining me here," he commented just to vex Brandy, knowing Camille had called to complain about the new commercial.

It worked, for Brandy's eyes glittered with blazing fury as she glared at him. "What you do with your own time is not my business, Mr. Winngate. But I will not have my home turned into a brothel to prevent your temporary loneliness. Neither your Camille nor any other lady friend is welcomed here. If you have need of some female's services or company, then I suggest you meet one of them in the nearest town for the coming weekend. Nigel is a frequent guest of mine; no, he's not a guest. He's family; he's like my very own brother. So you can wipe that lewd expression off your smug face and dismiss those vulgar thoughts. No matter, under no circumstances will you invite one of your women here! Those are my terms for our business arrangement, Mr. Winngate, sir!" With that tirade, she breathlessly stormed into the house. Brandy didn't stop; she walked out the front door. She rounded the house and headed for the stables. She would lose her anger and anguish with a brisk ride, the one his arrival had interrupted.

Both men stared at the door, neither knowing what to say or do. Nigel finally spoke up first, "Just to clear the air, Steve, Brandy and I are very close friends; nothing more. I know that story is utterly fictitious because I know her so well. She's like my little sister; we spend a lot of time together. But we've never been lovers, nor will we ever be. For one thing, she isn't like that. She's an old-fashioned girl who's struggling very hard to survive in a modern world. Don't attempt to place her into one of those molds for the many women you know; she won't fit. Brandy's different; she's unique and special. If you haven't realized that by now, then you'll never know or understand her." The displeased singer was sorry he had ever suggested this visit.

Nigel's tone became firm and cool as he went on, "I will issue you one friendly warning: Don't try to use her in any way. In spite of how strong and intelligent you think she is, she's very vulnerable and naive. Knowing the two of you, I think you're the very man who could either win her love or devastate her, so don't tamper with her emotions. Either keep everything on a business level or leave here right now," he advised the intense Steven, appealing to the man's conscience.

"You think Brandy might be romantically interested in me?"

"Yes, but I also think she's afraid of you and of herself. Perhaps that's why she didn't call me and cancel my visit— self-defense. I've never seen those lights in her eyes before, nor have I ever seen her so completely unsure of herself. The thing is, you two would make a perfect team; you're a great deal alike, and even your differences are compatible. Would you believe I was planning to introduce you two in Vegas? If it isn't presumptuous, I wish you would give yourself a chance to get to know her... really know her. I know from personal experience, a man doesn't want to remain the envied, carefree bachelor forever. But even if you're not romantically interested in her, get to know her as a friend. She's great fun, and she's mighty easy to be around."

"I was only teasing about Camille. You know I can hardly tolerate her more than two minutes. I guess I don't wear jealousy or defeat well. I know Brandy's unique; that's really why I'm here."

"I was invited before you, Steve. Brandy didn't call me home as her defender. I visit every few months. This is a great place to unwind and to rest. I've written some of my best songs here. Go easy on her, Steve. You could hurt her deeply."

"I fully intend to take your advice, Nigel. First I owe her an apology, then a few weeks of getting acquainted. I'm canceling the story on her altogether. I only used that ploy to get an invitation here. I wanted to meet the real woman, as you suggested countless times. But I did hope for privacy for my research," he said, teasing Nigel. "It's just that when I saw the two of you standing there like that, it blew my mind." Steven couldn't bring himself to expose their closeness.

"Brandy would never relax fully if I suddenly left you two alone. If you put on your best airs, she won't mind being left alone with you. A word of advice, don't try to charm her too quickly. She might doubt your sincerity. You do have a reputation as a heartless playboy."

When Steven went in search of her, he was told she had gone riding. He quickly changed into western boots and faded jeans. He laced his leather belt through the loops on his snug Levi's and fastened the large buckle: a brass lion's head. He hurried to the stables and requested a mount.

The foreman complied immediately. He also informed the genial, apparently easygoing man of where he could likely find her. Unaware of his slip, the foreman laughingly added, "Anytime she rushes out of here with *that* look in her eyes, she heads for the pond."

Steven grinned as he easily mounted up and headed off in the direction which had been given to him. He rode as agilely and smoothly as she did. He admired the strength and beauty of her excellent, expensive bloodlines. He had never given this breed of horse much thought until he had met her in Las Vegas. Since then he had avidly studied everything he could find about them. It had not taken long for him to understand her interest and her great love for them. But it was evident the Appaloosas were mainly a hobby; writing was her profession.

Steven eased back on his reins as he neared the pond. He quietly slipped off of the horse's back and tied the reins to a bush. He stealthily made his way through the trees until they abruptly ended to form a picturesque clearing with a mirror lake. Sure enough there sat Brandy on the grassy bank by the water's edge. She was absently tossing small rocks into the glassy water, watching the ripples which her action created.

The mischievous Steven leaned over and picked up a large, heavy rock. He threw it over her head into the water. It struck with a loud, heavy splash which sent sprays of water on her. Brandy gasped and jumped in surprise. She whirled to look up into his laughing face. He quickly hunkered down beside her. Between chuckles, he apologized and wiped her wet face with his handkerchief.

"I only meant to grab your attention, Brandy, not drown you. I'm terribly sorry," he said, still laughing in unleashed amusement.

His laughter ceased as he clarified, "Sorry for the water on you, and more sorry for my rudeness at the house. I was irritated at my service for giving Camille this number; I took it out on you. I was only teasing about asking her to come down here," he confessed. "I see plenty of her as it is. As you once said, she's one of those necessary escorts who fulfills my social obligations. Using her makes it easier than trying to train a different girl every month or so. With Camille, I don't have to worry; she knows she's strictly business. The trouble is, she's beginning to annoy and embarrass me with her animosity toward other female friends and with her unfounded possessiveness. There's nothing between us, Brandy. I don't even like her."

Brandy watched Steven closely. "Why did you say those terrible things about me and Nigel?"

"I was more than a little annoyed when I walked out to find you in the arms of another man. I thought perhaps you were playing some joke on me. I'm sorry."

"You said Nigel suggested you do this new story?"

"Yes, he did. Let's say it was a cross between a demand and a friendly suggestion. I must admit, the more I saw of you, the more I began to suspect he might be right. I considered assigning you to another reporter, then I decided the only one I could trust implicitly was me. Besides, the idea intrigued me. Not every man gets to rescue a dream, and then spend time alone with her."

She laughed with him this time. "What's that old saying about doing it yourself if you want it done right?" They laughed again. "Perhaps I was a bit hasty and rude myself, Steven. Do you suppose we could make another fresh start?"

He instantly extended his hand. "Steven Winngate at your service, ma'am," he drawled huskily, his eyes glued to hers.

She slipped her hand into his and gently clutched it. Smiling warmly into those blue pools of mystery and allure, she murmured, "Brandy Alexander..."

Their hungry eyes locked and fed on the sight before them. "I've missed you, Brandy. Why didn't you phone before you left town?" he asked seriously.

"I wasn't sure if you wanted to hear from me so soon. You did act rather cool after Camille's arrival," she reminded him.

"Sometimes I act like a spoiled kid. I was just annoyed with the change of plans. I would have preferred to spend the evening with you," he freely admitted, eyes glowing.

His hand captured a curl and savored its softness and vitality, traits which matched Brandy. "You aren't disappointed that I came, are you?" he questioned.

"Only disappointed you took so long to arrive," she confessed shyly.

His voice grew husky as he leaned forward and kissed her deeply and whispered, "I want you...."

She met his intense gaze and smiled. "I want you too...."

Their bodies sank to the grassy earth as they embraced and kissed greedily. Their senses soared as freely and happily as the hawk overhead. Steven's roaming hands tormented her aching body. His lips seared across her face and towards her ear, his warm respiration bringing tremors to her weakening resolve.

"Steven, wait," she urged him.

"Why? I need you, love," he coaxed, capturing her mouth with his.

When she could free her throbbing lips, she murmured raggedly, "I have men working the pastures today. We can't, not here in the open. Someone could ride up to water a horse at any moment," she reluctantly informed him.

He sighed heavily. "Later?"

A bright smile flickered over her enchanting face. "Later..." she cheerfully and eagerly agreed.

"If we can only talk right now, then you'd best keep your distance, woman. I can't control myself if I'm touching you or you're touching me," he playfully warned.

"I know what you mean," she said and sighed painfully.

Their gazes fused once more; they burst into shared laughter.

Chapter Ten

Steven and Brandy remained at the lake until a loud bell rang out persistently. They had laughed and chatted with such gay abandon they had forgotten the time. Her head jerked up at the muffled noise which was calling them to lunch. As they mounted up, they exchanged warm smiles, promising smiles.

"Race you back," he suggested with a twinkle in his eye.

"You're on, Steven," she quickly accepted his challenge, then kneed her horse into a swift gallop before he could even throw his leg over his saddle.

Within a few yards, he was at her side. "No fair," he teased as the wind whipped the laughter from his chest and carried it off behind them.

The carefree girl laughed at him, then snapped her reins to encourage Wildfire into a faster gait. Steven kept up with her only because of his skill and determination. They reached the stable at the same time. He quickly dismounted and helped her down. Their eyes met and briefly locked as her feet touched the grass and her hands slid down his shoulders and chest.

"You cheated, Miss Alexander," he taunted with a chuckle.

"I did not," she saucily replied. "Women always deserve a headstart. In spite of our past discussions, I am still a woman, and I dearly enjoy being one," she informed him amidst giggles.

"That's one fact I certainly won't argue. May I?" he inquired as he held out his bent elbow to escort her to the house. If the foreman of her ranch hadn't been standing there, he would have stolen a heady kiss.

"Yes, you may, kind sir," she drawled in a feigned Southern accent.

Nigel watched them as they approached him. He smiled. They certainly seemed to be enjoying each other's company. He could only hope for the best between them. If only they would stop being so guarded and distant with each other . . .

"Hello, Nigel," she said brightly as they spotted him sitting by the pool. Nigel called them over to where he was.

"It's about time you two came back," he gently chided them. "I'm starved! Mary has a fantastic lunch ready. I was just about to give you two up and dig in."

Brandy and Steven hastily washed up at the pool house as they chatted. She led the way into the large country kitchen. "You don't mind if we eat in here, do you, Steven?"

"Certainly not. It makes a real cozy setting."

That meal began their unpredictable and enlightening arrangement. Too unsure of herself and of Steven, Brandy cautioned herself to move slowly and carefully. For things to be right between them, Steven had to make the first move towards something more serious. She dared not allow him to think she was just like all other women—hotly pursuing him.

On his side, Steven was doing much the same. He planned to close in subtly on her, to avoid frightening her off or making her wary of his attentions. He determined to win her trust and confidence before letting her discover his feelings. If she was not interested in him in the same way he was interested in her, he would never let her learn of his growing love.

After lunch, Steven and Brandy took a long walk around the grounds. As they strolled along they talked, and talked, and talked. Nigel appeared content to laze by the pool and make notes on his next song. To foster his ploy, Steven questioned and photographed Brandy in various surroundings and on a variety of topics. Enchanted, Brandy cheerfully complied with Steven's gentle orders or playful suggestions. Steven was dazzled by this bright female, who could sway between an audacious child and a seductive woman. They laughed and joked about their uncanny meeting. He related things about himself and his businesses. They appeared content to simply be together. Nigel's eyes softened each time they sighted his two friends so engrossed in each other. The afternoon passed swiftly and tranquilly for all three.

Brandy had given Mary the afternoon off, saying Nigel could prepare steaks on the barbecue. While Nigel was getting the coals hot in the grill, Steven offered to help Brandy with the salad and with setting the table on the screened porch. Mary had scrubbed the potatoes and put them in the oven before leaving early. The kitchen was much too quiet and provocative and as a needed distraction Brandy asked Steven to select some music for the record player, which he did.

The sultry strains of Neil Diamond drifted into Brandy's ears as she withdrew the needed items from the refrigerator. When Steven returned to the kitchen, Brandy playfully teased, "Nigel might be offended you didn't put on his latest record."

"I've heard it umpteen times; I financed it," he cunningly retorted, handing her a glass of wine from her bar. "Besides, we have the real thing, if we care to hear him later."

Brandy laughed merrily. She thanked him for the drink. "You take the lettuce, and I'll do everything else," she sweetly commanded, enjoying this homey scene.

Steven accepted the knife, bowl, and green head of lettuce. When Brandy glanced at him, she doubled over with sidesplitting laughter. "You're murdering my lettuce," she wailed between giggles. "I can tell you've never seen a kitchen before."

A rueful expression met Brandy's grinning face. "You're right. Care to teach me how it's done?" he asked with a beguiling look.

"Like this," Brandy offered, taking the head of lettuce and gently tearing it apart.

"Why did you hand me a knife if I wasn't supposed to chop it?" he asked.

"To cut off the end," she purred softly, rising to kiss his cheek. "Think you can handle it now?" she teased.

"I can handle this," he murmured, closing his arm around her and pulling her against him. His lips tasted hers then moaned appreciatively.

"You'd better handle this later; Nigel will be screaming for his dinner soon."

"I feel like a phone always being put on hold," he muttered.

"Aren't you glad you don't have to remain on hold very long?" she boldly retorted, her hands roving over the broad expanse of his chest. "Get busy; I'm starved."

"How can you be starved after that marvelous lunch?" he asked skeptically.

"I didn't mean for dinner, Steven," she cooed meaningfully.

His eyes lit up knowingly. "I'm starved too."

They sighed regretfully and parted. Nigel joined them shortly to claim the platter of steaks. "Where's my drink? And who's that croaking on the stereo?"

Steven and Brandy exchanged looks and laughed. "There are other singers besides you, big brother. Get your own drink; you know this house as well as I do," she teased.

"Some service! You'd think I was a member of the family or something," Nigel joked easily, tweaking Brandy's flushed cheek.

Steven watched intently as Brandy flung her arms around Nigel and kissed him lightly on the lips. "Poor baby," she murmured.

After the food had vanished, both men helped Brandy clear the dishes and clean the kitchen. She glanced over at the two men and asked, "Anyone care to join me for some cream sherry on the porch?"

Both men accepted. Time passed as they talked and sipped their drinks. When Nigel noticed the way Steven and Brandy kept exchanging longing looks, he assumed they wanted to be alone. Nigel stood up and stretched lazily. "If you two don't mind my cutting out, I think I'll turn in."

"It's early, Nigel," Brandy stated halfheartedly.

"I know, but I'm beat. I think I'll get up early and work on the song that is nagging at me. See you two in the morning." With that, Nigel left them alone.

Steven didn't move for a lengthy span; he just sat watching Brandy. She suddenly seemed nervous and shy. He understood. Finally he stood up and stretched lazily, much as Nigel had done earlier. "Guess I'd better turn in too."

Brandy's eyes lifted to fuse with his entreating gaze. She didn't move or speak. Steven walked over to stand before her. His hand reached out in enticing temptation. "It's late, Brandy," he whispered softly.

She smiled, then placed her hand in his. He pulled her to her feet, his hands easing upwards to capture her head between them. He gazed into her softened eyes. They spoke without words. She reached for his left hand and led him to her room.

Steven walked inside the moonlit bedroom and halted to turn and look at her. Brandy was leaning against the closed door, watching him. He stepped forward. Their hungry eyes feasted; words weren't necessary at such a moment. His head came down to join their lips. The lock on her door clicked softly before her arms encircled his body.

The tender kiss became savage and fiery in an overwhelming surge of long-denied passion. His arms tightened possessively and greedily. His lips twisted over hers, parting hers and allowing his tongue to seek hers. His respiration was ragged; his body was consumed with need. Her name escaped his lips time after time between feverish kisses. His hands frantically roamed her back, wanting to feel her flesh against them. This moment had haunted him for weeks.

He halted the attack on their senses and led her over to her bed. He slowly unbuttoned her shirt and eased it off her body, tossing it to the carpeted floor. Her bra quickly joined it, then her jeans and panties. She stood motionless while he stripped off his own clothes and boots, as if hypnotized by his presence and what was taking place between them.

Moonlight stole into the room, shedding a soft glow on Brandy's body. Steven's eyes leisurely traveled from her tawny head to her bare feet. She was exquisite, desirable beyond belief. "I've missed you, love," he murmured huskily as his body seared against hers.

The contact was staggering. Brandy swayed and moaned. Steven's arms imprisoned her, his lips assailing her senses once more. A bronze hand cupped a breast and lovingly caressed it, the nipple responding to his heady touch. Steven halted to pull down the covers, then pushed her gently to the bed. "I've been thinking about this all day," he admitted hoarsely. "Damn, how I want you, Brandy."

"Steven..." she whispered against his demanding mouth, her arms going around his neck and drawing him to her.

Steven's tongue tantalized her as it circled her protruding nipple before hungrily encasing it within his torrid mouth. As if a fierce battle to please her was raging, his hands struggled against his lips to stimulate her to full arousal. Masculine fingers wandered freely over her body, caressing here and enticing there. He found sheer delight in drawing little sighs and groans from her. His hand slipped lower, to stroke her inner thighs, then to taunt her throbbing center within that tawny forest which beckoned him.

Brandy's head rolled from side to side on her pillow as she absorbed and responded to his stirring actions. She yearned to experience those wild and wonderful sensations once more. Her body pleaded for his. There was such firmness and strength beneath her roving hands as she explored his body. His body was smooth and hard, a blissful contradiction. It was cool and yet fiery beneath her touch. She craved to know every inch of it. Her hands traveled over his broad shoulders, down his furry chest to play in its black covering. Her fingertips circled his ears and she murmured her great need into them. A brave hand eased over his taut buttocks and around his slim waist. The brazen extension continued until it found a fiery torch which demanded to be encased and explored. He was so silky and warm, as if inflamed from within.

Steven groaned at her touch and his mounting need to possess her and to cool that same torch. Unable to wait any longer, he moved between her legs and entered her very gently. The moisture there allowed him to enter her without pain but not without notice. Brandy arched upwards to meet him.

"God, Brandy, be still a minute," he instructed apprehensively.

Brandy was past hearing Steven's tender warnings. Her body was a sheet of fire, flames which demanded dousing. He inhaled several times and sought to master the urge to ride her as recklessly and swiftly as she rode her stallion. He knew the danger of relaxing; he was too close to ending this ecstatic madness. When he gained some small measure of control, he began to move slowly, purposefully.

The tension built with each stroke. Soon Brandy was riding the crest of a powerful wave, one which stunningly threatened to sweep her away. Steven's mouth closed over hers to prevent her cries of potent release from being overheard by Nigel. Their mouths and bodies blended together as they rode the wave over surging rapids into a tranquil bay. Steven covered her face with kisses as the contentment of accomplishment settled in on her. He was breathing hard as he propped up on one elbow to gaze down at her. "I take it you're sufficiently fed now, love," he playfully whispered, grinning at her, his teeth white in the dim light.

"For now," she happily replied, hugging him tightly.

"Greedy little witch, aren't you? Hell, I'm not a kid anymore, woman. Take it easy on me, will you?" he teased quietly, trailing his fingers over her chest.

"You have only yourself to blame, Mr. Winngate. After all, you're the one who introduced me to this delectable treat. It's only right that you should be the one to feed me when I'm hungry."

"Is that a fact, my greedy hostess," he sighed contentedly.

"That's a fact, Winngate. I didn't forget to tell you you'd have to pay for your visit, did I? Nothing's free these days," she parried, twirling wisps of hair on his moist chest around her fingers.

"I certainly like your manner of billing and collecting," he murmured into her ear, then nibbled on it.

As his hands began to taunt her again, she chided, "I'm greedy? What do you call yourself?"

"Insatiable, where you're concerned, Miss Alexander. I might add, I'm a demanding guest."

"I hope so. Two weeks can pass awfully fast," she murmured wistfully.

"Then we'd best not waste a minute of them. Should I get my pad and take notes?"

"Just your mental one," she quipped, tugging on his sable hair.

"You know something, woman? I think I'm going to enjoy this job. Yes, sirree, I'm gonna have myself the best working vacation ever."

"You're a devil, Steven Winngate," she softly scolded.

"Incognito?" he came back at her immediately.

"There's nothing disguised about you tonight, love," she jested lightly, gazing tenderly into his bedeviling features.

His lips covered hers and his hands worked avidly to prove her right....

BETWEEN BRANDY and Steven, two days passed cheerfully in feigned businesslike discussions and photography sessions. Those same nights passed swiftly and passionately in unbridled joinings of bodies. With each passing moment shared, they both relaxed little by little. Nigel spent time swimming or writing his music. Mary worked, while furtively watching the ever-closing distance between the handsome stranger and her enchanted employer.

On the third afternoon of Steven's visit, he and Brandy went for a walk in the pasture. The moment they were out of sight, he reached for her hand. They strolled along in serene silence, their locked hands swaying with their movements.

"Watch out for snakes, Steven," she mischievously warned as he released her hand and raced towards the nearby cluster of trees, calling, "Beat you around the bushes" over his shoulder.

Steven braked so fast that Brandy filled the air with mirthful laughter. He whirled and looked back at her, scowling at her joke. "Woman!" he thundered in mock fury, then stalked towards her.

Brandy squealed and raced off in the other direction, towards the safety of the barn. She rounded the corner and rushed inside the enclosure. She agilely mounted the ladder to the loft and ambled over loose hay and hid behind stacked bales. She covered her mouth to suppress her giggles. Never had she enjoyed herself so much.

Steven was hastily in pursuit of the impish creature. After entering the barn, he glanced around with narrowed eyes. Sighting the wooden ladder, he surmised where his vixen was hiding. "Prepare yourself for a good spanking, my fetching damsel," he warned, grinning in amusement, feeling like a carefree boy again.

He steadily made his way up the sturdy rungs, then halted on the last one. There was only one hiding place. He moved towards it. When he headed around the bales in one direction, she raced around the other end, giggles following her departure. Within two steps, Steven had her captured and pinned to the loft floor on her back. "Got you now, my wily Kat." He began to tickle her.

"That's dirty pool, Steven Winngate," she shrieked, thrashing about on the golden straw.

"What about you, Miss Alexander? Snakes indeed."

"We do have snakes here," she hurriedly announced. "Look behind the barn. Clyde has the skins tacked up there, rattlers and all," she vowed truthfully. "If you don't believe me, just—"

"Telephone, Brandy!" Nigel called from the porch.

"Drat!" she panted.

"Are we expecting another protector?" he teased devilishly.

"I hope not," she quickly replied, then flushed. "Not unless it's Casey, but I haven't invited her, I swear," she promised humorously.

"Brandy! Where are you? Telephone!" Nigel persisted for a moment.

Steven rolled aside to let her up. She hurried to the loft window and yelled down, "Coming!"

Steven stood up, catching a rafter and swaying his body. He suddenly yelped like an injured puppy, slapping at his hand. He danced around, tossing straw this way and that, slinging his left hand. He forcefully smacked the offending wasp, killing it. As the black body dropped to the straw, Brandy observed his problem.

"Did it sting you?" she worriedly asked, coming back to his side.

The hand boasted of a rising welt, a fiery red area and a stark white center. "He got you all right. Come inside. I'll fix it," she coaxed.

"I got him back," Steven vowed triumphantly. "Dead as a dry well. That'll teach him to challenge and attack me."

Brandy looked at him strangely. The vengeful tone in his voice and the curious victory in his eyes stunned her. He looked and sounded as if he had just slain some powerful enemy and sadistically enjoyed it. *Men,* she scoffed mentally. *Everything's a war with you!*

Brandy and Steven headed for the house, with the annoyed man clutching his painful hand. "Are you allergic to insect stings?" she inquired, witnessing his vexation.

"Not that I know of. Never been stung before. The little devils haven't dared! Did you sic him on me?" he teased sullenly, meaning it as a joke, but it didn't sound that way to Brandy.

"Don't be silly," she scolded him, offended by his harsh words.

"It's Casey," Nigel informed her as she opened the door and entered.

"Tell her I'll call back in a few minutes. Steven tangled with a feisty wasp. I need to remove the stinger and put something on it."

Nigel went to deliver her message. Brandy guided Steven to the den and told him to sit down while she went for some tweezers and medication. He flopped onto the couch, muttering curses.

Brandy returned and skillfully extracted the tiny shaft of misery. She sprayed some Bactine on the same area, then smiled up into his stormy gaze. "All done. Feel better?"

"Not yet," he growled, wondering what Casey wanted, fretting over that call. "Snakes, bees, perils at every turn. Country life can be hazardous to one's health."

Brandy bit back her stinging retort. She smiled frozenly and apologized for his misfortune and misery. "I'd better phone Casey. Why don't you have a drink and relax? I'll be back soon." She left the room before he could respond.

"What's up, Casey?" she cheerfully asked when her friend answered.

"How's it going down there?" was Casey's first question. "Having fun?"

"You recall the story about the bear robbing the honeycomb and getting stung?" she teased.

Casey remarked in bewilderment, "What?"

"Steven just played the bear and his hand is smarting something fierce. I've doctored it, but he still thinks he's a grumpy bear."

"I see. Country life's not agreeing with our city boy?" she jested.

"Only today," Brandy commented. "Anything going on up there?"

"Just called to warn you," Casey began her explanation. Brandy stiffened until she added, "*Twilight*'s on the way to you. Devon wants one scene lengthened."

"Which one?" Brandy inquired.

Casey enlightened her. "I see," Brandy quipped, then laughed. "No problem. When do they need it finished?"

"Yesterday," came the reply she dreaded, but expected.

"I should have known. Always in a rush. When's it arriving?"

"Tomorrow, special delivery," Casey said.

"Yuck! Well, at least Nigel's here to entertain Steven while I fix it," she murmured miserably. "Anything else?"

Casey hesitated, then replied, "Not yet."

"What do you mean, not yet? Another problem?" she ventured.

"I hope not. Let's don't look for trouble, Brandy. I'm working on something; I'll call you when I have my facts straight."

With intruding work on its way, Brandy didn't want to hear any more. They spoke a few minutes, then hung up. Brandy sat on the edge of her bed in pensive thought.

Something had Casey on edge; what? *Oh, well,* she promptly decided, *Casey'll let me know when the time's right.* She returned to the den.

Steven was nursing a Scotch on the rocks. He glanced up when she strolled in, a frown on her lovely face. "Any problems?" he asked warily.

Brandy's gaze met his. "Just some revisions for Devon. They'll be arriving tomorrow. Seems *Twilight* isn't spicy enough for them," she sneered oddly. "Damn!" she blurted out angrily, then fixed herself a Scotch and water.

"If you disagree, why change it?" he asked curiously.

"I don't exactly disagree, Steven. The publishers know what sells. It's just the timing," she confessed sadly. "You and Nigel will have to entertain yourselves for a day or so while I doctor the manuscript."

"They want lots of changes?" he asked.

"No, only one scene lengthened," she absently replied.

"Why would that take so long?" he pressed in puzzlement.

"A writer can't just throw a scene in without rereading the manuscript. The whole story has to be fresh in her mind, or it won't mesh smoothly."

"But you know the whole story," he argued in rising confusion.

"I did when I wrote it. But with the revisions, it's hard to keep track of what's been changed. I can't refer to something which has been deleted or ignore something that's been added. It's sort of complicated," she added at his quizzical look.

"Evidently," he concurred.

"How's the hand?" she asked, changing the subject.

"I'll survive," he concluded, then chuckled. "Is that all Casey wanted?"

Brandy didn't catch the worried inflection in his tone. "She's not bringing the manuscript; she's sending it," she remarked saucily, winking at him, assuming that was the point to his query.

He laughed. "You know me too well, woman."

She met his beguiling expression. Did she? Or did she know him at all?

"You look worried, Brandy. Any bad news?" he asked, his concern showing in a different way. He stood up and walked over to where she was leaning against the bar.

"I'm not sure," she murmured thoughtfully.

"What do you mean?" he asked, stiffening imperceptibly.

"I can't put my finger on it, but Casey acted weird. Something's bothering her, but she wouldn't explain. She said she'd call me later, if she needed to."

"Then you have nothing to trouble that pretty head over. If something was wrong, she'd tell you. How about a swim?" he entreated to distract her. If she fretted, she might call Casey and demand an explanation. No doubt that cunning agent had gotten wind of his actions. He wished he could disconnect her phone for a few days; he couldn't.

Nigel's innocent interference made it impossible for Steven to visit Brandy's room that night. The inspired songwriter was working feverishly in the recreation area into which both of their rooms opened, working far into the wee hours of the morning. Steven thrashed about on his lonely bed as he impatiently waited for Nigel to halt his work and go to bed. Steven knew he couldn't reveal his relationship with Brandy by marching upstairs to her room, so he suffered in his guest room. Exhaustion finally overtook him, and he drifted off into restless slumber. Soon Nigel's song was completed, and he also turned in for the night, at three in the morning.

When Steven hadn't shown up by one o'clock, Brandy daringly eased down the steps and peaked into the open area of the downstairs den. Sighting Nigel as he worked diligently, she knew her evening with her beloved would not take place. Nigel was too much like her; when inspired, the clock didn't exist. Knowing how she disliked interruptions while concentrating so fiercely, she smiled and returned to her room. Long before Steven was asleep, Brandy was dreaming about him.

Early the following morning, Brandy knocked on the two men's doors. She was laughing gaily and playfully calling for them to arise, "Up, you lazy slugs! We're going fishing before it gets too hot. Anyone not up and dressed for breakfast in thirty minutes will miss a marvelous picnic," she threatened amidst giggles of delight.

She was dressed in olive green shorts which were made from army fatigue material. Her khaki shirt boasted of deep hunter green trees. She pulled the longer sections of her hair back and secured them with a bright yellow ribbon, letting the rest of her windswept curls fall into careful, casual disarray.

She was already seated at the table when both men joined her only twenty minutes later. Steven eyed her sleepily as he exclaimed, "Have you no mercy, woman? It's still night!"

"Night!" she shrieked. "It's nearly seven thirty. The fish won't bite after it gets hot. If you want to sample the excellent catfish in my pond, you have to supply them to Mary by two o'clock sharp. Otherwise, you might go hungry while you watch me and Nigel devour ours," she vowed as if totally serious. Only her glittering eyes and radiant smile gave her away.

She certainly looked chipper this morning! He growled sullenly, "Midnight fishing another of those hazards of country life?"

"Don't be so grumpy," she teased merrily. "Didn't you sleep well last night?"

"Somebody kept the light on all night, working," he stated.

"I know. I checked on you two about midnight to see if anyone wanted a late snack. Nigel had his nose to the grindstone and you were in bed," she remarked lightly, secretly winking at Steven, telling him she knew why he hadn't appeared and was so out of sorts.

Nigel grinned sheepishly. "Sorry, old buddy, it's that damnable creative flow. It just won't be controlled or halted. People like me and Brandy get caught up in it and have to go with it. Right, Brandy?"

"I couldn't have said it better," she perkily concurred.

Their mood contagious, Steven relaxed and grinned. He joined in that carefree spirit. "What if I'm the only one who catches any fish? Does that mean you'll go hungry? Begging?"

"Steven Winngate! Would you deny a starving lady in distress? From past experience, I think not," she teased boldly.

"I couldn't deny you anything. Neither could I ever refuse the role of Sir Lancelot," he vowed with his hand over his heart.

"You'll share your little fishes with us, won't you, Nigel?"

"Only if I catch more than five," he replied easily.

"You two are impossible. Eat up or be left behind."

Shortly they headed out to the lake. It did not require a genius or a long time to discover Steven was skilled at fishing. Brandy found herself wondering if there was anything he could not do or get. Was he perhaps too perfect, too demanding?

As time passed, it was a constant battle to keep her eyes and attention off Steven. His laughter would send shivers over her body. His warm, piercing gaze would inflame her blood and send all other thoughts fleeing from her mind. The last thing she thought about was delicious catfish for dinner!

Steven looked so sexy and relaxed in his western-cut Levi's and his emerald green knit shirt. When they took a break for lunch, the handsome rogue spread out the blanket upon the grass for her. She unpacked the fried chicken, potato salad, pickles, potato chips, sandwiches, and Tollhouse cookies. She smiled as she lifted the chilled bottle of white wine from the cooler. She placed red checkered napkins, eating utensils, and chilled wineglasses at three spots on the blanket, and then called the two men to lunch.

Steven's eyes widened in pleasure. As he took the plate which she was holding out to him, he grinned with genuine satisfaction and happiness. "This is my kind of picnic," he stated as an obvious compliment.

"See what you would have missed if you hadn't gotten up in the middle of the night," she jested joyously.

"You must be referring to that huge catfish I landed a while ago," he cunningly parried her joke.

"What else?" she swiftly shot back, then laughed.

"Perhaps the marvelous lunch and excellent company?" he murmured in a husky tone which sent thrills racing over her body.

They leisurely enjoyed the lunch which Mary had prepared for them. Their conversation was light and easy. Nigel entertained them with hilarious tales about some of his past performances. But it was Steven's stories about his African safari which captured her interest and undivided attention.

"If you plan to go again, Steven, I'd love to tag along. That would be a spectacular setting for a story."

"If you're serious, come with me this spring," he offered.

Her emerald eyes glowed. "Could I really?"

"Sure. Mary could tag along as camp cook," he jested.

"I don't think she would risk her life and limb on a jungle trek," she said, removing her socks and shoes, digging her toes into the grass.

"But you would?"

"Naturally. The heart of an adventuress beats beneath all of this fragile flesh and sweet charm."

His blue eyes softened as they traveled over her from sunlit head to bare feet. "Bring lots of insect spray; they'd have a field day with that delectable body."

She grinned and scoffed, "Is that a fact, Winngate?"

"Definitely!" Their eyes met and locked. She reluctantly pulled hers away, fearing the heat from his would surely singe her skin and sear her mind if she did not.

"Don't they have snakes in the jungle?" she inquired innocently.

"Of course," he responded.

"Can I bring one back to add to my collection on the barn?"

As their eyes met and their thoughts matched, they began to laugh. Nigel lay back and observed the looks and tones which passed between them. *Yes sir,* he decided, *this could be some match!*

Brandy could not control her giggles as the two men insisted on cleaning the fish for a blushing, also giggling, Mary. The men teased Mary until she returned to her kitchen to prepare another fabulous meal for the only man she could picture providing her little Brandy with a beautiful future. Brandy also went inside to bathe and change into a navy gabardine A-line skirt and yellow oxford blouse.

After dinner, the three spent hours playing chess. Each winner played the loser from the past game. Only once was that loser Steven Winngate. At last the hour was late and the three early risers were contentedly exhausted. They said good night and retired, still arguing over who caught the biggest fish.

Brandy denied her desire to work on the manuscript which had arrived that morning; a greater desire gnawed at her. She slipped between her periwinkle satin sheets, her naked body savoring the feel of sensuous satin next to silky flesh. It seemed as if Steven was awakening her senses to countless sensations. A soft moan escaped her lips as Steven's mouth closed over hers....

The next day, Brandy told the two men they were on their own while she tackled the *Twilight* revisions. Nigel was content to entertain himself, but Steven didn't look pleased at all. He scowled at Brandy when she suggested he work on his article about her. Instead, he spent hours on the downstairs phone...

Brandy curled up on the sofa in her cork-paneled office and started reading the edited manuscript. For once, her attention span was terrible. She couldn't seem to concentrate on the pages or the story. Her mind kept straying to the man who was around somewhere. Finally, with great determination, she poured herself into that story.

Mary knew Brandy was never to be disturbed, even for meals or calls, when her door was closed. Steven did not. When she didn't appear for lunch, he went to her office and calmly and ignorantly strolled inside. He moved so quietly that Brandy didn't hear his approach. He leaned over and nibbled on her ear.

She jumped and screamed, her mind engrossed in the torture scene which she was intensely reading. "Steven! Why did you do that?" she scolded him.

He grinned, still blissfully ignorant. "I thought you might be starving by now. Nigel's gone riding, and Mary's gone shopping," he hinted meaningfully.

"I'm working," she informed him, as if that explained everything.

"You skipped lunch. Why not take a break?" he persisted, nodding towards the door.

"I can't. I'm right in the middle of this work. If I stop now, I'll have to reread everything to this point," she said, politely attempting to discourage his amorous mood.

"So?" he speculated unknowingly. "What's the big deal?" he asked hazily.

"The big deal is a loss of concentration. Once I'm into something, I can't just stop and come back later. It's like keying yourself up. You let go and feel the action and moods. It's frustrating to stop and go. The creative juices get clogged. It's nerve-racking to be forced to turn off and turn on. It's like a swollen river during a flood; it's impossible to control. Every time I halt, I have to restart my engine."

"You look tired. You have to eat and rest," he coaxed.

"Not when I'm busy," she argued. "When you're working and concentrating, don't you skip meals or lose sleep? Do you like being interrupted or distracted?"

"That's different," he said too hastily, miffed by her refusal.

"Really?" she scoffed. "How so?"

"My work is—" He halted promptly when he realized what he was about to say.

"More important than mine?" she finished sarcastically.

"I have thousands of people working for me who depend on me, Brandy, their families too. If I don't work, they don't eat. What happens if you don't finish that book?"

"I have a contract, Steven. I have a deadline. Writing is my work, my love, my life. People depend on me to meet those obligations. If I miss a deadline, it throws off the whole schedule. Then, other people are involved, people who work and eat because of me and my writing: cover artists, publicity people, publishers, editors, agents, copyeditors, line editors, booksellers, buyers... There's a long list waiting for this work to be completed. My readers are also expecting it to be on the shelf soon. If I disappoint them or my book isn't available, they switch to some other writer."

He waited to see if she was finished with her dressing down. She sighed heavily. "I'm not used to having anyone around when I'm working, Steven. Mary knows when that door's closed, it stays closed. Writers have a saying— 'When the flow is on the go, stay out of its path.' We artistic people are sensitive, moody, disciplined. Sometimes I think writing a book is far easier than revising it. When you're creating it, the mood and reality are present. Once it's finished, so are the mood and reality. It's difficult to go back to that work and recall those feelings. Do you understand at all?"

"Yes and no," he replied honestly. "I do hate distractions and interruptions, but sometimes they can't be avoided. I just psych myself up again."

"With your kind of work, that's possible. You have notes and realities to deal with. I don't. It's all here, and it slips away if I keep staunching it," she stated, touching her forehead.

"But you have the book in front of you," he pressed for clarity.

"The book, yes, but not the revisions. They come after I read it and get into it again. Have you ever tried to retell an argument or frightening scene? Have you noticed how it varies with each telling? Scenes are like that, especially quarrels and perils. The first time they strike your mind, they're at their best. You try to record them as quickly as possible. When it has to wait until later, it never comes out the same, not as good. The characters come alive for a brief span. Each word, look, or action spurs the next character's. If I forget one of those, it spoils the entire scene. Once everything's mentally plotted, I record it as it runs across my mind, much like watching a movie. If the tape is broken, something's lost or edited when it starts running again. The losses are frustrating. I'm sure this isn't making any sense to you," she stated in exasperation. How did one explain inspiration, creativity, the writing flow, the intensity involved, the mental process?

"I understand writers don't like distractions, even stimulating ones. If you need any inspiration later, you'll call me, won't you?"

Her train of thought broken, she tossed her red pen aside. She stood up and flexed her muscles. "Perhaps a hot shower will refresh me. Care to join me?" she hinted, smiling at him. The work could wait a while....

"Sounds enticing, but Nigel just rode in. I think I'll take a ride. See you at dinner." With that casual dismissal, he swaggered out, whistling.

Brandy stared after him through the open door. He was gone, and her concentration was positively nil now! *Damn you, Steven,* she mused angrily. Brandy sighed loudly as she flopped down into her desk chair and stared out the window over it.

As Nigel encountered Steven, they exchanged smiles. "What's going, Steve?"

"Not Brandy. She's bleeding over her work in there," he snarled.

"You talked to her?" he asked in amazement.

"I tried to get her to take a break; she skipped lunch, and it's nearly dinner time."

Nigel shook his head of dark brown curls. "You've got a lot to learn, old buddy. When that door's closed, it's no-man's-land. It's an unwritten law, you can't break a writer's concentration." Nigel went on to deliver nearly the same lecture Brandy had just given him.

Coming from a professional male, somehow the explanation sounded valid, clearer. Of course Nigel's vivid parallel, that of interrupting sex during the intensity and involvement at a critical moment, clarified Steven's confusion. "Creativity is a unique and taxing gift, Steve, sometimes a curse. I can see her point. Hell, I've endured it. Some of my best songs have come to me when I couldn't write them down. Would you believe I can't recall half the words if I have to wait until another time to record them? It's as discouraging and infuriating as a flop record, or as mindboggling and satisfying as a hit. Try to understand, Steve. Show her some patience and consideration. Writers don't always choose their own schedules, or deadline. It's even worse when we try to fight our body-clocks. If we weren't here, she would be sleeping all day and writing all night."

BRANDY WENT TO HER ROOM and took a refreshing bubble bath. When she entered the kitchen, both men and Mary were surprised to see her. The strain was vivid on her face; she was exceptionally quiet. Nigel understood her mood; he ignored it, as did the perceptive and well-trained Mary. But Steven attempted to draw her out with conversation and jokes. Brandy halfheartedly replied, but didn't inspire further talk. She smiled faintly at his witty words, but the tension never left her somber eyes.

To Steven, Brandy appeared guarded and reserved tonight. He fretted over his innocent blunder. He had been making marvelous progress with her; he could detect her withdrawal and resentment. He had bruised her feelings as well as her ego. He had caused her to feel guilty and selfish; those emotions denied her sunny glow and happiness. Worse, he had implied her precious work was frivolous.

Brandy forced herself to remain with her guests until dinner was over and the men were playing chess in the upstairs den. She softly excused herself, then returned to her office. With sheer determination, she finished reading the manuscript and made notes for her revisions. But something was wrong; one scene just wouldn't flow, as if refusing to be written.

Steven had pulled out his briefcase and was working on some papers he had brought with him. Nigel offered to bring him a drink when he went upstairs. Nigel entered the kitchen just as Brandy was leaving it, a glass of iced tea in her grip.

Noting the look on her face, he cuffed her chin and asked, "What's wrong, love?"

"I can't concentrate, Nigel. That scene's being stubborn. Sometimes I wish characters didn't have minds of their own. They're refusing to do what Devon wants. How do I make them hustle when they demand to waltz?"

"Maybe you should pull back for a while," he suggested tenderly.

"I can't. Devon wants this change yesterday," she replied miserably.

"Don't they always want things yesterday?" he teased to lighten her heavy mood.

"This time it's true. Everything's finished. They caught something they didn't like after the galleys were printed. They feel it's worth the expense to change it before it's in final pages."

"You're forcing it, Brandy; we both know it won't work that way."

Nigel walked her back to her office. They sat down on the floor. Brandy rested her head on his comforting shoulder. They talked for a few minutes.

Steven gazed into the office; his blue eyes filled with jealousy and irritation. It was all right for Nigel to disrupt her, but he couldn't? Now he knew why his drink was taking so long to arrive! He left the tender scene which rankled him.

When Nigel returned, he found Steven sipping a drink. He glanced at the one in his own grip and the one in Steven's. "Give up on me?" he jested.

"I didn't want to disturb you and Brandy. I got it myself," Steven stated sullenly.

Nigel laughed. "I'd slap that little green monster off my back, old buddy. She was in the kitchen when I went upstairs. Something's blowing her attention; I can't imagine what," he joked pointedly. "Could be she'd rather be doing something else? I was just offering some brotherly solace."

Steven and Nigel exchanged probing looks. "You're crowding her, Steve," Nigel stated seriously. "She's under stress and pressure; don't add more."

The tone of Nigel's voice prevented a surly comeback. "Maybe I should have gone for the drinks," Steven declared huskily, then smiled.

"Too bad you didn't," Nigel agreed. "I think I'll call it a night."

"I think I'll take a walk," Steven said. He needed to unwind and think. Brandy was locked in her office, so he didn't change out of his satin robe in deep wine with black trim. He left the house and headed towards the pool. He perked up when he heard splashing.

"Don't you know it isn't safe out here alone?" he reprimanded Brandy, squatting beside the pool. Moonlight reflected off the gently moving water as she headed to where he was positioned.

"I thought you and Nigel were fast asleep," she murmured.

"I guess I'm not the only one who needed to unwind. Having problems?"

Brandy mounted the steps and tossed a large towel around her shoulders. "Sometimes a writer gets too close to a scene; she has to back off for a while, then try a fresh approach."

Something in her voice and expression said she was referring to more than her work. "That's true about many things," he ventured, smiling at her.

"Yes, I suppose it is," she agreed, returning his smile.

"Worked out all those kinks?" he inquired tenderly.

"Muscles, yes; brain, no," she replied honestly. "Want to take a swim? I could use some stimulating company and witty conversation."

"Like this?" he teased, patting his hand over his manner of dress.

"Is Nigel still up?" she asked oddly, glancing towards the house.

"Nope. Why?"

"Then why not? You modest, Winngate?" she boldly taunted.

He stepped close to her and gently seized her shoulders. "I can think of a better way to loosen taut muscles...."

"So can I," she laughingly declared, then shoved him into the pool. She knelt on the edge and mocked, "Is that any better, my fiery-blooded dragon?"

"I doubt this qualifies for a cold shower, my naive maiden," he parried, edging towards her.

Brandy giggled. "Do you need one?" she quipped playfully.

Before she realized what he was planning, his hand snaked out and yanked her into the pool. "I think we both need one," he stated triumphantly.

"I've had mine, this afternoon," she informed him sassily, revealingly.

"You don't need another one?" he hinted wickedly.

"I hope not. I've called it a night, in my office," she added bravely. Perhaps he needed special attention, reassurance.

A look of utter surprise flooded his features. He scooped her up in his arms and left the pool. He deposited her on the thick towel she had spread out beside the pool. His lips hungrily ravaged hers; his hands played over her receptive body. When the heat between them built to a fiery level, she whispered breathlessly, "We'd better go inside...."

"Why? We're alone. I like this romantic setting," he mischievously told her.

"But we're in view of anyone who happens by," she argued modestly, the idea exciting and stimulating.

"We're wet; we'll ruin your bed. How will you explain a soaked bed to Mary? As for me, I can't wait to dry off. I'm on fire, Brandy," he reasoned huskily.

"So am I," she promptly acquiesced, throwing caution to the gentle breeze which played over their torrid bodies.

As Steven's mouth took hers, he deftly unfastened the top and bottom of her swimsuit. He twisted to remove his clingy robe and silk bottoms, without pulling his lips from hers. Their wet bodies fused instantly, the drops of water evaporating from their blistering heat.

The union was rapid and urgent, restrained emotions set free. When they lay exhausted in each other's arms, he whispered, "How about that swim now?"

Before Brandy could answer, he picked up her naked body and jumped into the water. "Steven," she shrieked softly.

"Never swam in the buff before?" he jested. "Might be excellent research."

"You're a devil," she scolded him, snuggling against his hard frame.

"Comes naturally," he muttered against her wet hair, his hands slipping up and down her back. "I remember that day we had lunch when you told me about your demanding lifestyle. You're right. But don't you think you should allow time for yourself, Brandy? Don't you push too hard?"

"I don't normally have such a distracting problem as you, Steven. I told you I was selfish, that my schedule would be terrible and demanding on others. Now do you see what I meant?"

"Too clearly, woman," he said with a sigh.

"It's so complicated, Steven. Most people turn off their work the moment they leave their offices. Mine doesn't work that way; it's with me all the time."

"You need to learn how to shut on and off, Brandy," he advised seriously.

"I know, but that's easier said than done. The brain is a complex organ—a mind of its own," she speculated, then laughed.

"Believe it or not, but I'm learning that." He lowered himself into the water and tantalized her breasts with little kisses and nips. "But so is the body," he added.

Brandy shuddered at his enticing action. "Cold?" he asked.

"No, burning up," she replied candidly.

He stood up and gazed down at her. "Demanding little witch, aren't you?"

"I'd best take advantage of this break; it's back to work in the morning."

"I thought you worked all night and slept all day?" he hinted.

"I usually do, and I hope so tonight."

"You're going back to work?" he asked incredulously, knowing how late, or early, it was.

"No, to bed," she responded, then kissed him greedily.

"That's the best idea you've had all year, my lovely writer."

"Somehow I thought you'd approve," she murmured, hugging him fiercely.

Chapter Eleven

When Brandy sighed peacefully and stretched the next morning, she opened her eyes to discover Steven had returned to his guest room, as usual. Her following sigh was one of intermingled disappointment and longing. She asked herself why she and Steven were continuing this charade. They were adults; this was the eighties! She yearned to awaken with him at her side, to begin the new day on a delirious note.

Both were hesitant to reveal their closeness, even to their mutual friend Nigel Davis. It almost seemed as if unmasking it would subtract something special from it. Yet, Brandy was growing weary of this pretense.

She had slept late; the sun was high overhead. After a shower, she dressed and hurried downstairs hoping to see Steven before she locked herself in her office. Steven and Nigel were out riding. She shrugged, then carried her second cup of coffee into her office. Soon, the quiet house lent itself to concentration on the work still at hand.

Having learned his lesson well, Steven didn't disturb Brandy that day. Late that afternoon, Brandy leaned back in her office chair and gazed out her window. Her eyes touched on Nigel, who was lying in the grass beside the waterfall next to her home. His arms were folded and propped beneath his curly head. He was relaxing in deep thought, the

words of his impending song playing through his keen mind.
He looked so serene, an inviting sensation pulled at Brandy.

She had reached a temporary stopping point. She decided to take a walk, to chat with Nigel before he left, which
would be soon. With Steven here she had spent little time
with her close friend. She stood up and walked outside
heading for the fast-running brook and rocky cascade to
join him. She had glanced around, but hadn't located
Steven. Perhaps he was taking a nap, a walk, or a ride.

"I thought you came here to write music, not laze
around," she teased Nigel, dropping down beside her.

He chuckled, casting her a rueful look. "I did, but I'm
having too much fun to work around the clock.

"How's it going with you and Steve? Got that new story
done yet?" he asked, sitting up and gazing over at her.

"Fine. As for the story, that's his job."

"You best give him more attention, girl. Do whatever he
demands to protect yourself," he jested, winking at her, his
expression, but not his words, lost to the turbulent blue eyes
which were unknowingly observing them.

"I can't believe you're willing and eager to share me with
another man. You must want to protect my name as much
as I do," she quipped in return, grinning at him.

"You know what I told you, there's only one way to get
to a man like Steven Winngate," he reminded her of his
suggestion of friendship.

"I'm doing all I can, Nigel. It takes time. I can't exactly
throw myself at his feet. I was spending every available
minute with him, until that work arrived. I can only do so
much," she wailed amusingly to Nigel, but not to the worried Steven.

He leaned over and whispered wickedly in her ear, "Is
that where you want to throw yourself?"

Brandy surged forward to the stream and flung water on
her friend. "You're awful, Nigel Davis! Crude and vulgar!" she taunted laughingly, soaking Nigel from the waist
up.

"You little sneak!" Nigel exploded, his bare feet jumping into the stream to return her mischief in like kind.

For a time, they splashed and played as carefree as two children. Finally, Nigel left the stream and sank to the grass on his wet back. Brandy joined him, curling against his body and resting her damp head on his outstretched arm. Nigel's hand lifted and stroked her tawny mane.

Steven's rigid body stalked off towards the barn. A variety of feelings and thoughts were running through his mind and body. He halted by the corral fence and stared across the pasture where Brandy had been riding on that first morning.

"Are you sure you have to leave so soon, Nigel?" Brandy asked.

"Yep. I have an engagement in San Francisco. Besides, I think it'll be a good idea for you and Steve to have some privacy."

His tone of voice hinted at suspicion of their relationship. Brandy started to say something, then stopped herself. "Where is Steven?" she asked instead.

"He was sleeping by the pool. We took a swim earlier."

"I think I'll go speak with him before I get back to work."

"Not finished yet?"

"Nope. I have to complete it tonight."

When Brandy went to search for Steven, she noticed him standing by the fence, his outstretched hands gripping the top rail tightly. She smiled happily, recalling their blissful night. She headed toward him.

She ducked her head and passed under his left arm, to place herself between his body and the fence, between his strong arms. Her softened gaze lifted to meet his fathomless one. "Taking a break?" he asked guardedly.

"You did say I was working too hard," she teased, boldly laying her face against his chest and easing her arms around his taut body. "I thought you were napping by the pool. I was thinking about you, so I came looking for you."

"Thinking about me?" he echoed skeptically, remaining rigid.

"Yes," she responded warmly, her hands moving over his tight muscles, wondering at his coolness.

"Nothing like a man around to stifle the creative flow, huh?"

Brandy's head leaned backwards and she looked up into his unreadable expression. "Is something wrong, Steven?"

"Just tired. Too quiet to sleep here, or too noisy with those million crickets and frogs screaming at each other all night. Not much to do around here with my pet project working all the time."

Brandy sensed Steven wasn't venting his real feelings. "I suppose a man like you would find this kind of life boring and secluded. I'm sorry you aren't enjoying your stay. I guess I'm a terrible hostess." She dropped her hands to her sides and stepped back against the fence. "You planning to leave soon?" she asked very softly.

"I should be heading home; I have lots of work to do. Besides, you have Nigel to keep you company, when you finish your work."

"I was hoping to finish my work tonight. Nigel's leaving in two days." Brandy pondered the look—was it of unleashed jealousy?—on his face. "I was taking a break, so I thought I should spend a few minutes with him. I have been neglecting him since your arrival."

"Does he always drown his...*sister* in the stream?" he asked, glancing over her wet curls and clothes. "You two looked like you were having great fun."

"Why didn't you come over?" she questioned, knowing that sight had annoyed him irrationally.

"I didn't think you two wanted to be disturbed," he replied frostily.

"Don't be silly. We were just playing around."

"Are you just playing around, Brandy?" he queried oddly, his hands dropping to his sides and his gaze fusing with hers.

"I don't catch your meaning.... Are you jealous of Nigel?" she asked incredulously, candidly.

"Should I be?" he responded with another question.

"I'm flattered, but no. Considering our relationship, I'm confused by your doubts about me. You know Nigel and I have never..."

Brandy flushed brightly, clamping her mouth shut. "I'd better get back to work, or I'll never make that deadline," she stated hurriedly, then started to walk away.

Steven caught her arm. "Brandy, I didn't mean it to sound like that. I guess I am jealous. You're a mighty tempting lady, and I don't like sharing with anyone while I'm around. I'm sorry. I'm not bored or miserable here, just restless with you busy. I was thinking about *Glitter*. Once this mess is cleared up, perhaps I should sell it. I only purchased it to get them off my case; I seemed to be an obsession or favorite topic with them. If I don't sell it, I plan to change the format and content."

Brandy's probing eyes met his entreating ones. His words were not totally convincing. Why did he always act this way when they were getting close? Maybe too close for comfort? Was he worried she was reading too much into this stimulating vacation? Why did he draw her to him as a powerful magnet, then frantically switch poles to desperately repel her? Was Steven Winngate capable of feeling sincere jealousy? Possessiveness, yes; but real jealousy, no....

When she didn't respond, he asked, "Am I forgiven?"

"Sure, Steven. Why not?" she stated flippantly. "See you tomorrow; I'll be working all night." She struck a fast pace back to the house. She hadn't even replied to his mention of *Glitter* or its sale.

Brandy didn't appear for dinner that night. Steven fumed inwardly over his stupidity. Nigel was too mentally engrossed by his song-writing to notice Steven's black mood.

Around midnight Nigel went to the bar to fix himself a nightcap. As he passed Brandy's office, he could hear her berating herself. He halted and did an unusual thing; he opened the door and looked inside. Brandy glanced up and smiled faintly, motioning him inside. It didn't matter she had already showered and was dressed for bed in a satin nightgown; she was totally decent and concealed by her matching robe in magenta.

"Talking to yourself?" he jested, shaking his finger at her.

"Darn it, Nigel; I can't seem to finish this," she said in exasperation.

She was sitting on the floor and leaning against a small sofa, her work in her lap. He came forward and sat down. He pulled her into his arms and murmured, "Keep at it, love; it'll work out. Don't give up so easily."

"So *easily*," she scoffed. "It isn't working at all."

Nigel cupped her chin, lifted her head, and kissed her lightly on the lips. "You can do it, love. You always succeed."

"Do I?" she panted.

"Be kind to yourself, Brandy," he ordered.

"I'm sorry, Nigel. I just can't keep my mind on this when—"

When she halted, he laughed and speculated, "When you'd rather be with Steve?"

"Why did Devon need revisions at this time? I just finished one book and their other revisions. I wanted to rest and have fun before it was time to begin my next book. The way it looks now, I won't even have time to breathe, much less spend any time with Steven! He's planning to leave," she murmured softly.

"Did you tell him I'd be gone in two days? That could change his mind. I do seem to crimp his style," he jested.

Steven leaned against the wall and smiled as he continued his bold eavesdropping. "Steven Winngate is like mercury, Nigel, up one minute and down the next. He's the most infuriating, exasperating, unpredictable, complex man I've ever met!" she vowed.

"In other words, he's fantastic, and he's getting to you?"

"I honestly don't know how I feel about him. He has me so unnerved and confused that I can't think straight," she admitted.

"Then entice him into staying after I leave. What better way to get to know each other?"

"I don't think he wants to hang around any longer."

"Play your cards right, and he will," Nigel declared smugly.

"Spoken like a diehard gambler," she jested.

"I'll leave you to your work. Good night, sis."

"Good night, Nigel. You're the best big brother a girl could have."

Steven went into the den to carry out a stirring plan. Nigel left Brandy fretting over her work. Assuming Steven was taking a walk, Nigel turned in for the night.

Steven explored the bar's refrigerator and his eyes brightened when they touched on a bottle of champagne. He confiscated it and lifted two glasses. He headed for her office. He soundlessly opened the door. Brandy was lying on the floor on her stomach, facing the other direction. Her robe had been removed and tossed on the sofa. He watched her a moment, gathering his courage.

"Damn!" she snapped impatiently, then flung the pages and red pen aside. "Your concentration is zilch, Brandy!" she scolded herself, then laid her face on the carpeted floor. "Give it up for tonight."

Brandy didn't hear the lock on her door click as Steven made his daring move. He strolled forward as she pushed herself to a sitting position. "Think this will help relax you?" his mellow voice coaxed.

Brandy jumped and looked over at him. "Before you say anything, Brandy, I'm not disturbing you. I looked in first. You appeared at wit's end, so I thought this might help."

Brandy glanced at the champagne and glasses in his grip. Her smoldering eyes lifted to forge with his. She smiled appreciatively. "Your timing is perfect, Steven. Thanks," she stated honestly.

Brandy leaned against the sofa as he sat down on the floor beside her. "You sure I'm not interfering?" he pressed.

"Absolutely not," she murmured.

He grinned in pleasure, then opened the bottle. He poured a glass of golden liquid and handed it to her, then did the same for himself. He set the bottle aside and leaned against the sofa with her. "To a very talented lady, who brings great pleasure into my life, as well as into her readers'," he stated huskily, lifting his glass to her.

She touched his glass with hers, then drained its contents. "Is it too late to ask if I can lag behind when Nigel leaves?" he asked softly.

"No," she replied succinctly, grinning at him.

"Well? May I?" he pressed for an affirmative answer.

"If you'd like," she said, laughing happily.

He frowned amusingly. "I most assuredly would like to remain."

"Good," she purred saucily, then laughed as he filled her glass once more. "Trying to ply me with liquor, Winngate? Champagne goes right to one's head, especially on an empty stomach."

He chuckled and shrugged innocently.

"May I ask a crazy question?" she inquired, eyeing him speculatively.

He met her inquisitive look and nodded.

"Why are you trying to buy every book I've written, even those temporarily out of print?"

Steven went rigid; he paled slightly. How much did she know? he mused worriedly. "How do you know I am," he asked curiously.

"Casey told me. Why?" she pressed insistently, sipping her drink, his reaction passing unnoticed.

"I find you most fascinating and gifted. Now that I know you so well, I want to line a bookshelf with everything you've done. Naturally, I'm looking for first printings," he teased to disarm her. "If I have them delivered to you, will you sign each one?"

"I'm flattered; a whole shelf dedicated to Brandy Alexander. Of course I'll sign each one. But I doubt one shelf will hold them all; I've written over fifty books."

"Fifty-six, to be exact," he smugly informed her.

Her eyes widened in astonishment. "I've been checking around. I wanted to know all about you and your works," he clarified before she could question him. "I prefer to know my subject well. I've also viewed or read a copy of every interview you've given. Besides being talented and successful, you're an exceptionally likable person, and I'm awfully glad I met you." If Casey had told Brandy other suspicious actions, he wanted to innocently confess them before she demanded an explanation. "I hired someone else to do my investigative research. I hope you don't mind?"

"Mind? How could I? I'm honored and delighted you take such interest and care with your work and integrity. If you're dedicating a whole library shelf to me, what should I dedicate to you?" she playfully deliberated. "I know—my next book. Let's see..." she mumbled thoughtfully, sipping her third glass of heady champagne. "I could say, 'To Steven, who saved my life, and then taught me how to live it to the fullest.'"

He chuckled in delight. "If you mention my name, every woman around will be seeking me out to see what I taught you," he jested sexily.

"In that case, the inscription will read, 'To Sir Lancelot.'" She began to laugh at the expression on Steven's face. "No?" she hinted.

"Perfect," he responded. The bottle being empty, he took their glasses and placed them on the nearby table. "Need to get back to work?"

Brandy eased down to lie on the floor, her head spinning. "Nope! My characters don't agree with Devon's orders."

He reclined on his left side and looked down into her flushed face. He tenderly pushed a curl from her face and asked, "What does that mean?"

"You just being polite, or do you really want to know?" she asked, her eyes sparkling brightly.

"I really want to know. I'm learning a great deal about writers, and you. You sound as if your characters are alive."

"To me they are while I'm writing their book. I should say, they write their own story. If you try to make them do something they don't like, they balk and refuse. They won't allow anything which isn't logical and natural for them. I've read the manuscript several times, and they won't let me make the changes Devon wants."

"What does Devon want that they don't like?" he asked, but didn't laugh.

Brandy rubbed her tingling nose, then stated, "Devon wants a passionate love scene in a place where it doesn't fit. They can't just fall into bed after quarreling so fiercely. Her ship leaves in one hour when he shows up. They've been at each other's throats for days. He wants her to drop everything and pretend he's the only important thing around." Brandy halted when she realized how that scene was matching theirs.

"Go on," he encouraged, grinning knowingly. "I might be able to make some helpful suggestion so you can get this work out of our way."

"The hero is furious because the heroine won't rush into his arms and forget all else but him. She has something terribly critical pending. She's tried to reason with him time and time again, but he's stubborn and selfish." Their eyes met and locked. "It just doesn't seem logical for her to rush into his arms and make love when they've been verbally slicing each other to ribbons, when she's leaving within the hour, and when her mission is vital to her and others."

"We've been having our little verbal battles, but we still find each other irresistible. Anger's a funny thing, Brandy;

it can vanish as quickly as it comes. Let's just improvise a moment.''

Brandy watched and listened closely as Steven continued. "Say the hero is me. Say the situation is ours, past and present. Naturally you're the heroine. If my plane was leaving in one hour, would that halt you from making love to me?''

Brandy shook her head.

''We've been quarreling in a way. Does that prevent you from desiring me, even when I infuriate you?''

Again, she shook her head.

''You have this writing mission which is critical to you, but does it halt you from wanting me? Even when I'm an ass, do you hate me and reject me? No matter what happens between a man and a woman, it all boils down to needs and desires. Whatever we say or do, there's always a powerful attraction there pulling us together. If your hero's losing his woman, even briefly, he'd be desperate to love her one last time before parting. Even if she feels she must desert him, for any reason, she'd rush into his arms to show him how much she needed and wanted him. There is no greater sharing of oneself than by the joining of their bodies and spirits. To let them part in anger would breed destructive pride in both; each would wait for the other to make the next overture, like we did after our first night. Emotions, Brandy—they're powerful and complex.''

''But if she rushes into his arms the moment he enters the room, he'll think he's won their battle,'' she countered. ''If he uses a cunning seduction or brute strength to hold her there, she'll feel duped and used.''

''Why not let him walk into the room, close the door, then lean against it? Let him hungrily feast on her beauty and coming loss. Let her turn and meet his gaze, feel their need, then reveal her own in her eyes. When you want me, Brandy, I can sense it; I can see it. Let them walk slowly toward each other, to meet halfway, a compromise, a revelation of shared need. Once their eyes and bodies make contact, the rest is elemental. Passions take over, and the action flows naturally. He'll feel the depth and power of her love for him, as she'll absorb his. If she must still leave him, they'll part with something special between them. If you need a further misunderstanding to part them afterward, let them both suspect it was merely overpowering physical need which attacked them.''

"You should be a writer, Steven. You're right; it's perfect. I wasn't looking at it from that angle. It just sounded unrealistic for them to make passionate love under those warring conditions. But the way you explain it, it would be the most natural thing in the world. Thanks. Would you like a job as my research assistant?'' she offered playfully.

"Sounds most tempting and exciting. Do I need to apply or audition?''

She laughed. "Perhaps that isn't a bad idea.'' Brandy sat up and began to unbutton his shirt.

"What are you doing?'' he mirthfully questioned.

"I'm auditioning your chest. You have a most provocative body, Winngate. I love to snuggle up to you,'' she murmured, nestling her face against his hard and furry chest. "You smell divine,'' she stated, inhaling his masculine scent and stirring Old Spice.

"This wasn't the kind of application I had in mind,'' he informed her, chuckling. He eased his shirt off and embraced her cool and bare flesh against his warm and bare flesh.

Brandy's fingers wandered over his chest and arms, admiring the smooth surface which exuded such strength. "How can you be so firm and so soft at the same time?''

He chuckled again, trailing his fingers up and down her silky arms. "I'm glad you approve, Miss Alexander.'' Brandy's gown was deftly swept over her head to join her robe. He pressed her to the lush covering on the floor. His lips captured hers and enticed an immediate response.

Brandy's arms encircled his neck, her fingers entering his ebony hair. Steven kissed her lips, her eyes, her forehead, her chin, and the tip of her nose. When his lips nipped at her ear, he murmured, "I much prefer an audition."

"Then prove yourself, Winngate," she challenged seriously.

Steven slowly and seductively described his actions as he carried them out. Brandy was mesmerized by his tone and movements. She watched him as a cobra hypnotized by a snake charmer, as his hands fondled her taut breasts and his lips gently ravaged on.

His hand drifted downward. Brandy moaned with rising desire, his sensual movements erotic and stirring.

Steven's mouth devoured one breast as if trying to withdraw life-sustaining nectar from it. His hands deftly worked to tantalize her to instant surrender. Fires raged within Brandy and vowed to consume her. Her hand reached for the fiery torch which could torment her and also extinguish her blazing wildfire.

When her hand reached out for him she whispered softly, "Love me, Steven, love me now. I can't stand this torment."

Steven's lips seared over hers as he entered her. He set a wild rhythm as she clung to him and matched his pace. His lips were entreating and demanding. They covered hers to prevent her cry of release from shattering the silence of her quiet house. The struggle was easily won, the prize matchless.

Afterwards, they lay in the warm and inviting arms of contentment. "Well?" he hinted roguishly. "Do I get the job?"

Brandy's head moved to one side to meet his peaceful gaze. "You're hired, Winngate. No references needed. Would you care to read our scene tomorrow when it's finished? You did provide some stimulating insight. There is no power greater than passion," she teased.

Steven watched her closely, then smiled. A nagging dread entered his mind. Not even in the heat of passion had she said "I love you." Why not? *Was* it just physical attraction for her? Was it merely a romantic interlude? If only she would reveal her feelings ...

"You'd best get to bed, Miss Alexander. I want that work completed before dinner. Understand?"

"Yes, master," she purred merrily. "I suppose now that you've conquered me, I'm to be at your beck and call?"

"Naturally. All conquerors are heroes, Miss Alexander." As they parted, she grinned and whispered, "Good night, Sir Lancelot."

THE NEXT DAY PASSED in that similar frame of mind and tranquil mood. The manuscript was revised and returned to Casey. Nigel and Steven played tennis and took a lengthy swim in the pool. All three enjoyed drinks and snacks at the poolside and relished a marvelous dinner in the formal dining room.

The day before Nigel was to leave, Brandy gave a real Southern barbecue for her workers and two guests. Zack brought his fiddle and several other workers brought their musical instruments. They laughed, danced, and sang until past midnight. Brandy was so happy she wished this satisfying life could go on forever. Unbeknownst to her, Steven was wishing that same thing.

As Brandy and Steven sat in a swing slowly moving back and forth, she said softly, "I hope you haven't been too bored here, Steven. I know it's quite different from the life you lead in the big cities. Perhaps it's been relaxing and unusual?"

"Bored? Not for a single minute. If I were in your place, I would have to force myself to return to that rat race back there. This is real living, Brandy. You're fortunate to have this place. I can see how you save your sanity and replenish your energy now that I've tasted your kind of life here. Perhaps I'll buy myself a ranch somewhere. Then I might not have to cling to Lance Reynolds anymore. I envy you all of this."

Yet, his next innocent words dashed her new hopes, "Still, I'm a restless man who needs constant challenges to keep me alert and alive. That can only be found back there," he stated, hoping she would deny this and change his mind."

"You're probably right," she said, disappointing him. "Somehow I can't picture you as a rancher and farmer. I doubt there would be enough challenges around to satisfy that masterful, domineering streak of yours. For you, this makes a super nice vacation; but I don't think you would take to it permanently." She breathlessly waited for him to disagree; he did not.

They sat in strained, solemn silence for a time. Knowing Nigel was leaving in the morning, she excused herself to talk with him. Steven remained where he was in brooding solitude. She joined Nigel near the pool. Steven envied her total relaxation and easy communication with him, the warmth and closeness which they shared.

The following morning, they stood together on the long porch as they watched Nigel drive away in his rented car. Steven propped his elbow against a heavy post. "You two are very close, aren't you?" he asked in a muffled tone, one hand resting across his mouth, the other one tucked into the back pocket of his brushed denim jeans.

"Yes," she absently replied, wondering what to do and say now that they were alone. She tugged at the pockets of her yellow sundress, trying not to stare at him.

To their pleasure, they were soon enjoying their solitude and mutual company. For several days they amused themselves in a manner similar to the one which they had been doing before Nigel's departure, relieved the necessity for secrecy was past. The strain they had both anticipated did not materialize. In fact, the aura which now surrounded them increased in enjoyment and tranquility. Everyone except Steven and Brandy knew they were deeply in love!

Knowing Brandy would be uneasy during those first few days, Steven was careful to keep his amorous demands from panicking her. Yet, each hour which passed made him desire her all the more. In his rigid attempts to control his warring emotions and the enticing situation, he became restless and edgy. He resorted to long walks early in the morning and late at night. He knew if he remained too close he would besiege her at every turn. He cautioned himself to patience and to restraint.

Yet, his mood and reserve caused Brandy to feel and think he was actually becoming bored with her and with this life, but was too polite to leave early. The questions and picture-taking sessions halted the day Nigel left. She observed Steven's aimless roamings from her lofty bedroom window. Sadness flooded her body, for she knew he would soon be leaving. She feared their future contact would be slight or nonexistent. As much as she wanted him, she prayed she would not become so desperate to have him that she would resort to pursuing him from place to place.

She determined to constantly remind him of her existence and availability. If she was forced to become the carefree butterfly for a while, then so be it; Steven was surely worth that much effort! She threw her energy and imagination into making their remaining days together unforgettable and blissful.

One afternoon, they rode to the skeet range. They genially challenged each other to a contest; the loser would be the winner's servant for that coming evening. She matched him shot for shot during the first few rounds. The final one appeared to be heading for a draw. Determined to have her at his beck and call for a few hours, he tricked her.

Steven sighed heavily as he approached the line of fire. He then hesitated before giving her the signal to pull the release lever. He strolled over to where she was poised in her purple chinos and cotton blouse with its purple, yellow, and aqua flowers upon a creamy background. He grabbed her around the waist and muttered, "For good luck," then kissed her deeply and thoroughly, his tongue seeking and finding hers. When he finally let her go, she would have fallen backwards if he hadn't caught her and steadied her.

She simply stared at him, obviously shaken by his heated kiss. He was tempted to repeat his action, but did not. "Are you ready now?" she asked in a trembly voice.

He passed his tongue over his upper lip with a provocative slowness. "Um-hm . . . If I can hold my hands steady. You sure do taste good," he teased. He resumed his position, then glanced at her over his right shoulder. "Can the winner give any order he—or she—wishes?"

She was greatly tempted to say yes but from cowardice did not. Besides, she already knew who the winner would be and she dreaded to learn what that order would be. With her whole body vibrating with excitement and desire, she could never hit her next three clay pigeons! "Only within reason, Mr. Lecherous Winngate," she retorted with a grin and a dramatic tossing of her tawny mane.

He shrugged his disappointment, then declared, "Chicken."

"Pull!" he shouted three consecutive times, skillfully striking the target with each shot.

She watched closely as the first target exploded into many pieces, then the second one, and then the third one. Steven turned and engulfed her with a smug, triumphant gleam in his blue eyes.

Brandy slowly came forward and took the gun from his hand. She absently thanked him for reloading it for her. "Ready?" he called out almost instantly, having savored his coming victory long enough, planning to begin his enlightening move on her.

She glared at him, then grinned. "Be a gracious winner, Steven love," she taunted playfully. "No fair distracting me any more than you already have! If I weren't a lady, I might insist upon a good luck kiss myself!"

"I would be only too willing to oblige, my fair lady."

"I just bet you would," she scoffed pertly. She inhaled and readied herself as much as possible. She lifted the gun and called, "Pull!" To her surprise, she actually hit the target.

She shrieked her joy. She glanced over her shoulder and flashed him a mocking grin. "There're two more," he nonchalantly called out to unnerve her, planting his booted feet wide apart in an arrogant stance. Her gaze flickered over him.

"Pull!" she called out again. This time, she squealed and danced around as the clay target shattered and dropped to the dirt in many pieces. As she readied herself once more, he murmured close to her ear, "Sure you don't need a good luck kiss?"

The warmth of his breath caused goose bumps to cover her body. Her breath caught at the suggestive invitation in his husky tone. "No—thank you," she stammered, wanting nothing more than to toss down the gun and to throw herself into his waiting arms. But it was rash to reveal his powerful hold over her.

"Suit yourself, Brandy love. But my first order will be for a proper kiss of congratulations," he calmly warned her.

"Pull!" she called out weakly. Unnerved, she hesitated just long enough for the clay pigeon to pass her gunsight before she fired at it. The undamaged target fell to the earth and broke into two separate halves. She stared at the spot where it had fallen. She anxiously waited for him to claim his victory kiss, fearing what that devastating kiss would tell him.

The gun was gently taken from her hands and carefully laid upon the grass. He tenderly seized her shoulders and turned her around to face him. His hand grasped her lowered chin and lifted her head, forcing her to meet his softened gaze. "Congratulations are in order, Miss Alexander," he slyly reminded her of his past suggestion. Yet, he made no attempt to take his reward.

She eased up on her tiptoes and placed her arms around his neck. As she pulled his head down to hers, their gazes fused and locked. Just before her lips touched his, she playfully accused, "You cheated, Lance; you disturbed my concentration...."

The world began to swirl madly as did her senses. He pulled her tightly and possessively against his hard, lean body. All she could hear was the roaring of her molten blood as it surged through her fiery body and ears. She clung to him; she ardently returned each kiss and mentally pleaded for the next one. Not once did she consider pulling away from him. Not once did any other thought enter her dreamy mind other than about him and this blissful moment.

Pent-up, restrained emotions and feverish desires broke through her resistance and innocence. Intense hungers surfaced to shatter any will to refuse him anything. Her heart and body overruled any logic her mind presented. She had wanted him from the very first moment she had looked into those powerful blue eyes. Yet he was just as helpless to resist her or to control himself.

Painful reality returned in the form of heavy raindrops pelting her in the face. They welled in her eyes and slid into her nose. Steven's lips were searing a blazing path down her throat to the hollow of her neck. His back was soaked, but he never even noticed the wetness. Neither would Brandy if he had not been lying upon her supine body with her face skyward....

She began to struggle to get his attention and to halt their runaway emotions and this extremely dangerous situation. She feared one of her ranchhands would come riding by and witness this burst of unbridled passion. She did not even know how they had come to be lying on the lush grass, arms and legs entangled, mouths and senses united as one. His hands were moving over her body as if he owned it. Fiery kisses were being spread over her face, mouth, ears, throat. Soft words of persuasion and seduction were being fired into her eager and naive ears. Yet, as always, not one word of love or commitment left his lips. Doubts surged through her warring brain. If he felt anything serious towards her, he would have told her by now. Since he had not, it could mean only one thing. Her love for him stormed her. She could not continue this dangerous game. If she did, she could suffer greatly.

Steven was aware of her change of mood. Brandy began to panic at this total and frightening loss of control and at the powerful feelings which were savagely ripping away her reason. She felt as if she were being tumbled in the grass like some milkmaid by a demanding English lord. She tried to pull free, but his grip on her tightened. Each time she tried to cry out for him to stop this untimely onslaught on her senses, his mouth would claim hers and increase her uncontrollable flames and her fear. She began to struggle against him and her unrestrained emotions with this new energy and reason which her panic had born.

Brandy screamed at him and beat on his back with her fists to catch his attention. His persistence was intimidating, alarming. "Stop it, Lance; let me go!" she cried out at him as his lips forged another fiery path down her throat. She seized a hand full of his silky black hair and yanked with all of her remaining strength, for soon it would be too late to stop him. "Let's go home," she pleaded. "I have men working everywhere."

"What the—" he shouted in confusion and pain. He leaned back and stared down into her terror-filled gaze. "What's wrong?" he questioned through ragged breaths. His eyes were glazed with unleashed passion which she innocently mistook for fury.

His great strength of body and purpose only served to increase her fear and mistrust. He almost acted as if he would— She had to get away from him before there was no controlling or stopping his obvious intention to take her there in the meadow. But she was more worried and panicked by her mindless reaction and surrender to him. She had lost all sense of time, of surrounding, and of herself. In just a few more minutes...

Ashamed and frightened, she sharply panted, "I'm not some slut to be rolled in the grass! Let me go this instant! It's raining; I'm getting soaked!" she babbled foolishly.

Too impassioned to be kind or understanding, he glared down at her. "But, Brandy, I want you; I need you...now!"

He had left out the most important words. "No! Not here."

"Then why the devil did you lead me on this far if you had no intention of making love to me! Don't play the tease with me again! I might not be so generous next time!" he stormed at her, his blue eyes turbulent with the unleashed violence which flooded his hungry body and filled his eyes. How could she withdraw at a moment like this? He was almost tempted not to let her go; he was tempted to use his powerful allure to seduce her anyway.

Steven quickly rolled off her and sat up, painfully concealing his aroused condition. "Go home, Brandy. Don't make this any rougher on either of us. Next time, don't start something you have no intention of finishing. If you ever tempt me again..." He did not complete his wild threat.

Too scared to move, she simply lay there while the rain pelted down into her face and saturated her clothes. Brandy didn't want to leave him this way, but neither could she allow him to take her in such a selfish manner. Her chin trembled as tears rolled from her eyes into her already wet hair. Her body began to shudder with the full implication of her decision. God, how she wanted him too. If only she could be assured of privacy...If only he hadn't made it sound like an order...If only he loved her...

Steven turned and glared down at her. Even as he took in her vulnerable state and her anguish, he could not risk reaching out to her. "Get out of here before I refuse to let you go!" he snarled, his own anguish concealed by the gruffness of his tone. He fumed over her rejection. He wondered if she had been testing her power over him. He wondered why she always backed down when he was getting to her.

Brandy was propelled into motion with that new threat. She hastily jumped up and raced to her horse. She mounted up and prodded him into a fast gait. She did not dare look back. When she arrived at the stable, she called out for Zack to take care of her beloved Wildfire. She ran into the house and went straight to her room. Too wet to throw herself upon her couch or her bed, she walked through her sitting area in her bedroom and into the bathroom. She stepped into the tub and huddled there like some child frightened of a violent storm.

Brandy cried and shook for a long time. She sobbed as she noted the loud slamming of the back door following his much later return. When she could call forth no more soothing tears, she stripped off her damp clothes and took a long, hot bath which failed to relax either her taut body or her miserable spirits.

Brandy slipped into a satin nightgown—the silvery gray one which she had purchased in Las Vegas—and lay down across her bed.

She listened to the rolling thunder which made its nearby presence loudly known. She forced her attention on the steady pattering of the raindrops. She contemplated the power of the breeze which was swaying the tall trees near her windows. She tried to think about anything except Steven Winngate and this tormenting afternoon. Why had he treated her in such a cruel manner? Was he reaching for an excuse to be thrown out?

Brandy wondered how she could ever face him again. He had been right to be angry with her. In his eyes, she had led him on. She was new to such feelings, but she should have recognized their powers. How could he know how completely hypnotized she had been? How could he know it was only the rain falling into her face which had awakened her to reality? She would have fallen prey to his desires if that storm had not alerted her to the danger she was unknowingly entering; worse, the danger and humiliation of discovery by one of her workers. My Lord, couldn't she kiss him and hug him without making love each time? Did such expressions of tenderness have to lead down that passion-lined path each time?

If only she knew how he felt about her. He desired her, but why? She couldn't comprehend his violent temper and disregard for privacy! Guilt filled her as she comprehended the full reality of his physical pain and embarrassment. How could she make him understand? How could he ever forgive her?

Brandy began to weep anew. The thought that she had destroyed any possible hope for them to get together ravaged her tender heart. The hour grew late; the sky steadily darkened. Mary came to tap lightly on her door. Catching sight of her disheveled state, the pale face, and the puffy red eyes, Brandy knew she could not face Mary either. She rubbed her fingers over her swollen lips. No one could see her like this!

Brandy called through the door, pretending to be just aroused from sleep, claiming a terrible headache and a need for more rest. She asked Mary to take care of Mr. Winngate for her. Brandy said she would not be down for dinner. After promising to take care of herself, Mary returned to the kitchen to prepare Steven's dinner before leaving for the night.

Brandy stood up and went to sit on the floor near a large window. Time passed as she gazed out at the scenery without really seeing it. The clouds leisurely moved off toward the far horizon, leaving behind a star-filled heaven. She watched the yellow ball as it climbed higher and higher into that stygian sky until it was overhead.

Brandy did not know how long Steven had been standing there in the darkness behind her. She had not heard the click of her lock as he had expertly jimmied it. Her chin was resting upon her hands on the wide windowsill. She did not know if it was the sudden sensing of another's presence or if it was his scent or if it was his magnetic allure which slowly pulled her head around.

Steven placed a tray of food on the floor beside her. "I'm sorry about this afternoon, Brandy. I was out of line," he vowed huskily, then turned to leave, tormented by her loss.

"Lance! Steven!" she cried out before he was half way across her room. He halted, but did not turn around. He seemed to be waiting for some attack or well-deserved chiding. She suddenly realized he was assuming the blame, or most of it.

"You need not apologize; I was the one at fault today," she admitted just above a whisper. "But I wasn't leading you on, at least not intentionally. I didn't realize what was happening between us until...until it began raining in my face. Teasing isn't my style. Nothing is. I know I write a great deal about romance and passion, but I know little about its realities, only what you've taught me. I didn't come down to dinner because I was too ashamed to face you. I was afraid you would despise me for—for what I did to you out there. One of my workers might have come by; I just couldn't...I promise it won't happen again. Will you forgive me? Can we still be friends?"

Unaware of what she was unwittingly revealing to him, Steven smiled into the darkness. Feeling he had the answer he had come seeking, he inhaled deeply and then slowly released it. At his pensive silence, she lived through an endless period of doubt and agony. Was the damage irreparable? Did he hate her?

"I understand perfectly, Brandy. You have no reason to feel shame or embarrassment. It's obvious our timing wasn't right this afternoon. I suppose you know why I was so rude and angry?" he subtly and ruefully confessed.

"Yes. I'm sorry..."

"I'm the one with all the experience; I shouldn't have let things go that far. You're just too damn irresistible. Let's look at this afternoon as a lesson in self-control. I know you're not a tease. Eat your sandwich before it gets stale. We'll talk tomorrow. We have some matters to settle." Steven decided it was best if he allowed her some time and privacy to sort out her feelings and to accept them. He wanted to seize her and make passionate love to her; he feared to do so would only make it appear his interest was merely physical, which it wasn't.

Brandy yearned to rush into his arms and to shout her love for him, but his strange mood prevented it. She dared not endanger this new truce which he was offering. Somehow she had to entice him to feel more than desire for her. She had to prove she was different from all the women he had known and taken. She had to prove she was the woman he needed. She was elated when he asked softly, "Are you sure I didn't hurt you? I know how strong and persistent I can be."

"Thanks to you, I'm fine now, Lance, thank you."

He knew if he didn't get out of her room immediately, he would risk ruining everything again. She was willing to forgive him, and that was enough for tonight. He headed for the door. Just before closing it, he whispered, "Sweet dreams, love."

Her anguished heart began to sing with renewed hope and joy. He didn't hate her; if only she could somehow win his heart! She was suddenly ravenous. She wolfed down the sandwich and glass of milk. She flung herself upon her bed as plans for conquering him raced through her ecstatic mind.

Chapter Twelve

When the soft rays of sunlight began to drift across her bed and its shiny fingers began to play upon her face, Brandy suddenly sat up in her bed. She had forgotten to draw her blinds. Memories of last night flooded her mind like a rain-swollen river attacking a weakened dam. She flung back the covers and jumped out of bed. She hugged herself as she sighted the tray upon the floor near the window.

It had not been a beautiful dream. She danced around her room with great excitement and unleashed happiness, swinging her robe around in carefree exuberance. The wind which she playfully created caused a sheet of blue paper to tremble, then take flight behind her dresser.... She hurriedly showered and dressed in a lovely, white eyelet sundress. She checked her reflection in the mirror, smiling at the glow in her eyes and upon her cheeks. She rushed downstairs to spill her heart to him. No matter what he said or how he felt, she must confess this love which was storming her heart.

Brandy searched the whole house, but found no one. She nervously paced the kitchen floor while she waited for his return. She rehearsed her coming speech over and over. She had come to a point where she would accept any part of him, all or only a portion. She would go where he said, anytime he said!

Brandy could now comprehend how a woman could sacrifice anything for the man she loved. Nothing mattered to her, except having him and being with him. She wanted his company; she wanted his children; she wanted a life with him. She feared her heart would surely burst with love and excitement if he did not return soon and absorb some of it! Where was Mary? Perhaps she knew of her love's whereabouts.

Growing impatient and anxious, she called the stables to see if Zack knew where he was. She was stunned by his news. Mary had received a call from the farmer's market to come over and to check out their new arrivals for freezing and canning. But Steven Winngate had departed for the airport in Lexington shortly after daybreak! He told Zack he needed to catch a flight to New York at ten thirty.

Brandy glanced up at the kitchen wall clock; it was now eleven o'clock. She stammered her confused thanks and hung up the phone. He was gone! He had left without so much as a polite thank you or a friendly farewell! Why hadn't he told her he was leaving this morning? Not once had he mentioned his flight. Not a single word. Why had he run away like this? Why?

She covered her trembling lips with her shaking hands. Tears rushed down her ashen cheeks. Agony ripped at her tormented heart. How could he be so cruel and thoughtless? Only yesterday he had wanted...

Suspicion and doubt filled her anguished heart and turbulent mind. Since his arrival he had been persuasive and disarming. Resentment and anger filled her at his treacherous betrayal and her romantic foolishness. He had come to her room last night knowing he was leaving this morning. Had it been to taunt her or to punish her for her rejection at the skeet range? Why hadn't he made love to her last night?

My God, had he been making a complete fool of her? The ruthless tyrant! The cold-blooded, arrogant devil! The coward! Naive, trusting, gullible Brandy had blindly and recklessly allowed it. He had hurt her again....

She raged at his cruelty; she wept for the pain in her heart. No doubt he had laughed all the way back to New York City! Let that glacial, phony Camille have him; they deserved each other! If only she did not feel as if her very heart was being carved from her body with a dull knife. The anger, humiliation, and resentment were nothing compared to the cutting pain which sliced and pierced her heart, mind, and soul.

The door bell rang insistently. Brandy wiped her eyes and went to answer it. She opened the door to find a uniformed, special delivery man standing there, impatiently shifting from one foot to the other in open annoyance. He handed her a long, yellow envelope, telling her to sign for it. Assuming it to be contracts for a novel, she rapidly complied with his request. He turned and hastily departed before she could even tip him.

Brandy returned to the kitchen and placed the envelope on the table. As she sat down to reason out this drastic and unexpected turn in events, her eyes sighted the return label: *Glitter Magazine.* Curiosity filled her. Why would his magazine be sending her something by special delivery? He had only left here with his story and pictures this morning. Strange...

She ripped open the envelope and lifted out an advance copy of next month's issue. Her face drained of all color. She stared at the bold red print and the color photo of herself. He wouldn't...He couldn't...He promised...But the timing...

She scanned the index to locate the page number. She shook violently as she found that fateful page. She feared she would be physically ill or faint. As her misty eyes read the story and looked over the pictures, she mistakenly comprehended the reason for his hasty and abrupt departure. Now she recalled the phone ringing last night and Mary calling him to answer it: a warning?

She glared at the bold print in shock and disbelief: *"Will the Real Brandy Alexander Please Step Forward!"* by Laura

McGavin. He had lied, for he had not canceled the errone-
ous, malicious story. He had deceived her, duped her, betrayed her, and brazenly and cruelly seduced her.

She rushed upstairs. She hastily changed into a steel-blue
crepe dress. Her hands trembled as she loosely tied a pais-
ley scarf around her neck. She mindlessly tossed some
clothes into several pieces of luggage. She snatched up her
briefcase and tossed the magazine and the rough draft of her
present novel inside of it. She called the airport. Thank-
fully there was a flight which she could just catch if she
hurried. She called Casey's service and told her to be in her
office when she arrived there. She scribbled Mary a note,
saying her return home was indefinite.

WHEN BRANDY ARRIVED, Casey rushed forward to greet
her. "For Heaven's sake, Brandy, what's the emergency?"

Brandy opened her briefcase and threw the magazine on
her desk. "Check pages forty to forty-five. It came by special delivery this morning. He lied and tricked me! How can
I possibly do that publicity tour now! Change it to later, if
they still want me to show up after that trash hits the market. Every place I stop, those interviewers will be harping on
that story."

Brandy could not halt a new flow of tears. "I'm sorry,
Casey. I honestly thought I was halting it. He promised not
to print it. All this time I've been entertaining the devil in my
own home! And this is how he shows his gratitude! He
wants to destroy me and my name, plus my career. Why? It's
not even true! But you well know the public will eat it up.
I'm ruined, Casey...."

Casey's trained eye hastily scanned the story and pictures to assess their power and possible damage; Brandy was
right. She too was shocked and disillusioned. "Why,
Brandy? Is he still at your ranch? What did he have to say
about this vile story?"

"He *was* at the ranch. In fact, we've been having a wonderful time, or so I stupidly thought. The bloody coward left

this morning before I was up! No thanks or good-bye! He told Zack he was coming back here. As to why he did it, I have no idea. You know what he thought and how he acted after we met in Las Vegas, but I honestly believed he was being sincere. Somehow I've annoyed him to the point of ruthless revenge, but I don't know why or how to stop it. Do you know that he once offered me that story in exchange for the manuscript for *Valley*?"

"I know. He also offered Webster Books a million dollars for it. Naturally they refused; he upped it to one and a half million. Webster told him no amount could purchase one of your manuscripts," she informed the stunned Brandy. She went on to fill her friend and client in on her other findings and suspicions.

Brandy just sat there shocked. "Why?" she finally managed to ask.

"Would you believe I was convinced the snake was in love with you? What happened at your ranch?" Casey softly entreated.

Her mind spinning and nothing to gain by a refusal, Brandy glossed over Steven's traitorous visit, leaving little untold. "I must be the biggest fool born, Casey. I love him."

Casey felt this wasn't the time for advice on a broken heart. Her anger mounting against this vicious man, she declared, "We'll just go and see what Mr. Steven Winngate has to say about this and his deceitful methods! You coming along?"

"I'll never face that monster again! I'm leaving for the beach house right now. Don't call me unless there's an emergency. And please don't tell Nigel or anyone where I am. I need to be alone. I've got some mighty heavy thinking to do."

"Will you be all right?" Sympathy and concern filled Casey and flowed out to Brandy.

"I'll have to be, won't I? I might head on up to the Northwest until this story blows over; I have all my notes with me. That cold climate and juicy story should take my

mind off this tragic mess. I'll call you before I head out."
She paused at the door and glanced back at her friend and
agent. "I'm truly sorry, Casey. I did my best. In fact, I did
more than my best. Bye."

Casey smiled. "Don't worry about a thing. I'll take care
of this story and Steven Winngate," she vowed angrily. Both
departed in opposite directions for different purposes.

"SHOW MISS TREAVERS in," Steven stated over his inter-
com, wondering why Brandy's agent and friend had demanded to see him, calling it an emergency. Surely Brandy
wasn't upset about that letter he left on her dresser? Had she
sent Casey here with her response, a refusal? Did she know
about *Valley*?

Casey stormed into his masculine office of earthtones and
fearlessly approached his massive oak desk. She contemptuously threw the offensive magazine in front of him. She
shouted, "You filthy bastard! How dare you do that to
Brandy? You're the lowest form of life around! Worse than
that, you lied to her and tricked her. You led her to believe
you had canceled that piece of trash by McGavin. There's
no way to excuse or explain such treachery!"

Bewildered, he asked, "What are you talking about,
woman? I told her I wouldn't print that story. There won't
be an old one or a new one printed in my magazine. I just
got back this morning."

"Oh, I know what you told her! But I also know what my
own eyes see before them. How can you stand there and
continue this charade! The proof is right there!" She emphatically tapped the front cover with its bold print and
color photo.

His eyes followed her erratic movements. He gasped in
stunned fury. "Who the hell printed this lie!" he exploded
as his volatile temper was unleashed. He scanned the story.

Steven yanked up his phone and placed a call to the publisher. He snarled at the man who had blatantly disre-
garded his orders! "You're fired, Thompson! How dare you

go against my orders! I'm going to marry that girl if she'll even speak to me after this.''

They argued for a while, then Steven demanded he call the warehouse and halt any deliveries of that issue. "You'd better pray they haven't sent out a single copy. If so, I'll tear you limb from limb and burn down that place!''

Steven halted to ask Casey how she got her advance copy. When she answered him, his anger and dismay increased. There was a lengthy silence as Steven listened to Thompson's incredible explanation. "You're crazy! I didn't send you any such telegram! I told you not to run a story on her.'' He listened again. When Thompson said he had the telegram in his hand, suspicion began to eat into his mind. "See if McGavin knows anything about a telegram. Also have a Camille Blanchard checked out. From now on, no orders other than by phone or in person: Understand? I'll be in my office. Do what you have to do, but I want every single copy shredded today.''

After a brief silence, he shouted, "I don't care what it costs! If one copy hits the market, I'll have your head. I'll cover any expense necessary. While you're at it, burn every scrap of information on Brandy Alexander. Put a note in the files, no more stories about that woman unless I write them! Call when you can account for every copy!'' He slammed down the phone and muttered curses beneath his breath.

Suddenly recalling how Casey had gotten her copy, he whirled to face her. "Where's Brandy now? I have to explain this mess to her, if she'll believe a word I say now....''

"Needless to say, she's crushed by this deceit. She's canceled all of her publicity tours. Says she can't face anyone until this blows over. She left before I came over here. She refused to come along. Said she didn't ever want to see you again.''

"Was she headed back to the ranch?''

"No. That would be the first place anyone would hound her once this story hit the market. Let her alone, Mr. Winngate. I think you've hurt her enough. She won't even see Nigel."

"I have to see her, Casey! She's in love with me, or didn't she tell you that? Where is she?" he demanded.

"Yes, I know it. She has been since Vegas. It was written all over her face every time she mentioned your name. It just took her awhile to realize what that strange, new feeling was all about."

"Then tell me where to find her; please..."

"I can't; I promised not to tell anyone, especially you. Don't you think I know how you've treated her since Vegas? I also told her all about your devious investigation!"

"Did she discuss me with you?"

"Nigel dropped numerous hints when I asked him to protect her from you. Why else do you think he was there? He was going to cancel his visit when he learned you were going; I begged him to be there. I didn't trust you, Winngate; now I see why. He loves Brandy like a real sister. He wouldn't allow anyone to hurt her, including you. When he learns of this story..."

Before Casey could finish, the phone signaled a call. Steven quickly snatched it up, praying it was Brandy. He sighed loudly in relief as he listened to the news from the other end. "You're certain? Every copy?" He waited. "Excellent, Thompson." They talked for a few more minutes.

Casey wandered around his plush office. She halted by the leather sofa. She leaned over and picked up the galley of *Valley of Fire* from where he had been reading it. She whirled to confront him as he came up behind her, "How did you get this?"

"I have a friend at Webster who owed me a favor. I was told Brandy used me for the prototype for the hero; naturally, I wanted to see it before it hit print," he admitted honestly.

"Where would you get a crazy idea like that! *Valley* was written last year, long before Brandy even met you. It isn't even about the Valley of Fire in Vegas."

"I know that now. I've already scanned the galley. She's good, isn't she? From her style and vivid descriptions, I could almost see and hear her characters and settings. No wonder she makes the bestseller lists every time. I've been reading every one of her books I could obtain. As for *Valley*, I was mistaken, or maliciously misled."

"Is that why you've been harassing her? You thought she was using you for that story? That's why you wanted it!"

"Correct. When Derrick called last night to say I could have a peek at it this morning, I caught the first flight here. As for my deceptive visit to her ranch, I had to be certain about her before I proposed."

"Before you what?" she exclaimed in amazement.

"Proposed to her. Didn't she mention my offer of marriage? Seems I researched her a little too deeply and fully. I love her, Casey. There won't be another story about her, unless it's coverage of our wedding."

"What wedding, Mr. Winngate? She said she didn't want to ever see you again." It wouldn't hurt him to have some doubt inserted into that arrogant, smug attitude. Let him crawl to Brandy and beg her forgiveness for all he had put her through! He always got his way and his wishes; let him fret about this one very costly triumph!

"Where is she, Casey? I know you want to punish me, but don't torment her with the lack of the truth about me and this mixup. While I stew, her heart is needlessly breaking."

"Mixup? *Somebody* sent that telegram."

"I think I know who that was. I promise you I'll deal severely with her just as soon as I straighten out things with Brandy. Please, where is she?" he pleaded earnestly.

"How do I know this isn't some new deceit? Another trick?"

He pulled a black velvet box from his pocket. He opened it and stuck it under her nose. "Does this look like a trick?

I bought it this morning. I also have a return ticket on the afternoon flight to Kentucky. Would you care to see it?'' he boldly sneered, impatient to find his tormented love.

Casey's eyes stared at the three-carat solitaire engagement ring which was snuggled into the crevice in the midnight velvet box. ''You're actually serious! You do want to marry her!''

''If and when I can find her and clear up this mess!'' he replied, trying to curb his hot temper and to convince her to release the vital information about Brandy's hideout.

Casey laughed happily and boldly stated, ''I'll take care of this galley for you. I'll write down her address at Kiawah Island. I'll also send her a note that you can be trusted, if you'd like,'' she generously offered, convinced of Steven's past mistakes and future intentions.

She went to his desk and did just that. ''Make sure you explain why I betrayed her confidence and location.''

They talked as they planned his coming trip. Casey picked up the galley and headed for the door. She turned and vowed, ''You're a fortunate man, Mr. Winngate. You couldn't find a better woman than Brandy. She loves you, but she's hurt and confused; so go easy on her. Just get there before she heads out for the Northwest. It would take months to locate her there.''

Steven squirmed in the cushiony seat of the private jet which was speeding him to Brandy's side. He couldn't relax; he couldn't arrive soon enough to please him. He fretted over her hasty flight. Why hadn't she given him the chance to explain? What about his letter? His declaration of love? His proposal? After reading his letter, how could she believe he would be responsible for doing this vile thing, for betraying her and their love? How could she just run off like this?

He withdrew the velvet box and opened it, gazing at the ring, recalling how he had traced her size on a piece of paper using her dinner ring. He loved her; he needed her; he wanted her. There was a big stack of evidence against him.

Could he convince her it was all a terrible mistake? She had spoken the truth; *Valley* had nothing to do with them. If she truly loved him, why desert him? What if Casey was wrong? What if Brandy didn't love him? What if she was too proud or stubborn to listen, to forgive him? After witnessing and sharing her life-style, maybe she didn't want to change it, even for him....

Marriage, a husband, children—those were drastic changes. Children, the word and idea rifled through his troubled mind like staggering bullets. Neither he nor his naive Brandy had used or discussed birth control. What if— He beamed, a daring and persuasive argument dancing across his ecstatic mind.

Chapter Thirteen

In Brandy's troubled mood, the warm sun seemed to blaze down unmercifully upon her tawny head as she walked along the sandy beach. The lapping waves which normally played happily at her bare feet only annoyed her today. The azure sky seemed too blue and too clear while her mood was dark and cloudy. The air should feel tingly and fresh; it seemed to stifle and to irritate her instead. Today, when she was seeking to comprehend and to forget Steven Winngate, the elements joined to torment her, just as they had done on the first day she had met him.

Brandy could not seem to shake her anguish and loneliness, this agonizing feeling of betrayal of something rare and beautiful. Today had been the longest and most difficult day of her entire life. She did not even want to eat or to sleep. All she wanted was Lance Reynolds, and that was utterly impossible; he had made it impossible forever. She didn't even want to observe the splendid, colorful sunset which was in progress: It too reminded her of that first meeting.

She couldn't even cry anymore. Surely she had already used up her lifetime supply of that soothing treatment. For the first time, she had totally surrendered her heart and soul to a man...but one who did not want her. It was too late to take them back, for that demon had no doubt devoured them, bit by bit.

She slowly sank down to her knees upon the ecru sands. What did she care about the lovely scenery? What did she care about the expensive, crepe de chine dress she was still wearing? Nothing mattered now, nothing except somehow easing this terrible pain. She had walked for hours; she sighed wearily and dejectedly.

"Brandy..." a voice from the innermost reaches of her heart called out softly.

Thinking it was her traitorous mind taunting her, she cried out, "My God, is there no place to escape you? Everything reminds me of you! Damn you, Lance! Stop tormenting me!"

"Brandy love, how can I ever make you understand? I'm so sorry, angel," the deep voice murmured sadly beside her, an alerting shadow falling across her lap.

She whirled around, tossing sand onto the legs of his white deck pants and onto his bare feet. Her wide, doubting eyes slowly traveled upward. They went past his navy oxford shirt which was unbuttoned to his waist. They helplessly lingered upon the dark, curling hair upon that virile chest where she had rested her head many times. They briefly slipped over the gold rope chain with its noble lion's head. They halted hungrily upon his sensual lips. They roamed his striking face for a few moments, then settled on his vivid sea-blue eyes.

"Steven! What are you doing here? How did you find me? Did you come to gloat over your stunning, crafty victory? Or perhaps only boast of your cunning conquest of a naive girl?" she hotly accused, as tears began to ease down her cheeks. There was such pain and sadness within her eyes and voice. "You filthy bastard! Get out of my sight and life!" She jumped up and raced down the deserted beach.

Steven quickly and agilely pursued her. It was past time for a final understanding between them. His hand snaked out and seized the hand flying beside her in her hasty flight. He pulled her to a stop and caught her by the shoulders. Brandy struggled against his strength and flung curses at him, words she had only used till then in her novels. He turned her around and clutched her against him. She pounded upon his hard chest; she screamed at him; she threatened him; she cried in frustration and pain. When she was too exhausted to fight anymore, he loosened his steel grip only slightly.

"You're going to hear me out, woman!" he vowed in determination. "Shut up and listen!" he shouted over her tirade.

"Never!" she screamed at him.

As a crazed tigress, Brandy fought him wildly with her meager strength. Steven hooked his right leg behind hers and sent her to the sandy ground on her rear. They thrashed in the sand as he confined her legs between his and pinned her hands to the sides of her head. Still she desperately struggled for freedom.

"You're getting sand all over me! It's in my hair!" she shrieked foolishly at the resolved Steven. "Let me up!"

Brandy's order had no effect on Steven. "Look at me, Brandy!" he stated firmly.

"No!" she refused, twisting her head to one side. Brandy did halt her wiggling which was dangerously hiking up her dress towards her writhing hips.

Steven dragged her hands through the sand until he touched her head and imprisoned it with his thumbs and forefingers, burying them in tumbling silk. When she struggled to pull free, he refused to release her. "I know this might sound incredible, but I love you, Brandy."

"Love me!" she shouted at him. "How can you say that after what you've done to me? I trusted you! You lived in my own home! You slept in my bed! I entertained and befriended you while you were conniving to destroy me! How dare you come here with such malicious lies! Wasn't that last story juicy enough for you and your readers? My God, Steven, you knew it wasn't true! Why?"

"Listen to me, Brandy; I can explain ev—" he began.

"I just bet you can! More lies, Steven? More torment and betrayal? I won't listen to anything more you have to say. I won't be fooled or lied to again. Stay away from me! I never want to see you again! Never!"

"You will hear me out, Brandy," he declared confidently in a softened tone.

"No! There's nothing more to say! You liar! You coward!"

"At least give me the courtesy of explaining my side of this mixup! You owe me that much!" he stormed back at her.

"Owe you! You have the gall to come here and force your lies on me? I saw the magazine; I know about your treachery!"

"Damn it, Brandy! Listen to me for a minute! I had nothing to do with that story. Somebody pulled a fast one on both of us! Some little schemer sent a telegram to *Glitter* to release the first story and signed my name! I swear it wasn't me, Brandy. Casey brought that advance copy to my office. She and I put our heads together and did some fast talking and tracking. It won't hit the market; I ordered all copies destroyed this morning. If you don't believe me, call Casey and ask her! I ordered them to destroy all information they had on you. I forbade them to do another story about you."

"You got rid of every single copy? But that would be a huge loss, a fortune!" she argued skeptically.

"But you would be a bigger one, Brandy love. The money isn't important, but you are," he replied in a tender and entreating tone.

"Me? What are you trying to pull now, Steven?"

"I love you, Miss Brandy Alexander. I have since that first moment I pulled you from your car and held you in my arms. I think I knew even that moment you were the woman I'd been waiting and hoping for. I was just too damn stubborn and blind to realize it sooner. So many things kept coming between us, things I couldn't understand. I couldn't take the chance you weren't for real. If necessary, I'd sacrifice every cent I have to prevent your loss. I swear to you all of those issues have been destroyed. Didn't my note tell you anything?''

''What note?''

''The one I left for you on your dresser. I explained where I was going; I told you I'd return soon. Why didn't you wait for me? At least confront me and give me a chance to tell my side!'' he snarled angrily.

''I don't want to hear your side, or anything you have to say!''

''You've put me through hell, woman; and by God, you will listen!''

As he began to talk, Brandy squeezed her eyes shut to close out his face. She began to hum loudly to drown out his stirring voice. Steven's anger began to rise. He sat up, capturing her hands beneath his legs. He pulled a black velvet box from his pocket. After removing a ring, he tossed the box aside. He held up the large diamond and growled, ''I went to New York to get this!''

He grabbed her hand and slid the ring on her finger. Brandy struggled again. ''Don't you dare put that on my finger, Steven Winngate!''

''I'm asking you to marry me. If you say no, I'll never ask you again. If you take that ring off your finger, it'll never be put on again!'' he thundered his warnings.

''You think by marrying me you'll stop me from suing you for every cent you have! The old wife-can't-testify-against-her-husband routine?'' she sneered doubtfully.

''You're a blasted fool, Brandy!'' he stormed, his blue eyes glittering ominously.

''So are you, Winngate!'' she purred acidly.

''You shouldn't look so surprised. I asked you to marry me in my note!''

''If there was a note, I never saw or read it!'' she challenged. ''Just as there was never any story! You liar! It was all a cruel trick!''

''You're partly right; there never was any story. I only used that ploy to get an invitation to your ranch. You gave me the idea that night on the terrace. I wanted to get to know you better so I could decide if you were for real. Damn it, Brandy! I've never met a woman like you before. You scared me to death with all these crazy, new emotions. I knew I wanted you, but I was afraid to reach out and claim you. At first I saw you as a challenge to my ego. I was angry because I thought you were only using me for hero research for that new book of yours. When Officer Connelly told me your accident appeared awfully suspicious, I assumed you arranged our first meeting. Then when I came to visit you, Ross told me all about you. When he said you were fighting some story in *Glitter,* what was I supposed to think? When he said he'd read your notes about me and our escapade, I was furious! It looked like a setup to meet the owner of *Glitter.* Officer Connelly practically said the accident was faked!''

''Faked!'' she shot into his explanation. ''What are you talking about? I almost died out there, and you believed I was only trying to meet you? Of all the egotistical nerve. Thank God you didn't think that out there and leave me behind. I don't care how it looked or sounded, I'm innocent!''

''I know that now, Brandy. But I didn't know you then. Ross was the one who told me about Tom's show and *Valley.* I was furious with you. You didn't tell me your name or job. My God, Brandy, I thought you were creating a fantasy and then selling it. I thought you were exploiting me and our meeting in that book. That's why I wanted it.''

''You can't be serious. I never use personal experiences! Landis Rivera does sound like you, but I wrote that book long before I ever met you. *Valley of Fire* is located on a tropical island, not in Vegas. It was eerie when I went there, even when I met you. I didn't exploit you, Steven; I would never do that. In fact, I had a suspicion you had something to do with my accident.''

"Why?" he demanded. "You know—"

"Quiet, Winngate; I'm not finished," she stated when he opened his mouth to deny that charge. "I know how upset you were because I had innocently detained and humiliated you. I also know you were furious about your bike, and you blamed me for everything. Officer Connelly got a real charge out of filling me in on the details of how you rescued me and how you resented it later. Since the beginning, I've been nothing but one big joke to you! You've resented me and tormented me for—for some unknown reason. There were plenty of times when I knew you were lying to me, but I didn't know why. I couldn't understand what game you were playing with me—one minute nice and warm; and the next, nasty and cold. I couldn't understand you or your actions. I think you've finally made yourself very clear."

"When I came to the hospital a few days after your arrival, Dr. Ross told me who you were. He saw your notes, Brandy. What was I supposed to think and feel? He said—"

She injected. "Ross! That vile snake! How could he know who— Of course! So, it wasn't my imagination; someone *did* search my room and briefcase that day. You never came back after that second morning," she argued, catching a past statement.

"But I did. I was utterly bewitched by you. I was waiting for the police to question you, then I hoped my outrageous behavior wouldn't damage what I had discovered as a mighty tempting situation. When Ross filled me in on your identity and the book you were writing about me and the Valley of Fire, I was furious and hurt."

"But I haven't written any book about you or us! Nor do I intend to do so. Why do you keep accusing me of exploitation?"

"Ross said the *Valley of Fire* was about me...us."

"But it isn't! I would never use you in any way."

"While I'm confessing my sins, I might as well lay all o my cards on the table. Another reason I so hurriedly lef your ranch was to reach New York in time to see the galle of *Valley* before final printing. I even tried to purchase th draft from Webster weeks ago. I know it has nothing to d with me or us. I also know when and where it was written. know just about everything there is to know about you Brandy, personally and professionally. I have every inter view you've given, a tape of each television appearance, an a copy of every single book you've written. So if you thin I have any doubts or qualms about you, you're wrong. Thi might sound insufficient and late, but I'm sorry I didn' trust you completely. But I had to make certain I was no mistaken about you."

Those stunning confessions slowly and incredibly sank i on Brandy's whirling mind. She gaped at him in astonish ment.

"I went to New York to settle this matter once and for all and to buy that ring," he went on.

"But why did you leave without a single word? I didn' know what to think. Then, when that magazine arrived—'

"I told you before; I left a note in your room. At least yo could have come to see me or called me. You owed me th chance to give my side of this. The letter didn't mean any thing to you?"

"I haven't seen or read any note or letter from you Why?" she asked in bewilderment.

"It explained everything. I put it on your dresser befor I left."

"Then it disappeared. I never saw any letter or messag from you. Not even a good-bye or a polite thank you! Wher the *Glitter* arrived, I assumed it explained your hasty re treat!"

"Then you really don't know why I left? What it said?"

"I know nothing of this mystery letter!"

He threw back his head and sent forth peals of hearty an relieved laughter. "What's so funny, Winngate?"

"That so-called mystery letter contained my proposal of marriage. I told you I had some business to take care of in New York. I asked you to consider me as a husband while I was out purchasing this," he said, pointing to her finger.

He grinned and murmured huskily, "Since you didn't get that mystery letter, I'll give you the gist of it: I love you. Will you marry me as quickly as possible? I can't survive without you. I feel as if you've forced me through my own mental Valley of Fire."

She simply stared at the dazzling three-carat engagement ring. She tried to absorb these new facts and to reason out some of the old ones. Steven continued at her silence, "Thanks to Ross, Connelly, and Camille we've had a lot of interference and misunderstandings. Too, I could blame my own pride and suspicious nature for some of the trouble." Should he reveal his daring ace-in-the-hole?

"Camille? You mean that little joke you two played on me?"

"I never intended for it to happen that way. Fact is, I was a little too carried away to even notice anyone or anything. I'm sorry I hurt you and embarrassed you, more than once."

He sighed heavily and went on, "I think she's the one who sent the okay for the story...or Laura McGavin. I have someone checking it out now. Whoever it is will rue that day."

"Revenge is a mighty costly product, Steven. Forget about her. Besides, trouble would only draw attention to the story. Ross had his reasons; I embarrassed and spurned him several times. As for Connelly, that was pure mischief. You wouldn't believe the things he told me about you! I was literally terrified of you! You kept confusing me with your unpredictable behavior. I couldn't tell if you liked me or hated me."

"The truth is, I love you and want to marry you."

"Why didn't you tell me yesterday? Or last night?"

"I had to clear my own head. You're like some potent drug, Brandy. I knew I had to get this ring and marry you immediately. I've given you lots of reasons to despise me and mistrust me. To tell the truth, I've been petrified you'd refuse. Do you know how hard it was to stay away from you when you were so close and vulnerable? I wanted you at my side every minute. It was sheer delight when old Nigel left."

Steven relaxed his grip, then released it. He eased back on his knees before her, waiting for her response, his heart drumming wildly.

Brandy sat up, staring at the ring on her finger. Slowly she eased off the sparkling diamond. She looked up into Steven's shocked and tormented expression. "You once asked me if I had ever loved a man. The answer is yes; I loved him the first moment I met him, and I still love him with all my heart. I doubt I will ever love another man, if I lived forever. You also asked me if I'd ever received an irresistible proposal; the answer is yes. I fully intend to accept it."

Steven swallowed with great difficulty. He stared at the ring between her fingers. His very soul threatened to explode with the anguish building there. Brandy smiled. She held out the ring in her right hand, then offered her left one. "If you don't mind, Steven, an engagement ring goes on the left hand, third finger, not on the right hand."

Astonishment flooded his face. Her point and answer struck home. He laughed and followed her soft order. "You scared the hell out of me, Brandy," he admitted.

"That makes us even. I was terrified of the things you made me feel and think. I've written that same scene many times, but I've never lived it. I don't think I even honestly thought such emotions were real or possible. Yet, the only reality I knew was you. I wanted you so much. But I didn't know how you felt about me. When you came to see me last night, it took every ounce of willpower I could muster not to tell you how I felt. I was so afraid it would shatter what we had. I was going to tell you this morning, but you had gone."

She laughed as she tenderly caressed his tanned cheek. "I love you, Steven Arthur Winngate, alias Lance Reynolds. I have since that first moment when I looked over Ross's head and gazed into those pools of blue. I could hardly complete my last assignment for thinking and dreaming about you. Do you really want to know why I selected a blond alien with amber eyes? I didn't want you or anyone to know how deeply you had affected me. I made certain he was your exact opposite! I had never met or known anyone like you. You walked into that room, and no other man ever existed again. Not before or after or during . . ."

His hand reached out to stroke her satiny cheek and slip into her silky, tawny tresses. "Why don't we drive through the Valley of Fire on our honeymoon?"

Her emerald eyes melted into his sapphire ones. Her fingers laced through his raven black hair. One hand then slid down his finely chiseled jawline and moved across his proud, cleft chin. "There is no one more captivating than you, Steven." Her finger teased over his sensual mouth and brought a smile to his face. She studied the entrancing blue eyes as she jested, "You cheated at the skeet range. You knew a kiss would devastate me and my aim. Every time you touch me or look at me, I want you."

He chuckled lazily. "I think you missed on purpose just to collect that kiss."

"Naturally. I love you. I can hardly wait to marry you, my love."

"Then how about tonight? If not, don't kiss me. I feel as if I've waited so long for you; I can't wait any longer."

"How can we get married on such short notice?"

"We can use the jet I borrowed from a friend and fly to Vegas where this all began. With the time change, we can be married before this day ends."

"I don't dare give you the time or chance to think twice. Give me a few minutes to change and to pack."

"I could think about this a thousand times and never change my mind. Get packed, my love. You can change clothes on the jet. It's outfitted with everything: bathroom, lounge, bedroom, and bar.''

She looked up into his happy, relaxed features. He added, ''Everything, once you're aboard....''

''I'll pack right after a much deserved and much needed kiss and embrace, Winngate,'' she murmured.

He pulled her into his arms. His lips leisurely moved over her face, eyes, throat, and mouth. The last kiss deepened to one of total love and commitment. She clung to him tightly, knowing her dream had finally come true.

He reluctantly set her away from him, eyes blazed with passion. ''We have to pack and leave here right now, Brandy love, or not at all tonight,'' he warned playfully.

''You call the airport and have the pilot ready that jet. After all, you did say it was fully equipped . . . with everything.''

Their eyes met and locked in mutual understanding. ''Five hours in the air, all alone, is a mighty long trip, Mrs. Winngate-to-be. Do you trust yourself to be alone with me that long?'' His blue eyes gleamed with passionate mischief.

''Yes, it is a very long trip, isn't it? I love you, Steven, and nothing else matters now. Nothing.''

She could not resist claiming one more kiss. He pulled her tightly to him. His mouth came down on hers, erasing everything from her thoughts except him and their fiery future. As Brandy's arms eased around his neck, the diamond sparkled in the vanishing sunlight, blazing as brightly and clearly as their love and passion.

Readers just can't seem to get enough of
New York Times bestselling author

Sandra Brown

This May, a mother searches for

A Secret Splendor

(previously published under the pseudonym Erin St. Claire)

Arden Gentry is searching for the son she was forced to give
up. But finding him could resurrect all the half-truths, secrets
and unspeakable lies that surrounded his birth. Because it
means finding the man who fathered her baby....

Find out how it all turns out, this May at your favorite
retail outlet.

See what happens when two lovers are

Tempting Fate

By National Bestselling Author

JoAnn Ross

Donovan Kincaid—absentminded professor, rakishly charming, last seen wearing one black shoe and one brown....

Brooke Stirling—sophisticated college administrator, determined not to let the relationship she'd once shared with Donovan affect her new job. But sometimes fate takes an unpredictable turn....

Look for TEMPTING FATE this May at your favorite retail outlet.

Somewhere over the
MIDNIGHT RAINBOW
love is waiting

LINDA HOWARD

Priscilla Jane Hamilton Greer had always been given
the best by her daddy—including the services of
Grant Sullivan. Grant, one of the government's most
effective, most desired agents, was given two orders—to
find this high-society girl being held captive in Costa Rica,
and to bring her home.

Alone in the jungle, fleeing armed gunmen, the two
battle fear and find a love that teaches them to put the
demons of the past to rest—in order to face the demons
of the present.

Available at your favorite retail outlet this May.

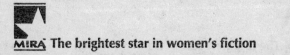

MIRA The brightest star in women's fiction

MLH3